D0113854

EVE IN THE CITY

OTHER BOOKS BY THOMAS RAYFIEL

Split-Levels

Colony Girl

EVE IN THE CITY

Thomas Rayfiel

Ballantine Books • New York

Eve in the City is a work of fiction. Names, places, and incidents either are a product of the author's imagination or are used fictitiously.

A Ballantine Book

Published by The Random House Publishing Group

www.ballantinebooks.com

Book desgn by Julie Schroeder

Library of Congress Cataloging-in-Publication Data
Rayfiel, Thomas, 1958–
Eve in the city / Thomas Rayfiel.—1st ed.
p. cm.
ISBN 0-345-45516-9
I. Title.
PS3568.A9257E94 2003
813'.54—dc21
2003045303

Manufactured in the United States of America

First Edition: September 2003

10 9 8 7 6 5 4 3 2 1

This book is dedicated to

Nancy Rayfiel

and

Betty Durbin

sisters

EVE IN THE CITY

CHAPTER ONE

They say the city never sleeps. It does. Just before dawn you can hear it snore. Light hangs in the air, directionless, not yet pressed into rays. The smell of a hidden sea soaks through stone. The streets themselves have that booming emptiness of a shell held to the ear. Everyone is dreaming. It's when I began to wander, that time in between. I had been in New York a year, and even though I worked until five, five in the morning, still I couldn't close my eyes. I had the urgent sense something was happening, something important, the very reason I had come here in the first place. I felt there was a secret structure to the city, a true form, and if I gave myself up to it, became one with the seeming chaos, then I could master it and, I don't know, attain magical powers, become who I was destined to be. I was seventeen.

"Eve is looking for God."

"Actually, I'm fleeing the Devil."

"It is the same thing, yes? Takes you to the same place."

I stumbled but kept walking. That couldn't be right, could it? But like everything Viktor said, it made a kind of twisted sense.

"Get in the car, Eve," Brandy yawned.

"No cars in the Bible."

Then was the way to God through the Devil? To head right at him? At Him?

"If you were wiolated," Viktor called, "I would feel personally responsible."

"If I was wiolated, you probably would be personally responsible," I muttered.

"What?"

"Nothing."

He acted as if it was one of the big benefits of the job, that you got a ride home. Door-to-door service, he called it. But if she wasn't careful, whoever he dropped off last got more like door-to-bed service. Besides, I had brought my sneakers. I wanted to walk. I wanted to be alone. After seven hours at the bar, I felt like an ashtray.

"You know, honey, it really isn't safe," Nora said.

She was nice, older, maybe thirty, with dark maroon hair and this throaty smoker's voice. She sat up front. Brandy and Crystal were in back. Viktor kept rolling alongside me. I knew all I had to do was turn, go on a one-way street, and he wouldn't be able to follow. But I didn't want to be rude. He was my boss.

"I'll be OK. I promise. I like to walk."

"Let her go, Viktor." Brandy was getting mad.

He stopped, and I obediently stopped, too.

"Why?" he asked. "Why do you like to walk?"

I shrugged. It was nothing I'd ever considered.

"I guess because I like to think."

Brandy and Crystal cracked up. They were both drunk. I never drank at the bar. That's how I made my money. When a customer bought me a drink, I got water and pretended it was vodka. That came out to more than my tips, most nights.

"She likes to think," Brandy gasped.

I was red. Even Nora was smiling at me in a kind of pitying way. Crystal couldn't stop giggling.

"Shut up," Viktor said.

They did. We always did what he said, when he spoke in a certain way.

"I'm sorry." Why are you apologizing? another part of me asked. "It's just that—"

And then he took off. It was so typical. He had to leave me standing there, breathing the taste of his burnt rubber. What he couldn't take was anyone walking away, turning their back on him. It wasn't about me personally, I realized, which was certainly a relief. I watched the car get smaller and smaller and felt this Wait welling up in the pit of my stomach. Wait for me! I loved the way we would all slide against each other when he turned, how he accelerated so fast you were pinned to your seat and the whole evening, all the bad smells and ugly looks, got blown out the window, got left behind.

But it only lasted a minute, that feeling of wanting to belong.

Later, I don't remember how long after, I stood in the middle of Madison Avenue. With no traffic, the signals revealed their pattern: red, green, yellow, red again, rippling down out of Harlem. In a store window, male mannequins modeled suits. They had no hands. Cuffs sprouted, perfect tubes, around each absent wrist. A trick of reflection placed me among them. If you asked, I would have said I had no destination, that I was only obeying the lights, that I was as subject to forces as the sheet of newspaper blown across my path. I had nothing to do, nowhere to go. The green finally reached me and I began to walk.

At Seventy-third Street a couple was making love. Her feet were off the ground, clamped to the waist of a struggling, bare-buttocked man. His side was this S that kept clenching and unclenching, trying to straighten itself out. I wanted to look away, but couldn't. I was mesmerized. My feet were glued. Here was something that was such a crucial part of life, and I had never actually seen it. I mean, never from the outside. Why wasn't that allowed? Maybe because if this was what love really looked like I was going to join a convent. She let out a cry. Or maybe he did. It was punishment. They were urging each other on. I couldn't tell who was obeying whose will, or if they were both in the grip of a power bigger than either one of them. And then something changed.

Is she getting raped? I asked.

Because now that I thought about it, that's exactly what it looked like. I did this flip, this mental maneuver, and in the same exact scene I had just been watching, one thing became another, all because of what was going on in my head. The way her hands were frantically pushing, how her feet, which just moments before I thought were trying to stay up, now seemed to be fighting to get away. What should I do? Should I scream? That's what she had been doing. But screaming . . . why? Anyway, she wasn't screaming anymore. Whatever it was, was finished. They slowed, then stopped. In silent agreement, he let her down. I must have made a sound, a cough, or scraped my shoe against the pavement, because she turned. I glimpsed a face packed tight with anxiety—a bud, cut open—then white legs in black stockings. Her heels echoed in on themselves. She was walking away. She was gone. Like she had never been.

And I was still here. Alone. With him.

"I'm sorry," I called. "Was it my fault?"

He didn't answer. He was propped against the wall, pants still down around his ankles, penis pulling him stiffly to one side, like a dowser's divining rod or a bad shopping cart.

"I didn't know what to do," I went on. "Stop, or keep going."

He made a noise, halfway between a sigh and a moan, then fell.

I walked to the curb, staggered once, adjusting to the new height, then kneeled. The lights threw conflicting shadows. The streetlamp, high overhead, outlined regular features, straight nose, square jaw, while the DON'T WALK sign, lower down, made a mess of his stomach, a muddy shape that was still in flux, still forming. I reached to steady myself, and part of it came off on my hand, hot.

"Oh," I said stupidly, seeing now, planted deep down in his belly, not a penis after all, but instead, wagging in crude imitation, the rubber-coated grip of a hunting knife.

"Oh my God," I corrected, as the pool of blood moved toward my shoes.

The city spun. I was running, but it felt more like my feet were busy staying on top of things while the ground jerked this way and that, changed directions and height, tried to throw me off. I had to find a place with lights, not signs or signals but the warm glow of cloth lampshades, of thick candles. Someplace where humans might be. There were no all-night stores, just locked buildings with doormen sleeping inside. I finally found a Korean fruit stand and after babbling incoherently got them to tell me where a police station was. By the time I got there I was exhausted and panting, my mad dash turned to a crawl. I pulled open the heavy metal door, squeezed in, and plodded to a high desk where a man in a uniform sat reading a newspaper.

"Yes?" he asked, without looking up.

I opened my mouth, then shut it.

"Are you here to report a crime?" he asked.

A crime. What just happened? It didn't go with words. It came from another part of my brain.

"If you're here to report a crime, you have to see a detective. But there's none available right now. I can give you a form to fill out and a detective will call you later."

"I saw something."

He closed the newspaper.

"You're a witness?"

"Yes," I decided. "I'm a witness."

I opened my mouth again, then asked, What did I see? It wasn't so clear. What I'd seen. It also wasn't so clear what I should do about it.

"Miss?" the policeman asked.

What actually happened?

I heard myself saying, Yes, I saw a robbery. Two people struggling. And then someone getting stabbed. Of course. That's what it was. A robbery. I was making it up now, lying my way to a new, better truth. A cleaned-up version. And then I ran away. Yes. It all made sense. I didn't say anything about what couldn't be, what I had actually seen. While he wrote things down and talked to someone on the phone, I glanced at my hand. I had been frantically clawing it against my side, so the stain, if there had ever been one, was gone. There was just skin, rubbed raw.

"What's your name, honey?" he asked, still working on the form.

"Eve."

"Eve what?"

"No last names in the Bible."

He didn't get it. This was going to end badly. I could tell. Just the fact that he believed my story was a frightening sign. I could feel me beginning to believe it, too, believe the reasonable lie over the impossible truth. And why not? You slap labels on what you see that don't even begin to describe reality, labels that paper it over. And then you work on fitting those labels into a nice little life, the life you're told to have, the life the world offers you, if you want to have a good time, if you want to stay normal. And meanwhile, underneath, what it's all based on, is this insanity where you can't even tell what it was you saw, where things change from love to rape to maybe murder! Without changing at all.

He was looking at me, pen still in his hand.

"I don't have a last name." I stared back, trying to look tough. "I'm Native American."

Eve Needs-a-Drink, I added silently.

Someone was frying steak for breakfast. Its smell climbed the winding stairs, past the fifth floor, up a little hidden passageway at the other end of the hall, to "the attic," my landlord called it, when he showed it to me; "servants' quarters," Viktor had scowled, clinging to the banister, out of breath, the time he tried to get in. It felt like the steps would never end. Even at the top I wasn't home yet. Getting to the top was just the beginning. I held on to the worn steel banister. All habit had been stripped from my life. The key fit in the lock. It was a miracle. I let the heavy door bang shut and break something inside me. The anxiety of the night that I had kept so carefully sealed came flooding out.

"Wait," I told myself.

My hands trembled as they popped ice cubes from the tray. I poured bourbon into a glass.

"Wait," I said.

And I did. I waited for the ice to melt. Because I knew this was serious. I took my time. I waited so long I almost didn't want a drink. The moment was past. Almost. But as soon as I took one sip I knew I had to have a lot more.

It never happened. That's what I decided. Of course. It was so obvious. I had dreamed. I had fallen asleep, and kept walking, sleepwalking, right into that world I had been thinking about, where everything gets mixed up. It had seemed real, sure, but dreams do, until they fade. And now I could feel it fading. I was washing it away, soaking it out, like a stain. There. It was gone. Completely gone. I was back. Sane Eve. See? All it took was bourbon. And people wasted all that money on psychiatrists.

When you let the ice melt, I told myself, it tastes better.

That was my problem. I was impatient. I rushed things. I gulped when I should have sipped, ran when I should have walked.

"Screwed when you should have kissed," a voice added.

"Shut *up*."

I whirled around but of course there was no one. What shocked me wasn't so much that I talked to myself. I was getting used to that, living alone for the first time. But the words I used! Words I had never said out loud before. And the things I said! Things that weren't even true. There was other stuff, too. Horrible insults, bad advice, whole scenes I played out with people who weren't there. They kind of fascinated me. They were clues. I was my own oracle, telling me things about myself I didn't know, or didn't want to admit knowing, so they appeared as these unexpected bits of craziness. For example, just now, "Screwed when you should have kissed," where did that come from? Did it mean I really *wanted* to sleep with someone? (And there was only one someone, unfortunately.)

But I didn't. I took this inventory of my soul. Every lust, every itch. Every wish, every hope. And Viktor Kholmov didn't figure in any of them. For one thing, he was shorter than me, which I hadn't thought biologically possible, but even with his ridiculous shoes he only came up to my forehead. And he was a horrible human being. He saw men as things to get money from and women as things to get sex out of. I don't know if he saw much of anything past that. Brandy thought he was nice. She was "in love" with him. Why? I'd asked. She thought that was the stupidest question, so stupid she couldn't answer it. She rolled her eyes. I swear I could hear the echo they made in her big empty blond head. "He has nice shoulders," Crystal said. "Yeah, I suppose he does." I suppose he did. I had never really noticed them before. Maybe the fact that he left them naked most of the time made me look away. He wore undershirts, not real undershirts but the colored ones that are meant to be seen. One was even tie-dyed. So I was always trying not to stare at his hairy armpits and this mole under one that was like a black egg. I kept expecting it to burst and millions of little six-legged Viktors to come scuttling out and swarm all over the bar. "And the mustache," Crystal added. I nodded like it was famous. The Mustache. He was always touching it, stroking it, making sure it was still there.

No, I didn't want to sleep with Viktor, I confirmed blissfully.

By now I was eating the bourbon, tearing off chunks of it like bread. I looked down and saw ice cubes melted to thin discs. It was a shape I had seen in some book. Platelets. What blood came in. My blood, at least. A transfusion. I gave myself more.

At eight o'clock, the one patch of sunlight my apartment got glittered at the bottom of the tub. I slid deep under the water and stared up. My ankles were black, just from walking. It was amazing how dirty the city was. I scrubbed and scrubbed.

"Why don't you shave?" Viktor had asked me earlier.

We wore hot pants at work. And stockings. He liked that look. To see you all encased like a sausage. I changed as soon as the bar closed. I was the only girl who did. Sometimes Nora threw a sweater over her leotard, but no one else seemed uncomfortable except me. Still, even when I had gotten into loose shorts and a baggy T-shirt, he reached from his stool and ran a hand up my thigh.

"Stop it."

"Hairy women. In my country they were always Party Officials."

Why don't *you* shave? I realized I should have said. But of course it was too late.

"Don't you want to be a woman?" he went on.

"You mean if I shave my legs I'm a woman?"

"It is a rite of passage."

He would use words and phrases that were so precise. Because his accent was strong, you thought he didn't know the language, but he did, maybe even better than you. In a different way, certainly. He used English like a scalpel, like it wasn't part of him, so he could make it do what he wanted. Nothing ever just came from his mouth. It always had a purpose. And that purpose was usually to make you uncomfortable. I pried his hand loose. Brandy was pretending not to see, banging around the tables in front perched on her monster heels. She was already tall. I don't know why she had to be taller. It was insecurity. Or maybe she thought he liked it. Anyway, I knew I was just being used to drive her crazy.

"If I shave my legs, what grows back will be different."

"What do you mean? What grows back will be hair."

"Not the same kind of hair. Don't you know that?"

"Know what?"

"Never mind."

"Wait."

But I had worked myself free.

Now I looked at my leg, stuck straight in the air, trying to intercept the shaft of morning that streamed through the bars of my bathroom window. Beyond them was the roof. I had a razor. It lay in the corner where the tub met the wall. It was my temptation every time I took a bath to shear away my childhood and start fresh. I knew that once I started I'd have to keep going, keep shaving, and what grew back would be that black bristly stuff, not the soft down that lay there now. On the other hand, on the other leg, as I raised it and got rid of more dirt, when I did shave, it would be smooth, smooth like a baby, like those girls men call Baby, and his fingertips would slide over me, not drag against the reality of my flaws, not get bogged down, stuck, and sink in. I would be hard and slick, at least on the outside.

I didn't get dressed. I never went out, after. Everyone was running around with their heads down and this haunted look in their eyes. I could hear it happening out my window, the buses and horns, the buzz of people you never noticed unless you worked nights, so you were used to *not* hearing it. There's a beautiful silence to the city, but it's obliterated most of the time. I put my shades down so I wouldn't have to see the bricks. Daylight made me feel like bruised fruit. I turned on the lamp, lay on my stomach, and read. I loved buying books, not from bookstores but from men on the street, the ones who laid them out on card tables or the sidewalk. I didn't go by titles but by how the book looked and felt. I liked small paperbacks you could jam in your back pocket, ones that had been read so often the covers were flexible and the paper mushy. They were so cheap. Everything else was expensive. People tried to charge you for a glass of water. But each book was only a dollar. I bought whole armfuls without looking. Why not? I didn't know what was good. I was so ignorant. I piled them on the floor and opened them like presents, presents to myself.

It was also my way of eating, because I didn't like to eat. I got incredibly hungry, but the urge set off this panic in me. I was afraid if I ate, I wouldn't stop. I would immediately get old and gross and . . . *there,* in a way I wasn't now. I felt as long as I stayed empty inside, then none of this was really happening. I could still go back. (Though back to what? And why would I want to, when I had come so far to escape?) So I ate with every other part of my body. I wolfed down liquor. My feet chewed up whole blocks. And at night, which was morning, I lay on my couch, which was also my bed, squeezing down into the cushions like an animal flattening itself against the ground, and read. I was starving for words. I read actresses' memoirs, diet books, how-to manuals. It didn't matter. Whatever looked and felt a certain way. I was going by instinct for the first time ever, in every part of my life. It was the only way to explain the mess I had gotten myself into, that it was my mess, and because I had chosen it, because I had let it happen to me, it must be important and necessary. That's what I told myself, yawning and reading and very drunk, I guess, although I didn't feel it particularly, the rest of the city gearing up just as I was slowing down.

Around noon, I turned off the light and looked at myself, examined my body. It was a different kind of shadow than at night, where neon signs and headlights gave everything sharp angles. The dark had this caressing quality. I touched myself, to make sure I was still there. I had to keep planting my hands just to make sure I was me, because the rest of the time I was so busy trying not to be there, not to be the girl they saw. Usually I fell asleep that way, sprawled on the cushions, with no blankets, splayed out, offering myself up to the heat. But this time the phone rang.

"So," he said, and let that hang a moment. "You are alive."

"Of course I'm alive."

"I tried you earlier."

"I must have still been out. Walking."

"Walking and thinking, yes?"

"I was just about to go to bed."

"Alone?"

"Of course alone."

"Why 'of course'?"

I had the phone pressed to my ear. I wanted to hear where he was. There was always noise when Viktor called. Sometimes it was arcade sounds, machines dinging and ringing, racking up meaningless point totals. Once there was music so loud I could barely hear. He was calling just to make me jealous that he was at some happening scene, a party he had found in the middle of the day. As if I cared. Viktor didn't have an address or number. Nobody knew where he lived. People called him at the bar, but he never came to the phone. You had to leave a message. He called you. Lately, though, it was always from the same empty-sounding place. I could hear deep echoes, like in a warehouse or a high school gymnasium.

"Where are you?" I asked.

"Not far. I could be there in five minutes."

. . . which meant an hour. It was such an obvious trap. That was the thing about Viktor. He was so obvious. I kept thinking there had to be more to it. That he couldn't really be so wrong for me. That this was all part of some deep plan he had. But maybe it wasn't. Maybe he was just some sleazy guy who talked funny and ran an illegal bar. End of story.

"I can barely hear you."

"Eve." He let that hang there, too.

I had made him call. He was responding to some psychic distress signal I had sent out. It was ridiculous, but I felt in control, like I was influencing him, even though from the outside, in the real world, it was Viktor who bossed me around. But I was making him do that, too. Even though I didn't want to.

"Brandy hates me."

"Brandy loves you," he corrected. "Crystal hates you."

"Crystal? No. Why should Crystal hate me? I like Crystal, a little."

"You don't know nothing."

"Where are you?"

"Conducting business."

There was another vibrating, echoing sound. The airport? Was it a plane landing, taking off?

"Who did you go upstairs with, this morning?"

"No one."

"Yeah, right."

"I take the girls home, Eve. That is all."

"I'll bet."

"You just have a very conventional sense of home, that is the problem."

"I don't want to go home."

"Of course not. You are still in flight."

And you are trying to shoot me down, I answered silently.

"Considering your background, it is perfectly understandable," he went on. "All this is new to you. Perhaps I know what you are going through, more than the others, since I, too, was raised in a cult. The cult of Communism."

My brain was already loose from its moorings, drifting, getting slapped back against the dock but no longer tied to it, knocking once and then sailing out, a little further each time.

"Eve, are you asleep?"

"Of course not."

" 'Of course,' again."

"What do you mean, conducting business? Aren't we your business?"

"You? You bring in almost nothing. You in particular, with your lying cheating ways. I see you secreting funds in your pants pocket."

"We don't have pants pockets."

"Yes, exactly. Why do you think I have you dress that way? Most women would be too modest to pad their buttocks with filthy dollar bills. But in answer to your question, the bar at best breaks even. I could make ten times more having you all sit in a room providing phone sex."

"What is phone sex, anyway?" I yawned. There was this blurry boundary where today became yesterday. I was surrounded by it now. This fog. "I've always wondered."

"Phone sex is something remarkably similar to this, if you must know."

"Why do you call me, Viktor?"

"To see if you are all right."

"And am I? All right?"

"To see that you got home."

"I don't want to go home."

"You sound strange. Did something happen?"

"No. I was dreaming, that's all."

"Sleep, Eve."

And then I thought he—I know it sounds crazy—I thought he kissed me. It was just a sound, that soft touching of the lips. It could have been anything. What I wanted to hear. What I feared hearing. The only reason I knew the call was real at all was because when I woke, hours later, drenched in sweat, panicked, in the late afternoon, the cord was wrapped around my throat, strangling me, and the telephone was making that siren sound, with a lady's patient voice repeating over and over, "The receiver is off the hook. Please hang up. The receiver is off the hook . . ."

It was an Opening.

I climbed the steep steps to the second-floor gallery. Someone had sent me an invitation. I didn't understand how that was possible. It was the first piece of personal mail I had ever gotten. I came to find out who sent it. Otherwise you couldn't have dragged me there. I didn't like art. I had been to the museum and seen all the famous paintings. They were pretty, I guess. But it was obvious that what made everyone stand around gaping was their being worth several billion dollars. "You can go on the street," I felt like announcing. "Go anywhere and see visions far more magical. People breathing. The sun on a pigeon's neck. And you can really have those. They can be yours alone, for nothing. All you have to do is tear your eyes away from money!"

After a while, someone came over and explained I was in the Gift Shop, but when I got to the real thing I felt the same. It was Idolatry.

I looked at the name printed on the wall just inside the door, the same as the one on the postcard, which wasn't even a real name, just like, when I went in farther, the paintings weren't even real paintings.

"I took a picture of my vagina," this woman was saying, "and had it blown up, poster-size. Then I rented advertising space in five subway stations. I left the photos up a month, until they were covered with graffiti, then took them down, had them framed, and hung them in the gallery."

"You took a picture of your vagina?" someone asked.

"And blew it up, poster-size," she said. "Then I rented advertising space in five subway stations."

I kept walking. There were lots of people. They were all talking to each other, trying not to make eye contact with the "art" they had supposedly come to see. But there was a sculpture in the middle of the room, too, so their looks kept running this optical obstacle course, shifting everywhere, then flitting nervously away. I found myself pushed to that one open spot made by everyone else's turned back. It was a display of soap dishes, the porcelain kind that are built into the bathroom wall, but they were chiseled out and sat on pedestals with the soap still inside, not fresh bars, but used, different shapes and colors. I had no idea what it was supposed to be. At least they smelled nice, all the perfumes, and that one green detergenty kind.

"You're next."

I looked up. The person wasn't talking to me but to this guy standing next to me. I mean *right next* to me. He had just appeared. He was tall and very thin so you could imagine him moving without a sound, even over the creaking shiny wood floor. But what made me jump was that he was suddenly so close, way inside that invisible border you put up.

The man who was talking to him looked like a jerk. The tall guy must have thought so, too, because he didn't even answer, just nodded.

"Are you done? Have you even started?"

It took him a long time to think of what to say. And then he just came out with, "Not yet."

The questioner walked away. I thought he was going to talk to me now, because he was practically standing on my foot, but instead he stared at the soap. So I stared at him. He was lanky. I never really understood that word before but somehow I knew this must be it. He was made of parts that fit together, one after the other, and they moved smoothly, like they were very well oiled. Two long legs, a narrow waist, a torso, two arms, all separate somehow, but perfectly matched. Oh, I thought to myself. A body.

"That's mine," he said, without looking up.

"Of course it is." I thought he meant his hand, which I couldn't take my eyes off of. It had these . . . fingers.

"That's my soap."

He pointed to a round one, the smallest of all, just that

last bit in the middle that doesn't dissolve anymore, that you can't get rid of. I tried to think of a profound comment, to show what a deep thinker I was.

"You must be very clean."

He had sandy hair and mild eyes. He was one of those people who have never been worried in their entire life, who have seen everything coming from ten miles off and are just waiting, patiently. For you.

"Marron came to my studio with a hammer and screwdriver and asked if she could use my bathroom. She didn't say what for."

"Who?" I asked, but casually made it sound, through this peculiar talent I have, like, Want to go out sometime? He had the most beautiful haircut I had ever seen. Different parts of him kept revealing themselves. His kindness. His generosity. It was nothing special, the haircut, but it was amazing. I could see every hair. They were all the same length. I was afraid I would reach out and touch it but then realized I already had, in my mind. I was rubbing against it like a cat.

"Marron." He nodded somewhere. "She didn't even tell me what she'd done. I just saw the hole, later."

"You have a studio?"

He nodded like, Doesn't everybody?

It was sandalwood. I bent over, pretending to admire the display of soaps, and his soap in particular, but really because I was afraid I was looking as naked as I felt. All at once I understood that what I had been smelling all my life—from one minute ago when he stood so close to me, closer than any human being has ever stood to another—was sandalwood.

"Are you a friend of Marron's?"

The problem was that, even though I was ready to give

myself to him utterly, I couldn't understand a single word he said. Was he a foreigner?

"What. Is. A. Marron?" I asked slowly.

"Marron McKee. The artist. She's over there."

I looked past him. It was the same woman I had gone by on my way in. She was pretty, with dyed blond hair, like a cake that has really fancy icing but isn't good to eat.

"I took a picture of my vagina," she was saying.

It was amazing how she could say "vagina" over and over again without getting embarrassed.

"No. I don't know her. I don't know anyone."

"Marron's very talented."

All right, so he had a flaw. But being intelligent just got in the way, most of the time. I would do the thinking for both of us. It would be this delicious burden.

"Horace."

He stuck out his hand. He was formal, but not shy.

"So you're an artist?"

"I paint."

"I love painting."

Oh, Eve, I thought.

I wish I could say we had this great conversation, but it was the opposite. He asked about me a little, which was nice, but I totally ran down what I did, made fun of it. I must have sounded like the most uninteresting person on the planet. There was this tension, which was actually the best part, this stumbling awkwardness we kept trying to overcome. Not boredom or that desperate urge to get away, at least not for me. I couldn't tell what he was thinking. He was very polite and had an atmosphere to him, a world you could walk into, if you took just one more step. I kept sneaking quick breaths and holding them, like he was a drug.

"What do you do when you're not working?"

"I just lie around, basically."

. . . with no clothes on.

He nodded like that was a perfectly acceptable activity, doing nothing.

"But why am I here?" I went on. "That's what I have to find out. I got an invitation. This postcard."

"What's so unusual about that?"

"I'm not supposed to get mail. Everything else that comes is just junk, or bills for the person before me."

He frowned.

"See, I don't really exist. In the city."

"Apparently you do."

"But I don't know anyone."

"You must be on the list."

"What list?"

"Everyone has a mailing list. Whenever they're in a show, they send out invitations. Marron has almost a thousand names. She's very focused."

Right, I thought. On her vagina.

"Would you like to meet her?"

Are you out of your mind? I smiled, which he must have heard as "Sure," because he started walking over, going in front of me.

I reset my face, found a new expression, a bored, unblinking, challenging look like, I love your lover. I found strength. It was surprising, because the rest of me was falling down a hole, but on the outside I was putting on this act, walking the walk and talking the talk, I hoped, of a New Yorker. This girl, Marron, I finally figured out (I had this incredible lag in understanding, it was probably already tomorrow), it was her artwork, her Opening. She stood in front of a huge black-and-white-speckled photograph that was covered with scribbles, stains, swear words, even dirty drawings in Magic Marker. It was exactly what you looked through, not really noticing, when you were reading movie posters, waiting for a train. She was dressed very properly. I knew the type. Guys found her attractive because, without their knowing it, she looked just like their mothers once did. But when she turned, I almost took a step back. She had serious eyes. There were flowers at her feet. People had brought bouquets. She was standing on them.

"Marron, this is—"

Before Horace could blow it, say something in front of her that would give away the incredible power of our new relationship, that he loved me so much he couldn't even remember my name, I saved him. I stuck out my hand and said, "Eve."

"Eve what?"

"Just Eve."

She stared at me.

"Do you model?" she finally asked.

I had heard that line so many times from guys at the bar. Usually it made me laugh. But coming from a woman, it completely tripped me up.

"Me? No."

"You look like someone."

"Well, I'm not. I mean, not anyone in particular. Maybe I'm trying to look like some model without realizing it. You know how you see an ad in a magazine and then how if the person looks even just a little bit like you, you make this big effort to look more like her? Because she's in a magazine? So by the end you can't tell if . . ."

. . . can't tell if what? I panicked. I didn't know what I was talking about. What was happening? At the bar I was usually considered the smart one, at least by me. Plus, as usual, it wasn't even true. I had never done that, seen a picture in a magazine and then thought it looked like me. I didn't even read magazines anymore. They were evil. Then I realized she was joking, making fun of me. Do you model? And I had taken it seriously. I tried changing the subject.

"So, didn't it fog up?"

"What?"

I pointed to the big photograph.

"The camera. The lens."

She turned and looked with me for a moment. She had a nice head, on a very long neck, like a swan, which are actually snakes, I remembered thinking, the first time I saw them. Swans were snakes that had grown feathers and turned their ugliness to beauty, but they were still creepy. A creepy beauty, that's what she had. And anyway, what kind of name was Marron?

"I wanted them to respond," she said, as if I had asked a completely different question. She had these memorized speeches. You could tell by the way she delivered them in a singsong voice. "To respond without knowing it. To manipulate a response. I mean, it doesn't look like me. It's completely abstract when you enlarge it that much. Just dots. But look how sexual what they wrote and drew is. Like they were enthralled."

"Who's they? Men?"

"Men and women. The Male Gaze. We all look at things through the eyes of men. Whether we admit it or not."

"I don't."

"Then you do, if you think you don't. It's only when you realize you do, that you might not. I wanted to show a glimpse of the world. The world we live in, not the world we make."

I had no idea what she was talking about. I was the foreigner, I realized. Our eyes met. Or rather, mine looked into hers, which were just these empty suckholes, devouring everything. Then they turned away. I didn't exist anymore. They'd gotten what they wanted, which was the admission that I was an idiot, I suppose. More people came. With roses. Calling her a genius. She took the flowers and cradled them in her arms. I watched the thorns rub against her skin. It was a contest, who was going to scratch who. While they talked to her, I managed to slip away, but just as I reached the door I heard her call.

"Eve!" It surprised me, that she remembered my name.

I waved like I had to go, which suddenly I realized I did. I was late. It's weird how lies, the lies I told myself, at least, really turned out to be the truth. Did that mean the things I took for granted as true were really lies? She gave me one last ultra-intense stare.

"Scc you," she said, then smiled, like she wanted to be friends.

It wasn't until I was outside, three blocks away, that I stopped dead, so suddenly the momentum pitched me forward. She had hypnotized me! She had made me walk out forgetting all about him, the love of my life, the handsome man who was tall and smelled of sandalwood. What was his name again? Horace. How could I have done that? And where had he gone? While I was talking to that cold bitch whose cunt was all over the subway, he had disappeared! Just as miraculously as he had materialized by my side in front of those bars of soap. I shook my head. He had been trying to ditch me. That's why he led me over there. I must have been boring him stiff with my talk about lying on the couch all day doing nothing. I thought I had been in love, for maybe fifteen minutes, but now I saw it was more like a seizure. I had wanted to love so badly that I had taken it out on some innocent bystander. Like those crazy people who go berserk and shoot up a commuter train, except I did it with my heart, and to myself.

Bars are just rooms. That's what most people don't realize. They think they're these special places, full of possibility. Viktor's was a cellar, though when I once called it that he was annoyed. "This? This is a garden apartment." He looked over the place proudly. It was a cellar. You went down steps to get to it. It was in a house on a side street off Times Square, ordinary from the outside. Tourists were buzzed in and then had to duck, so they had this bowed, hunched quality when they appeared. There was one big space with tables, chairs, a jukebox, and, instead of windows, posters of the city. The Empire State Building. The Statue of Liberty. There was a bar, but no register, just an adding machine with a roll of tape, and a cash box. It would have been so easy to steal, except Viktor watched. Even when making drinks, he stared. You got the sense he was monitoring every transaction. Our big claim to fame was that We Never Close. Which wasn't true. But we did stay open way past the last legal places that had signs, and doors on the street, and liquor licenses, until five, sometimes six in the morning. Viktor paid those bartenders to tell their customers where to go. Sometimes they came in, too, the bartenders. They got to drink for free. But mostly it was conventioneers from Kansas City, college kids, French people or Germans. We were a tourist trap.

I got there in a bad mood, a little late, not much, and no one else had come before me. Still, he was furious. The room in back was stacked with cases of beer and boxes of liquor bottles. You could see through a dirty window to the "garden"

Viktor had talked about. It was this completely wild junkyard, about the size of a postage stamp, with big chunks of cement overgrown by three-foot-high weeds. People hung their clothes on lines or off fire escapes. From that far down I could look straight up and see underwear flutter, glow, in the night.

"Eve!"

"I'm coming."

I tried not to look at myself. There was no mirror, but I tried to not even look down. The heels were the worst. I hated the sound they made, like I weighed two hundred pounds.

"I don't like you looking," he called.

"Well I don't like you looking."

"I don't look. I—"

I opened the door. He was blocking my way. Whatever he was going to say he stopped, then stepped to one side.

"What?" I asked.

"You look nice," he said.

"Yeah, right."

I swept past him.

It wasn't fair. I wanted to choose. Was that such a crime? To want some control? It seemed to me that if you loved someone they should love you back. I mean it was just common courtesy. But reality was almost the exact opposite. Loving someone pushed him away, and then when he withdrew he left this vacuum and Mr. Wrong got sucked in, liking you because you were busy loving someone else. It made no sense.

Viktor got back on his high stool, his little throne, and watched me do chores, set out ashtrays, wipe off the smudged top of the jukebox. I knew all the songs, not by title but by what buttons to push. B11. J18. M2. It was like quoting

Scripture, the snippets of music that went through my head. I smiled, thinking how far from God I was. Though everything I did—it was all so ritualized—still had for me a religious significance. Even the feeling of Viktor's stare as I bent over to wad napkins under a shaky table leg.

"What?" he asked.

"Nothing."

"I said you looked nice."

"Exactly. I look nice to you."

He scratched his arm. He was such an unattractive man. It was almost a selling point. You knew you weren't being blinded by beauty.

"Look at me," I said, straightening up, forcing myself to do just that. Here, mirrors were all over, reflecting each other, to hide the ugly surroundings. Everywhere you looked you saw a million of you getting smaller and smaller, being minced by a giant knife. "I'm dressed this way, in clothes you picked out, and you said I looked nice."

"So if I said you looked bad, that would be a compliment?"

"Yeah. I guess." I looked around for something else to do. I really wanted to quit. I think he sensed it, too. I was tired of losing arguments.

"It is a job," he said gently. "You dress in provocative clothes. It has nothing to do with anything."

I was trying not to cry. A bottle had rolled into the corner. We'd missed it, cleaning up last night. It lay there. I focused all my attention on it.

"Where I come from," he went on, "there is a flower you pick. It is quite common. It is used as a symbol. A message. You put it in your hair if you are a woman. In the lapel of your jacket if you are a man."

"And what does it mean?"

"That you like to be fucked up the ass."

I started laughing. I don't know why. Viktor maintained this perfect poker face, but I could tell he was pleased. I couldn't stop. Brandy came in. First her heels, then her legs, then, much later, the rest of her.

"What?" she asked. "What's so funny?"

I tried to breathe, but that just made it worse. Tears were rolling down my cheeks. I was so far from God.

"What is it, Eve?" Brandy demanded.

"Eve is happy," Viktor said.

When I first came to the city, I hadn't been anywhere besides a tiny religious colony in the middle of Iowa since I was seven years old. I knew there were all these mistakes I could make, all these traps out there, waiting for me. I also knew I had come for a reason, that I was on a mission, though a mission to do what I couldn't have told you. So I wasn't scared. It would descend on me, a sense of purpose, of vocation. All I had to do was live my life.

I started looking for a job right away. Even stocking shelves at one of those fake drugstores, the kind that doesn't have a pharmacist in back, sounded exciting. You got to use a price gun and wear this blue smock with a nameplate. EVE. I really wanted to see my name in raised letters. But when they asked, "Eve who?" I didn't know what to do. Lie, of course, part of me said. Look around and choose something, anything. Eve Candy. Eve Wart Remover. Eve Incredibly-Gross-Looking-Boss. But I couldn't. My mind went blank. I was so good at naming the world, but I couldn't name me. That had to come from outside. Anything I chose would diminish me, make me less special, more like them. "Just Eve," I repeated, and they looked. I saw this wedge being driven between my life and the normal daytime world. But I couldn't help it. I couldn't betray me. Not for $5.50 an hour.

That's why, when Viktor came up in a coffee shop and started talking, saying how he saw I was looking at the Help Wanted ads and that he knew about a job, my heart gave a little leap.

"It is not regular," he warned. "It is off the books."

"What does that mean?"

"It means I do not want to know about you."

"I already told you, I'm Eve."

"Yes, but that is all I want to know."

"Why?"

"For legal reasons. We pay cash at the bar. Nothing exists on paper. I do not want to know your last name, your zip code, your age . . ." He looked me over. "Especially your age."

"I'm sixteen."

". . . or anything else personal. In fact, it would be better if you came up with another first name entirely."

"Like what?"

"Something sexy. We already have a Brandy and a Crystal. The girl you are replacing, her name was Amber. Do you want to be Amber, too? That would be convenient."

"I'm Eve," I reminded him.

"Yes, I see that."

I could tell he was already having second thoughts. I needed the money. I had been wasting my savings on the dormitory room of a scary hotel. I was almost broke, so I went on quickly, "What do I have to do on this job, anyway?"

"Nothing you don't want."

"How do you know what I want?"

"I said nothing you *don't* want. What you do want is another area with which I am not concerned."

"But you came over here," I pointed out. "You're the one who decided to talk to me."

"So I did."

And that was how I got started, how I found my way. Before, New York was all locked doors and shut faces. Once I began to work at the bar, everything else fell into place. I heard about an apartment that wasn't legal either. It was too high a walkup for fire code regulations, so there wasn't a lease or a security deposit. It even had electricity and a phone, from the last tenant, which I continued to pay. To me it was perfect. I was here and not-here. The first week, I cleaned and decorated. I felt like I was discovering my true self. I began to go out and walked for miles. One day I looked up and the city wasn't a maze anymore. It was an island. The streets ended in sky.

"It has to do with past lives," Crystal explained. "See, there are these points where something in your present life connects with something in your past. A face. Or the way someone talks. And then it's like a door you go through. Suddenly you're existing out of time. It's a portal."

"Portal to what?" Viktor wanted to know.

"The Infinite."

"You mean past lives like when you were a kid? Or past lives like ancient Egypt?" I asked.

"That depends."

"Depends on what?"

"How evolved you are."

She put three bottles of beer on her tray and walked off. Viktor shook his head.

"Crystal is a Buddhist."

"She is not." Brandy was very loyal. "She's a Scorpio."

"But that can't be falling in love," I argued. "Then it's totally random. Just a big coincidence. Someone looks a certain way, or does something special, without even realizing it, and you fall in love because of that?"

More people came. I got up. Customers had to be led in. That was the rule. They usually hesitated when they actually saw the place. It was so run-down and unexotic. Just candles flickering in bowls, posters, the jukebox, and their fellow tourists, eyeing them as they arrived, thinking maybe these were the real Manhattanites, the subterraneans coming out after midnight and living wild lives of sexual perversion. Personally, I would have thought encountering one of us, a bored, bleary-eyed girl in gold nylon pants, black stockings, and a scoop-necked top, would have been the last straw, that they would have run up the sagging wooden steps two at a time back to their nice clean hotel room, which at least had cable and a little refrigerator and more opportunities for genuine sin than anything they could find here. But they never did. Viktor told us to walk up to them, not say a word, not smile, just turn right around again and lead them to a table. "And don't look to see if they are following." The first few times, I was sure they had left, that I was making a fool of myself. When I got to the table I was always shocked to see them right behind me.

"It is the Air of Mystery you project."

"You mean it's my ass," I had realized by then.

He looked hurt.

"Why talk that way? You say 'hips,' don't you?"

"We say 'hips' but we mean ass."

"Ah. Well, then I say, 'Air of Mystery.' And don't you think I should know? After all, I am a man."

But I wasn't sure about that. He liked to hang out with us and listen to our conversations. He liked to talk about things, which I wasn't used to in men. American men. I took the new people's orders and came back.

"Then you have no control. It's all just a big accident, like a car crash."

"It's fate," Crystal said. "You're fated to love someone."

"But are they fated to love you back?"

She had thick shoulders. It was funny she acted so mystical because she was actually the toughest, most take-charge of all of us. Her legs were always set slightly apart like she was daring you to try pushing her over. She put her hands on her hips a lot. She had this piggish look of defiance. She thought we were making fun of her, though we never did. She had enormous breasts and guys stared at her.

"It isn't about *him*," Brandy tried to make me understand, like I was the idiot.

"Of course it's about him. He's everything. He's how you're going to live, and where, and even what kind of meals you're going to eat at night. He is the *color* to every object."

The jukebox was playing. S15. I noticed because no one else was talking. They were all looking at me.

Finally, Nora announced, "I need a Rob Roy."

"Who," Viktor asked, not turning, "ordered a Rob Roy?"

"No one. I said *I* need a Rob Roy."

"It is not a drink with which I am familiar."

"Just give me a scotch."

She stared across at me. She didn't usually talk. She was so much older. None of us understood what she was doing here, either from her side of it or Viktor's. She couldn't have made much money (when customers bought her a drink she drank it, a double), and he couldn't have gotten much satisfaction bossing her around. She did what he said, but acted like she didn't have to, like she was humoring this little boy. When she got up, even after sitting for just a minute, she always stretched, a long yawning stretch like she had just woken from a really great dream. She was still spectacular-looking. She really could have modeled, even though guys never tried that line on her. But her face, beautiful as it was, had this tragic-roadmap look to it. You could see all the broken promises, the bad decisions, a whole season of suffering.

"So anyway," Brandy went on, which you'd think would have been the start of a sentence, but you would have been wrong.

She teetered off to lead in another customer. The place was beginning to fill up.

"And of whom do I remind you?"

"What?"

I had fallen asleep. It happened, even after all this time. I wasn't totally on nights. I would close my eyes, skid off into a dream, then jerk awake, usually in the act of tumbling off a stool or walking into a wall.

"Clearly I remind you of someone. That is why you react to me so wiolently."

Crystal had gone off, too. Nora was there, but he talked this way in front of her. I noticed that if you didn't make any noise yourself, people acted as if you weren't there, like if you couldn't talk, you couldn't hear, either. I fantasized about being one of those silent mysterious types, but I could never keep my mouth shut.

"Why did you pick me, anyway?"

He took it the wrong way.

"I did not pick you for nothing, missy."

"No, I mean for working here. Why did you offer me this job?"

Brandy came back with an order.

"Just a minute." Viktor held up his hand like a traffic cop. "You were trembling and desperate and reading the Employment section of the newspaper upside down, as I recall."

"That's not what I meant. I mean why me? Everyone else here is pretty."

Nora was still sitting, sipping her drink, looking right past me, through the wall, through the dirty window, to the junkyard garden in back.

"I need a Long Island Iced Tea," Brandy said.

"Go to your station," he snapped.

"My station?"

Maybe I just wanted to be scared. Maybe that was the attraction, if there was one. There was this anger in Viktor, bristling like the hair on his shoulders or his stupid mustache, and I was the one who made it come out. It was my specialty.

"I suppose," he actually considered, "I chose you for your gamine quality."

"My what?"

"Shit! Doesn't anyone in this country receive an education? Because you look like a boy, of course."

"Oh. Well, thanks a lot."

"Where I come from, that is high praise."

"Where do you come from, anyway?"

He would never tell. I had assumed it was Russia, but once he corrected me. It was one of those "former Soviet republics."

"You could not pronounce it."

"Try me."

"Someday," he threatened, scooping ice with his hand.

I watched him. He knew more than I did. About life. I could learn from him. Steal his knowledge. If he didn't steal something of mine, first.

But what if our dreams are aware of each other? What if they interact, inhabit a World, just as our waking moments do? Then there would exist a true "night life" of fear and fantasy, memory and premonition, ruled by laws so unknowable it would be wishful to call them laws at all. A parody of day. Or maybe its blueprint.

A truck went by with no back, a big open cube. It slowed. A man inside pushed out bales of something. They landed softly, tumbled a few feet before coming to a stop. Another man, in a knit cap and a long white robe, emerged from a newsstand and gathered them in. He frowned, seeing me reach into my pocket for money, then took out a razor and slit the plastic strip. The papers, no longer under pressure, rose. I took one. The newsprint was cold and fresh. I peeled back the first page.

"What you looking for?" he asked.

"I don't know," I said, checking all the sections.

A murder? A rape? A dream?

I had this composition book, the kind kids used for school, with that black-and-white speckled front. I bought it to write letters, but when I opened it saw I had made a mistake. It didn't have lines. It was just blank pages, more like a sketch pad. Still, I tried.

Dear Mother,

That was usually as far as I got, words slanting across the open space. This time I went further:

I was going to write you. I was going to begin, "No, I haven't fallen off the edge of the earth," but now, looking around, I think maybe I have.

CHAPTER TWO

"So whenever she opens a present and says something, the maid of honor writes it down. Like, 'It's just what I wanted,' or, 'It's beautiful.' Then, when the shower is over, they give her the list, and those are the things the bride is supposed to say to the groom on her wedding night."

We all nodded. Except Viktor.

It was Brandy's birthday. We had stayed, the four of us, after work. At 5 A.M. there was no place else to go. We brought things. I was very proud of my contribution. Viktor had scooped himself some but wasn't eating.

"It's called trifle. I got it from a recipe, sort of. Except I couldn't find raspberries. So I had to substitute."

"Substitute what?"

"Frozen artichoke hearts."

Brandy was sitting with her shoes kicked off. For once she wasn't flipping her hair like she had this private wind to contend with. She was tired from the night's work, the center of attention but not really up for it. It made her seem sweet. One of us. Or maybe I felt like one of them, for a change.

"How old are you?" I asked.

"Eighteen, I guess."

"You guess?"

"Yup. Eighteen." She drew it in the air with one finger. "And I always will be, as long as I can stay awake."

"Oh."

I got it. So tomorrow, about to happen any minute, was her real birthday.

Crystal gave her the present.

"We all chipped in."

I listened for what Brandy said.

"That is so sweet."

That is so sweet, I imagined saying, seeing my husband naked for the first time.

"It's wild!"

It's wild! I mouthed, as he took me in his arms.

"If it's too big, you can return it."

"Too big? Are you crazy? It's perfect!" she screamed. "I'm never going to take it off! Oh my God, I'm going to die!"

"Look at Eve."

Viktor finally took a bite. His teeth crunched on something. I hadn't completely defrosted the artichoke hearts because I thought they would keep it cold.

"Incredible," he pronounced carefully.

"I like frozen foods. They're so manageable. The way they come in individual plastic packets. Or in boxes with those beautiful pictures on the outside? These ideas of meals.

Three things on a plate, not touching, not running into each other, so at the border they don't form a fourth thing, and then a fifth thing, this whole meal of glop that dribbles through your fork. I mean that's more like what happens in real life, don't you think?"

"You look, when you blush, like a rose red."

"Jesus, Viktor."

He had been drinking. Which was unusual. But this was a special occasion. He took another bite. I listened. *Crunch crunch crunch.*

"I was married," Nora said.

We all turned. She was nursing a white wine. She'd made Viktor open a bottle. She held her glass by the stem, with two fingers, and tick-tocked it back and forth. The wine swished from one side of the rim to the other, but never spilled.

"Did you have a shower?"

"Kind of. My husband tricked me. He knew I wouldn't want one, so he said we were going someplace. His sister's house. He opened the door, let me walk in first, and shut it behind me. Then he drove away. I remember hearing his car." She paused, hearing it. "My car, actually."

"A surprise shower." Brandy held up her bracelet. "How romantic."

"Did they do that trick?" I asked. "Writing down what you said after each present?"

"All they gave me was a Bible. The kind that zips."

The Word of God, I imagined saying, as he forced me down on the bed. Forced? No, that wasn't right.

We danced. Just the girls. Viktor put the jukebox on a free setting where it played all the selections, in order. We'd moved the tables to sweep up, so there was space. I don't know who started it. Nobody, really. It was spontaneous. Crystal bumped me, on purpose, in a kind of aggressive, friendly way. And Brandy got this sudden burst of energy.

"It's my birthday," she kept saying, trying to convince herself.

It wasn't an orgy or anything, but we were all dancing with each other. I remember Nora's hair, my face passing through it, we were so close, this thick, strange-smelling forest. Henna. Nile mud. Crystal's way of moving was to try and bulldoze you off the floor. I leaned forward, against her, and stopped us. She looked up, surprised at how strong I could be. Brandy stood in one spot, bopping her arms and legs, eyes closed, nodding her head, sinking deeper and deeper into herself, into this trance. We all ended up dancing around her, like priestesses.

"What are you going to do the rest of the day?" I asked later, while we waited upstairs for Viktor.

"Oh, I don't know." Brandy was back to her old self. She looked around, harassed, trying to avoid photographers. "There's this yoga class we go to sometimes."

"We?"

"Crystal and me."

"Do you change?"

Brandy looked down at me like I was crazy.

"Well, don't they wear the same kind of clothes in a yoga class as we do here?"

"Of course we change, Eve. What kind of nut do you think I am? It's completely different, yoga and here."

"I know. But the clothes—"

"For one thing, we wear leg warmers. Don't we, Cris?"

Crystal smiled.

"You're the one who's so weird about changing."

"I'm not weird. I just like to get back into my own clothes, after. What's so weird about that?"

"Listen to you. 'My own clothes.' These *are* your own clothes, silly. I mean, you paid for them, didn't you? And you wash them, right? Anyway, you didn't change today."

"No," I said. "Today I forgot."

We were waiting between the inner and outer doors. When Viktor's car finally appeared, we ran. None of us wanted to be outside. We were sea creatures hurrying between one shell and the next. Once we were in the backseat again, we relaxed.

All these possibilities, I thought, watching Nora's shoulders bounce going over a pothole, feeling Crystal's body, smelling Brandy's perfume. Their presence was so strong. They were these paths to take, ways to be. Even though I knew I couldn't take any of them myself. I couldn't be anyone but the freakish mutant I was. But still, just having them around was comforting. I loved them.

"So maybe I'll do yoga, too, sometime."

"Sure. If you want."

Nora adjusted the mirror on her side.

"Why do you do that?" Viktor complained.

He was very touchy about his car. She blew a long stream of smoke against the windshield so it clouded right back.

"There's this great instructor. What's his name?"

"Krishna," Crystal supplied.

"The Hero of a Thousand Faces," Viktor called.

"He can sit on his nose."

Her eyes were staring straight at me. Nora's. In the side mirror. It's just a coincidence, I told myself. But she had twisted it that way, so we were seeing each other, even though her back was turned. I couldn't understand why. It's not like she was being friendly. Does she see herself in me? I wondered. That was a chilling thought. I wouldn't want to be her. Although part of me did. If I could be her without paying the price. To be past everything without having suffered. But that was impossible. While they talked, Crystal and Brandy and Viktor, we tried watching each other, keeping this single, unbroken look, both of us bouncing like crazy over the bad streets. He was driving too fast. We kept moving our heads, bracing ourselves, to stay in touch. It was a game. When he slowed down, so did our gaze, until we were perfectly still, locked into each other.

"See you, Eve," a voice said.

"See you," I answered, still staring.

Brandy and Crystal were getting out. Fresh air rushed in.

"Happy birthday," I remembered.

"I'm getting out here, too," Nora announced.

"I'll drive you."

"No, I'm meeting someone."

"Here? Who?"

She slammed the door. They slammed theirs.

"Hey," I said.

Viktor gunned the engine. I was alone with him. How had that happened? He blasted off like a rocket and I was thrown back.

You could see sunrise in the exhaust of other cars. That was the difference between here and the Midwest. Out there, light changed on the horizon. It came at you slowly, in order: purple, red, pink, orange. Here, you were suddenly in the middle of everything. Sunrise was all around, right outside your window. Every color at once. You could reach out and grab a handful, if you weren't going ninety miles an hour.

"Viktor, stop it!"

"Move up. So I do not feel like a chauffeur."

"How can I move up?"

He took a turn so hard I crashed against the door.

"Just climb over the seat."

"I can't."

"Why not? Crawl over the top. As you did when you were a child."

"We never rode in cars when I was a kid."

"Ah yes, I remember now. 'No automobiles in the Bible.' You act as though you are performing some task ordered by God. But mostly what I see you doing is running away."

I came tumbling down and hit his elbow. The car swerved.

"See," he said, "how much better is the view?"

I hadn't ever ridden up front in Manhattan. The city came to life the instant you turned onto a block. Whole scenes appeared, then vanished. Steam came out of a manhole cover. Nora had left her window open. The car was filled with that strong summer morning smell. Really it was fall, middle September, but the air held on to a late, lazy August. What was that smell made of? Coffee. Butter. And something else. We weren't talking. There was a silence, but it wasn't a good silence, it wasn't relaxed. The euphoria of the night, if that's what it had been, the feeling of togetherness, had left along with the others. Now we were back to our own sad sorry selves and I could tell that we both didn't want to be. For a minute, for a whole hour, there had been this melding of personalities.

"How come you keep turning? Why don't you just go up Broadway?"

We were getting stuck at every light, snaking through narrow side streets.

"Shortcut."

"Really? Because it looks like it's taking us longer."

"Shortcuts often do."

"Take longer?"

"In the short run, yes. But in the long run, no. It all depends on where you are going."

"Home."

"I thought you did not want to go home."

"Well, I do now."

More boring sexual tension. I would probably like Viktor if it wasn't for this. Or hate him. But at least I would know where I stood. It was all so complicated and all about nothing. We were one of those knots you pull tight and it disappears, becomes a piece of string.

"I am not a citizen."

I yawned, grateful to him for changing the subject. Although really, the subject was all in my head, wasn't it? Nothing had been said. It's not like we'd ever done anything. I couldn't be light. Lighthearted. That was my problem. People talked about flirting like it was this totally acceptable form of behavior. Like it could be fun. Or dating, which was apparently this carefree laugh-a-minute time you had, in which case I had never been on a date, because for me it instantly turned into a matter of life or death. Mostly death. Why was I making such a big deal out of this? Viktor acted the same exact way with the other girls. I just took it too seriously. I glanced over and saw, in the morning light, how much older he looked. His mustache was dark, but some of the hairs on his shoulders were already gray.

"I came here years ago. As a student."

"A student?"

"I still consider myself one, in essence. A student of human nature. But not affiliated."

He tapped the steering wheel. He wore a ring. With this hideous, plastic-looking stone. I'd never really looked at it before. Guys shouldn't wear jewelry, I thought.

"Not affiliated," he repeated. "So I never got a green card."

He said it like "blue sky."

"What's that?"

"It is a card so you can work. Legitimately. It is why I started the bar. No one would hire me."

"Same here."

"Hardly. You exile yourself by choice, not necessity. For me it is question of status."

I yawned again. We were almost home.

"Thank you for eating my trifle. You're the only one who did."

"It was good of you to make food yourself. Everything else was store-bought."

I smiled.

"Could we be friends, Viktor? I could really use a friend."

"Will you marry me?"

He made a wide sweeping curve and my street appeared. By magic. I looked for me on the sidewalk, then remembered I was here, in the car.

"It's halfway down."

"So I recall."

We pulled up to the curb and stopped. He turned off the engine. We sat.

"You heard me?"

"No." I shook my head. "Not really."

"It is a formality, on one level. By marrying you I would automatically receive citizenship. But of course there are other considerations."

"Is that why you've been nice to me? Because you wanted to get married?"

"Well." He looked confused. "It is a good reason to be nice, yes? Because you wish to marry someone?"

I sighed and wished I could keep on sighing until all the air went out of me. I wanted to collapse in on myself, get small, invisible.

"That's the stupidest thing I ever heard," I said, while another voice, inside me, the voice that monitored things on a kind of delay, was whispering, Wait. He asked you to *marry* him.

For legal reasons. Or illegal reasons, really.

No. He said that was part of it. *On one level.*

Oh, give me a break.

"We don't even like each other, Viktor. Why don't you ask Brandy? She's crazy about you."

"You do not marry someone because you like them."

"You don't?"

"Your language is incredibly obtuse when it comes to love and like. Half the time you use them interchangeably, and half the time you make them distinct. When it suits you. It is the reason for your high divorce rate, I think."

You see? the voice went on. It's this way he has of pretending he doesn't care. That it's all some scam. Because he can't bring himself to say it. But in a way, that proves he really feels it.

Really feels what?

That he's madly, passionately in love with you.

I got out of the car. He got out, too, and came around. My heart sank.

"Eve!"

"I'm going upstairs."

"But you haven't said no yet."

"Oh, so you knew I was going to say no the whole time." That got me mad. "Then why did you even bother to ask?"

"I assumed you would say no, at first."

"At first. And then what were you going to do?"

He kissed me.

I burned myself once. On a stove. It had electric coils. I was used to gas. I leaned back and put my hand down and, instead of jerking away, the way it would from a flame, my flesh just sank in. That's what this reminded me of, how he took my wrists, pulled them behind my back, and burned himself into me. Before I had a chance to know what was happening.

"Mingrelia," he pronounced wetly, in my ear.

"What?"

"I am from Mingrelia. On the Euxine Sea."

I was pinned against the front of his car. His hands were all over me, but they couldn't get in, which was his own fault. He had picked the outfit. I sighed and thought, we better go upstairs or I'm going to bend his precious hood ornament and then he'll be furious. It's funny, but I actually would have slept with him, right then and there, based on not damaging a little chrome statuette, if someone hadn't cleared his throat. Loud. We tried ignoring it, but whoever it was did it again. Right next to us. To make us stop.

An angry-looking man in a suit and tie was standing in front of my building. He was black, with a shaved head. I hadn't noticed him when we parked.

"Miss America?" he said.

"What?"

"You are," he accused, looking right at me, "Miss America."

Oh, great. A lunatic.

I pushed Viktor away. I'd had it. Hearing voices? No problem. Admiring giant photographs of a vagina? I could handle it. Marry a man I found physically and morally repulsive? Why not? All those things were kind of normal, when you thought about it. Part of growing up. But being called Miss America: for some reason, that was going too far.

Even stranger than this crazy person standing there was Viktor's reaction. Instead of going over and punching him, which is what I was afraid he would do, or maybe what I was hoping he would do, he just stood, shifting from one foot to the other.

"It's OK, it's OK," he said nervously.

"No it isn't. Did you hear what he just called me?"

"Eve—"

"I am *not* Miss America."

"Shh, Eve. Of course you are."

He put his arm around me. I knocked it off. Kissing was allowed. Gross pawing, even, was allowed. Hand-on-the-shoulder was not. Why?

"It is *politsiya*," he explained.

"It's who?"

"I'm Detective Jourdain," the man said. "New York Police Department. You reported witnessing a robbery last week?"

Viktor was actually sweating. I had never seen anything like it before.

"Oh. That was a mistake. I didn't really see anything."

"We've been trying to get in touch with you, Miss America."

"I haven't been answering my phone."

"Which is why I came in person. Couldn't find you on the buzzer, either. So when I heard your friend here say 'Eve,' I took a chance that you were—"

"It's not 'Eve America.' I told that policeman I was 'Native American.' "

He looked at me.

"Not that I am, really. That's just what I told him. Of course, I guess we're Native American. In a way."

He took out a pad.

". . . except him."

I nodded at Viktor, who was trying to slip back into his car.

"Bye," I called. "Thanks for the ride."

"Yah," he said.

He was playacting. He gave this stiff, phony wave. I leaned in the open window. He was having trouble with the key.

"I'll think about it."

"Think about what?"

"You know."

"Oh. Right." He'd forgotten. "Good luck."

Good luck?

He drove off extra slow, like he didn't want to get a ticket.

The building had thick cement steps. Usually there were kids hanging out, but it was too early. This man—I still didn't believe he was a detective—unbuttoned his jacket, sat, and started writing. I breathed in the warm air. Rotting garbage. That was the other smell of summer in the city. Coffee, butter, and the trash, before it was picked up, cooking in its cans.

"These aren't my clothes."

I looked down at my barmaid outfit. The one time I hadn't changed.

He kept writing.

"I work nights. I just got off. That was my boss. He was giving me a ride home."

I waited. What was he writing?

"You shouldn't have come. That's why I haven't been answering my phone. I didn't want to talk about it. I realized later I didn't really see what I saw."

". . . which was a man and a woman, and he was assaulting her?"

"Well, no. I mean it wasn't clear."

He went back to writing.

In a minute I was going to start to giggle. I could feel this hysteria coming. Which was usually terrifying, but somehow, after what just happened with Viktor, hysteria seemed entirely appropriate. Plus, there was the fact that I was standing here, in gold hot pants, watching this guy scratch notes in a little pad, asking about a dream I had.

"Excuse me, but are you a policeman or a psychiatrist?"

"What did you see, Miss America?"

"Stop calling me that!"

"I apologize. America is a common name, in Spanish."

"It is?"

"I didn't mean to offend."

I felt this tightness in my chest. Now he was going to ask for my real name and it would start all over. The lies. The refusals. But he didn't. He just looked up from the steps. His head seemed extra big because he had no hair. His eyes were bloodshot and his nose was bent to one side, like he'd been punched, long ago, and not healed right.

"Tell me what you saw."

"Nothing, really. I had a dream."

"A dream?"

"Kind of a waking dream. And then . . ."

I thought about it.

"I'm a crank!" I suddenly realized. It was exciting, this great discovery. It answered so many questions I'd been having about myself. "I'm one of those people who go to the police and report things that never happened. I'm sorry. And I got you out here so early, too, just to talk. I suppose that's why we do it, because we're lonely. We cranks."

"Just tell me what happened."

"How can I? When nothing did?"

He looked at me.

I was used to being stared at. Not because I was good-looking. The opposite. Because I was dressed like I was supposed to be good-looking, so there was this gap. Guys either tried making me into more than I was, tried pasting some face or body on top of mine, and then had this sad, disappointed look when it didn't work, when I couldn't support the weight of their fantasies, or, more often, they tried to make me as ugly as possible, magnifying my flaws until I was nothing but a big, red, seething mass of pimples, so they could feel superior to me, I guess. So they could say, She's nothing special. At least that's what I imagined they were thinking, if they were thinking anything at all. But this policeman looked at me in a completely different way.

"Guess what? I just received a proposal of marriage."

"I heard."

"So what do you think? Should I say yes?"

He closed the book and spread his palms on his knees, ready to get up.

"I feel like I'm coming loose," I added hurriedly. "Like the rest of the world is this carved panel in a church, and somehow I've broken off. Like I don't have the wall behind me anymore."

He stopped. I was holding him there. Which I realized was my aim. But I didn't know what to do. I never did. I never knew why I wanted what I did, and when I got it, by accident, I never knew what to do next. Why I didn't want him to go, for example. All I knew was that suddenly, desperately, I didn't want to be alone. I wanted him to look at me that way again.

"Maybe it's because I've been staying up at night and sleeping in the daytime. So I don't have this shared experience of an eight-hour sleep to lean back against. To connect me with everyone else. Instead I feel like I'm becoming a sculpture. Freestanding. Not just a bump in someone else's view of things. You know what I mean?"

I wanted him to say, Yes, he understood. Which was more than I did. But why him? He was nobody. Just this glaring man whose time I was wasting.

"What did you say your name was again?"

"Detective Jourdain." He got up and dusted off the seat of his pants. I'd lost him. "I'm giving you my card. In case you remember."

"Remember what?"

"Well, only you can say what it is you remember. Isn't that right?"

"I guess."

I watched him walk up to Broadway. I liked it that he wore a suit. It was unusual. The kind of men I met didn't wear suits. I kept waiting for him to turn, to look back at me. Even after he was gone.

* * *

"Waiter? There's a roach in my martini."

You have got to stop drinking, I told myself. Especially *before* the date.

I watched the bug struggle through freezing currents of gin, ribbony Gulf Streams of vermouth, toward the Isle of Lemon Peel, those yellow cliffs, always receding.

"Something wrong, miss?"

"No. Nothing."

A mark of authenticity, I decided. Tequila had its worm, a New York drink its roach. I bent low and felt tiny legs kick frantically against my lip.

This was all wrong, from getting to the restaurant on time, going in and asking for him, to letting them seat me, pull out a table, have me balance on one of those uncomfortable cushioned benches. Then they walled me back in so I couldn't move, so I had to wait. What was I doing here? I had wanted to borrow clothes, but none of the girls at work fit me. I wanted it to be someone else's taste, I was so unsure of my own. Finally, I found a thrift shop that was open in the morning. It had dresses downstairs, hundreds of them, all black, and one light cotton jumpsuit, in red. I tried it on and knew. It wasn't so much how it looked but how I felt. Like some kind of superhero. Which was what I needed now, a magic Shield of Confidence. I sat as the minutes passed, watching the flowers in the crystal vase, on the thick white tablecloth, wilt.

He had come to the bar. I didn't even recognize him at first. I just thought, There's a guy who's in the wrong place. But when Brandy went to lead him in, he didn't follow. Instead he talked to her. She came over.

"He says he's a friend of yours."

"Yeah. Right."

I thought she was joking. Then I saw. It was Horace.

He didn't sit. He didn't make any small talk. He didn't seem capable, or maybe he just sensed I couldn't handle it. Standing there, at the foot of the stairs, he asked me if I wanted to have dinner some night. In front of everyone. I didn't even say yes, just wrote down the name and address of the place where we were supposed to meet, totally flustered, like it was a drink order. He didn't seem interested in the bar or what I was wearing, thank God. Not that I could tell. Mostly what I was aware of was this scarlet flush starting at my neck and going all the way up to the tips of my ears. And everyone's eyes on me. When I finished writing, he smiled, said goodbye, and went back up the stairs. I watched *his* ass, which was a switch. His Air of Mystery. Except he really had one. The whole thing couldn't have taken more than two minutes.

That had definitely been the best part. That would definitely *be* the best part. Especially since it looked like he had kept right on going, up the stairs, and then back to SoHo or Paris or wherever hip New York City artists went when they wanted to stand a girl up on what technically might be considered her first and last date, ever.

You could leave, a voice told me. How much does this drink cost? You could leave a twenty and get up. You're still thin enough to squeeze out that passageway before the next table. You haven't eaten anything yet. If you wait until you've eaten, then you'll be trapped, forever.

And where will she go? another voice asked.

Well, I got the jumpsuit, I chimed in. That's the most important part of this adventure. I could just go be in the jumpsuit. It doesn't matter where. Someplace where I'm not the only person alone in the whole room.

But you're always the only person alone in the whole room. No matter where you are or who you're with. So why is it bothering you now? Maybe because you're scared you won't be alone much longer, if you stay.

If she stays much longer she's going to fall asleep, which will be a really great way to spend her night off, passed out in the middle of a fancy restaurant with a fork up her nose.

"You're such an idiot," I snarled.

"Sorry I'm late."

"Oh. Hi."

I tried to stand. The table shoved me back down, making a really deep bruise across my thighs. Silverware clinked. The vase wobbled. I reached out and saw my glass was empty. Which is worse, went through my mind, to hallucinate a non-existent cockroach or to swallow a real one? It seemed like a very key question, at the time.

"I was working," he said.

There was this silence. I looked around for a conversational opening. Something witty that would explain who I was, that would hint at my hopes, my dreams.

"I've been getting drunk."

"Good."

"Not really. It's three o'clock in the morning for me. I'm totally disoriented. I mean, I was even before. I mean I would be anyway, being here, no matter when. With you."

He was dressed the same as before, slacks, shirt, a jacket. I know that sounds like nothing, but that's the point. His casual was formal. Even though he couldn't have been more than twenty-five, he was a grownup and I was in a red jumpsuit that, I suddenly noticed with horror, was see-through. He was a person and I was something else. That's what was wrong. For starters. He was also way too handsome. His face was lean, like his body, but not dry or pinched. And when he looked at me, it was just too intense. He made me uncomfortable.

"So your day off really begins later. Past midnight. And early tomorrow morning."

"I guess."

"So you never go out."

"Of course I go out."

"But not with people."

"Not with people," I repeated. I hadn't thought of it that way. But then what was this?

"I'm honored."

"Just don't expect me to be interesting."

He didn't smile when I said things. He got them, he understood, but didn't feel this need to react. He took them in, nodded, like it was another piece of the puzzle. He was serious.

"It was the same for me, too. When I finally found where you worked."

"You said you asked someone."

"I asked about twenty people. All you said was an after-hours place near Times Square. That wasn't the first night I tried to find you. When I got there I was wiped out. It was past 2 A.M. Just like it is for you, here. I could barely keep my eyes open."

He could now. I felt them working their magic. It was nicer this way, a slow softening instead of being paralyzed in the gallery, or frantic and embarrassed when he had come to the bar. Were those the only two times I had ever seen him? No, that was impossible. But when else could we have met? Oh, right. In a past life. I began to see what Crystal meant.

"But why? Why were you looking for me?"

"You left the Opening so fast."

"I had to. I was late."

"We didn't get a chance to talk. You ran away."

"I did not. I'm just on a different schedule, that's all. I'll always be on a different schedule."

He thought about that.

"So we'll never see each other at our best."

We were staring. It was really nice. I know "nice" sounds like such a silly word but that's exactly how it felt. The more we agreed there were these reasons not to like each other, the more amazing it was that we did. When the waiter came over and asked what he wanted, he looked at my empty glass and said, "I'm drinking what she's drinking."

Three children, I thought, spaced two years apart. Girl, boy, girl. No. Girl, girl, boy. That way the girls can help me take care of the boy. Because boys are harder.

We walked back to his place. I was deliberately not noticing where we were going. It was such a relief not to have to think about that. Instead, part of me was high up, watching the two of us go down the street, this short person in a red jumpsuit trying to keep up with a tall guy's long legs. The other part of me was intensely physical, blindly registering every time we brushed against each other and then flew apart. There was no in between. No day-to-day me.

"He was raping her?"

"I don't know."

"Was she a prostitute?"

"It was just a dream. It didn't really happen."

"A dream you had on the street. Walking. That you reported to the police."

"The dream police. This guy came with a book and wrote everything down."

"Maybe growing up in that place you were telling me about, that . . . Christian community, makes it hard for you to tell what you actually see, out here in the world."

"Or maybe I see things as they really are," I said. "Because I haven't been fed lies from the moment of my birth."

Maybe that's what you like about me, I wanted to add.

The city fell away. There were no more corner stores, no subway stations or one-block parks or Chinese restaurants. Trucks sat backed up to loading docks, idling, filling the air with exhaust. We came through the other side and I saw what I had never seen here before: a DEAD END sign. The road actually stopped. It had been so long since I'd gotten to the end of anything. There was a boarded-up building, smaller than the ones we had passed. It had two cast-iron domes on either side of a locked garage, to absorb the impact of a runaway truck. Or maybe a runaway horse cart, it looked so old. It was a heap of brick dust, held together by habit, cemented in decay. He led me up a tilting staircase to a hallway on the second floor, then into a room with windows all along one wall. There were fluorescent lights hanging overhead on thin chains. They took a while to turn on. When they finally did, with that metallic ping, I gasped.

"They're grow lights," he explained. "The place used to

be a hydroponic garden. They grew marijuana here. At least, that's the rumor."

It was the biggest space I had ever seen. You could have fit six of my apartments there. No, ten. Or more. But it wasn't just the size. Or the windows. It was the bareness. The floor and ceiling and walls were all stripped back to exactly what they were. Pipes were visible, the plumbing and steam, coming up out of nowhere to make a sink, or snaking along the baseboard to meet a register. There was a mattress in one corner. A door that led to a bathroom. A hot plate. A portable refrigerator. A coffee maker. And that was it. I had this vision of a room as the inside of a person's brain. So mine was this tiny cluttered dark afterthought, this space at the top of a building that no one knew what to call, that didn't even exist, officially. And this was Horace's brain, beautifully organized, everything for a purpose. A big table stood in the middle. He had obviously made it himself. Thick, nailed-together pieces of wood. Another, the kind that tilted, a drafting table, was off to one side. Then there were metal shelves with all kinds of equipment, paints, brushes, jars, some art books, running along one wall, and canvases against the rest, all with their backs turned, except one. A big one.

"Did you clean up for me?"

"It gets dirty. Grit floats in from the highway. The windows don't seal. I mop every other day."

He nodded to a real mop, the heavy kind with a tangle of thick strings, in a steel bucket with that powerful squeezer attachment to wring it out. I wanted to be that mop, have him use me, purge all this dirty ugly black liquid from my body and leave me pure.

"So you *did* clean up for me?"

I had just been joking.

"I cleaned."

The floor was painted, that was another strange thing. It was this glossy white, a blank picture we were entering.

"You can come in," he said.

I was still standing at the door, scared of all the space. Also, I didn't want to look at the painting. It's not whether I would like it or not. I really didn't care. I was afraid of what to say, how to act.

"You look tired. Why don't you sit? Here."

He wheeled over a chair, the kind of high adjustable stool that's in sections, with a little panel that pushes against your back. But I went to the mattress, instead. The bed was made, with sheets so tight you couldn't imagine just slipping in. It had his smell. That was reassuring. Sandalwood. There was a book and clock next to it. From down here, the floor stretched away, this unbroken expanse. I got a flash of how he felt, how lonely he was. Lonely in a different way than I was. Lonely inside himself.

"Eve, wake up."

"I'm not asleep."

"Why are you crying?"

He sat next to me and squeegeed this tear along my cheek. It was such a professional gesture, catching this dribble of paint before it ruined things, pinching it off. I felt a distant shiver.

"What's the matter?"

"What you said before. That we'll never see each other at our best."

"I meant because one of us will always be tired."

"I know what you meant."

"So, really, each of us will see the other at his or her best," he worked out. "Just not at the same time."

"Wow." I finally pretended to notice the painting. It was hard not to. The thing was the size of a billboard.

"I started it tonight. Before I came. That's why I was late."

My vision was flickering. I had drunk so much coffee it was backing up on me, making me queasy. My head was having trouble staying on its neck. There wasn't really much to see. It was mostly bare canvas, huge, with a few colors. I tried to see what they made but I couldn't. Or maybe they didn't make anything. But they were pretty. Like him. He was pretty. Can a man be pretty? He was. I was getting confused, this low down. I was having a love affair with gravity.

You haven't said anything, Eve, a voice reminded me. Say something about the painting. Quick!

"Do you believe in the divinity of Christ?"

His hand had slid under my hair and was holding the whole back of my skull, palming it the way those incredibly sexy black guys in the playground can do with a basketball. I smiled. It was funny, comparing Horace to a black guy. He was so pale. It never occurred to me it was funny comparing my head to a basketball. That's exactly how it felt.

His voice came from far away. His fingers were doing the real talking. They were all along the outsides of my brain, feeling it, pressing it, probing.

"I hadn't really thought about it much."

"Because I think I may be Him. A female Him."

His fingers kept doing what they were doing. It irritated me that he didn't react. Did that mean he wasn't listening, wasn't taking me seriously? Or that nothing knocked him off his calm center?

"Why?" he finally asked.

"Well, for one thing, Christ's mother was a whore."

"Wasn't she a virgin?"

"Oh. Right." Great, I thought. A nitpicker. "The point is . . ."

I waited. And then I realized I was still talking. I mean I was supposed to be. But I had run out of words, finally. It's like you lay tracks, with your eyes down, not looking where you're going, just throw them in front of you and steam along, and then you run out of tracks, reach for the next one and it's not there. You look up and discover where you are, where you've taken yourself, and realize, This is where I was heading all along. This is my fate.

But it wasn't. Not yet, at least, because after a few more minutes he saw how tired I was and said he was getting me home. I didn't understand. I still thought it was just a question of where we'd end up, together.

"No, no, let's stay here." I tried picturing how I'd left my apartment, every single piece of dirty underwear either hanging over the back of a chair or on the floor. "You cleaned up for me, but I didn't clean up for you."

"It's my fault. You've got to sleep. I should have realized what your schedule was like. I didn't think."

Don't think! I felt like screaming.

The next thing I knew we were on the street, walking again. I was exhausted. He practically carried me. Then I was alone, in a cab, heading home. I watched the city stream by. It was so glamorous. I even liked the way the total on the meter kept going up. That seemed very New York, that all this beauty cost something. But when I dug into my pocket, the driver said it was already taken care of.

"What do you mean?"

"The gentleman," he said.

* * *

"He's gay."

"He is not gay."

"He's gay and you're a slut. It's a match made in heaven."

"Ladies."

Krishna, the instructor, held Brandy's ankles, one in each hand, looking back and forth, lining them up.

"Perfect!" he announced.

Even though we were standing on our heads, I saw she managed to give her hair a little flip. Then he walked right by me like I was invisible. I wanted to stick out my foot and trip him, but my foot was tucked behind my ear. I should have taken the karate class, I thought. Instead of this retarded grope session where a bunch of horny women in Danskins waited for a yoga dude in a loincloth and shoulder-length hair to come over and "correct" them.

"It's gross," I complained later. "His hair was brushing right up against you, wasn't it?"

"Why is that gross?" Crystal asked.

"I don't know. It just is. And I am not a slut. I told you, we didn't do anything."

"But you wanted to." Brandy lay back against the wood with her eyes closed. "On the first date, too. So you're a slut in your mind, which is the worst kind."

"It sounds like he was being nice." Crystal yawned.

"Thank you," I said. "That's exactly right. He was being nice."

She wore a towel. Three of them, actually. Brandy was naked. I didn't know what to do, so I compromised, half sitting on one and kind of draping it over me but then letting it slip.

"What's the point of this again?"

"To make you sweat."

We were the only ones in the sauna. I thought it would be like her birthday party, all of us bonding, but even better. Nora was older and not so interested. Viktor was the cause of all our trouble, all our discord. But without those two, without work around us, it was awkward.

"Like Native Americans." I thought of that policeman, Detective Jourdain, calling me Eve America.

"Who?"

"Indians. They have sweat lodges. Where they go. It's supposed to help them meditate."

"Are you going to see him again?"

I let the towel slide more.

"I'd go out with him again, if he asked."

"So you're just going to hope he comes back to the bar?"

I wished I could be Brandy. Her limbs were tumbled back, eyes closed. She had dropped all her irritating movements. She was channeling her true self. I wished I could be her or I wished I could be Crystal. She had made a tent out of towels and was camped inside, protected by this thick wall of Attitude.

"Call him," Brandy said.

"And say what?"

" 'Come to my place.' " She sprawled the length of the bench. " 'Come to my place and we'll make love on my roof.' "

"I can't get to my roof."

"Well, then on my bed."

"I don't have a bed, either."

We were all innocent. That, I finally realized, was what we had in common, why Viktor had picked us. Even Nora, who looked so tragic, so ruined by all sorts of excess, had this amnesia when it came to men. Brandy and Crystal, they were so into talking tough, into being big experts, but that's all it was, talk. I folded the towel into a pillow, then, keeping my eyes shut (maybe other people were going to see me naked but I wasn't), reached back to put it under my head. I lay down, felt my body unfurl, took a deep breath, and blew out, hard.

"Just think of a reason to get together," Crystal's voice came. "An excuse. It doesn't matter what."

But it did. When I called Horace, I wanted it to be for the right reason, not a tawdry little lie, an excuse. I wanted it to be something that would lead us down the path to true love.

Someone giggled. They were making fun of me. They could read my thoughts. That's what went through me at first. Then I wondered if I was dirty or I had funny-looking feet like in those subway ads. HAMMER TOE. INGROWN NAIL. PLANTAR WART.

"What?"

"Nothing," Brandy said.

"If you were getting raped," I asked, "what would you do? Fight? Or just go along?"

The sweat was collecting on me, forming rivers, pools. I reached down and smeared my hand across.

"Go along?"

"You know. Play dead."

"It depends."

"He has a knife at your throat," I added, more confident now, really seeing it. Except not in images. Feeling what happened. Trying to imagine. I knew I would keep feeling it as long as I kept my eyes closed.

"I don't know," Brandy said. "I guess it would depend."

Crystal snorted.

"Depend on what?"

"A lot of things. It's a stupid question."

"Don't tell me you haven't thought about it."

"Of course I've thought about it."

"Well?"

"Just because I've thought about it doesn't mean I know what I'd do. Nobody does."

I couldn't breathe. There was a blade at my throat, choking me, burning, heated by my own fear. I couldn't swallow. Inside me, I felt this awful force, like my spinal cord was being cut.

"And what about after? Would you tell?"

"No," Brandy answered, almost before I got the question out, strangely sure.

"Of course I'd tell," Crystal said. "Why wouldn't you?"

But almost as if to illustrate the point, Brandy didn't say.

"I'd tell everyone," Crystal said.

Maybe not in words, I tried to imagine Brandy saying. But in how I acted. How I saw men from then on. We all acted as if we'd been raped anyway, whether we had been or not. Just the possibility, the fear, dictated how you faced things.

"Is that a tattoo?"

I frowned and tried raising my head while keeping the rest of my body flat. This solid black bar lay across my upper thigh.

"That is when I tried to get up at the restaurant. When he came in and I was sitting against the wall. The table made that. It's not a tattoo, it's a bruise."

"You better call him." Brandy laughed.

And then it came to me: I had to find her. The woman on the street. I didn't know why, but suddenly it was clear that she held the key to the mystery. Not just to what happened that night, but to what was happening right now and what was going to happen in the future. My future. I moved one leg so it sealed against the other, then raised them both high.

They were the tail of a fish. I was a mermaid. I tried following myself in toward the center, where my body changed from fins and scales to flesh. But I couldn't. There was no clear point where I switched over. What would I do, once I tracked her down? What would I ask? That wasn't important. It was the idea of a quest that appealed to me. To find the truth.

CHAPTER THREE

The sixties. Mother kept one dress from then, a fabric printed with hundreds of red-white-and-blue circles. They were supposed to be election buttons. Each had KENNEDY in the middle, except where they got cut off at the seam. Then they just said KEN.

"We made them ourselves," she explained. "The campaign didn't have a lot of money. They gave us the material and told us to be creative."

It was short. I watched her in the mirror and thought, I do not have nearly as good legs. Dad, whoever he was, must have been a midget.

"Didn't he die?"

"Who?"

"Ken Kennedy."

"Bobby. He was my great love."

"You knew him?"

She turned and looked over her shoulder, examining her back.

That's it! I was the President's daughter, sent by my father to go among ordinary mortals, until one day, discovered, I would reveal my true nature and—

She took it off. I looked away. I didn't like seeing her naked. She was so casual. I slept in a T-shirt that came down to my knees.

"You want it?"

"Want what?"

She was folding it up. She folded really well. Things stayed together. She could do those paper animals. Origami. My clothes looked so perfect after a wash. It was only when I put them on that they got ridiculous. I watched her tuck the dress behind all my shapeless uniforms, hiding it. From who? From her. She had to teach me both parts, the rebel and the rule-keeper. Because there was nobody else. Because both were inside her, battling away. And I never said thank you. I just accepted things, grudgingly. They were these burdens I was taking off her hands, off her conscience. But I must have sensed how special the dress was. It was one of the only things I took with me. And now it lay here, this package, smaller than I remembered, a little decorative animal. A crane. A giraffe. I hesitated before undoing it. Maybe there was some secret message inside. Of course there wasn't. I put it on and tried smoothing ancient folds. The dress was the message, all by itself.

Horace didn't understand.

"What are we doing here?"

The corner was different in daytime. People walked right over the spot. I felt like shouting "Look out!" every time a man's shiny shoe or a woman's heel splashed down where the puddle had been. I could even see the tracks that were begun, all from this central point, bloody footprints, radiating out. Nobody stopped. It didn't even slow them down, that they were trampling this sacred patch of cement. They would have trampled me, too, if he hadn't been here, by my side.

"I don't know. A clue, I guess."

"What kind of clue?"

"Well, I was reading a first-aid manual, and it said wounds in the abdomen usually have a lot of blood. So I thought maybe there would be this trail we could follow."

He looked at me. I was following all the imaginary footprints.

"But it looks like the trail leads everywhere." I shook my head. "Everywhere and nowhere. See, then I was reading the Triple A Roadside Assistance Guide, and they said—"

"Wait. You were reading a first-aid manual, and then a book on how to drive?"

"What's so strange about that? They're both about solving problems. About how to live."

"But—"

"And they only cost a dollar. I didn't go to college, like you. This is my college, right here."

"So what did you learn?"

"When you hit a patch of ice," I recited, "when you lose control of your vehicle, *turn in the direction of the skid,* and keep going."

He waited.

"That way the wheels straighten out. By heading right into the disaster. I'm not sure how. And then you regain control. So that's what I decided to do, by coming here. I'm turning in the direction of the skid."

"You've lost control of your vehicle."

"Yes. And I called you."

Why? Why had I called him? Because I thought it would be a really fun date? It suddenly occurred to me that maybe the best way to get a man interested in you was not by repeatedly describing this vision of seeing some guy almost get his penis cut off.

"Are you sure it was a dream?" he asked.

"Yes, I'm sure."

"But dreams happen in your head. You don't come back to them. Not to a place."

"This is where it happened," I insisted.

I was about to crumple, inside. He must have sensed it, because he stood in front of me, blocking my view.

"You want to come back to my studio again?"

That was a good idea. Pick up where we left off. Was that what I'd wanted all along? Was this just a very complicated way of me asking him out? I could have invited him over for dinner. But then I would have had to cook, and after my disaster with the artichoke trifle I wasn't going to risk that again.

"Maybe you shouldn't read so much," he suggested.

Down in the subway, it was rush hour. The train was packed. We pushed our way in and he took my hand, kept us moving, until we got to the end of the car. Then he slid open the door and motioned for me to go out. I thought we were trying the next one, to see if it had seats, but instead he held me. We were in between, outside. There were two metal platforms, just big enough for one person each. On the glass window was the back of a sticker. SRAC NEEWTEB EDIR TON OD.

"Have you ever done this before?"

"Done what?"

He was standing on one side. I was facing him, on the other. When the train started, we rose and sank at different times as our separate cars negotiated the track. Big springs, hanging off chains, covered in rubber tubes, bounced on either side of us. There was the soft sound of steel clashing, groaning, pulling away, then hitting again, and that smell, of hot dust, I guess, and electricity. His hands were on my hips, steadying me. It was the same way he had appeared that time at the gallery, been past my defenses without my noticing. As a special favor, he put me in a position where I didn't have to say yes or no. He touched me, but not in some gross way, not bullying, dominating, like I had seen Brandy thrill to with her studly yoga instructor. In fact, his hands were perfectly still, just holding me so I wouldn't fall, keeping me safe, letting the vibration of the ride, the swoops and shudders of the two cars as they struggled to stay together, all that motion, translate into what he was doing, something between a massage and an incredibly erotic caress. This went on and on. I leaned into him. He had that same serious expression as when he was looking at art, or asking about my life. His hands were this power flowing through me. They held me up, but only because they made me want to fall. I'd heard that saying about someone making you "weak in the knees," but never knew what it meant, until now.

Of course it helps that you're wearing a dress ending three-quarters of the way down your ass.

It's her dress. He wants her, not me.

You are her. Part of you. Half her.

Half her and half Ken Kennedy, the short fat midget-dwarf.

President Ken Kennedy, to you.

"It's so great we can't talk," I finally shouted, ruining it. I had to, for some reason. It was so good it was scary.

"What?"

"I said, It's so great we can't talk!"

The train slowed. He nodded, that I should open my door. I didn't get it at first. What he was trying to say. We had been communicating so perfectly, but only about what we already knew, which was that there was something between us. It was almost like the perfection of that mutual desire made every other part of our relationship, even the smallest things, full of misunderstanding.

"We're here," he said.

I nodded. Of course we were. Here we were. In love. It was so beautiful.

"This is our stop. This is where we get off."

"Oh."

When we got up the steps, he didn't take my hand again. He didn't have to. He wasn't leading me. We walked at the same exact pace. We settled into a rhythm. There was this deepening. The air had turned violet. Traffic lights were ice cubes at the bottom of some really fancy cocktail. He was so clean and light and right. He brought out the healthy side of me. He would lead me out of darkness, out of my own unhappiness. And I wanted to do the same for him. He was imprisoned, too, in a jail of his own making. We all were. I wanted to bust him out.

"How's the painting coming?"

He frowned, surprised, like he didn't remember telling me that's what he did.

"The big one. For your show."

"Slow," he admitted.

I wanted to reach out and touch him, but that would destroy this beautiful sound we were making, our feet, on the pavement, in harmony.

"Listen, don't you have some fantasy? Something that you've always wanted to do, but been too shy to ask for?"

He coughed.

"I'm serious."

"I've never been asked that before."

"Sure you have. Just not out loud. That's what everyone asks everyone. That's really all we have to offer each other."

"Is it?"

We kept walking.

"If I did," he finally risked, "that's all it would be. A fantasy."

"Well, I thought maybe we could—"

"Fantasies are like those stones you find on the beach that look so beautiful and special. That glow. But if you bring them home, they turn into dried-out pebbles." He was all disapproving. "You have to leave fantasies where they are. You can't bring them into the real world."

"Why not?"

"Then they're not fantasies anymore."

"So you want to go to Coney Island?" I tried understanding.

We walked more, in silence.

"I want this."

"This what?"

"To be here. Now. With you."

It wasn't some grand declaration. He didn't stop, or look at me, or say it any differently than he'd said anything else. It was just this matter-of-fact remark, like, I want a glass of water. But it hit me so hard. I'd never heard anyone say that.

That they wanted to be with me. I never realized that's what I wanted to hear.

I found the belt loop in his pants, hooked my finger through, and tugged, hard.

I wasn't going to answer. I wasn't going to respond in any way. I was going to let the moment collect and thicken, let the tension build until it was unbearable. I was going to be the kind of girl I always wanted to be, mysterious and silent and intriguing. This was going to be a Great Love. We were going to climb that tilting staircase, cross his endless empty space, lie down on his low, low mattress, and watch all the clean white sections of floorboard shoot away.

Oh my God, I thought, this is actually the way it's supposed to happen. For once.

He opened the door to the studio. Marron was there.

"Wow," she said. "Cool dress, Eve."

"You're early," Horace called.

"Did you get that at a vintage clothing store?"

He wasn't next to me, anymore. My finger was closed around air.

"We were going to Openings tonight," he explained, from the kitchen area.

"I guess I'm early."

I noticed she didn't say, I'm sorry. And then I realized she was inside, waiting. So she had a key.

I tried not looking at her. Meaning I stared. She was all in black, sitting at his drafting table chair but turned around so her legs straddled the shiny metal stem that came up the back. It was such a lounging around, I-own-the-place pose. The chair was on rollers. I wanted to walk over and give it one sharp shove, so she would wheel across the rest of the room, hit the wall, and flip right out the window onto the West Side Highway.

"You going to come with us, Eve?" she asked. "You want to look at art?"

"No. I have to work."

"That dress is so hot."

"It was my mother's."

"Really? Did she sleep with him?"

"Who?"

"John F. Kennedy?"

Right. And then he gave her this dress. This really subtle memento. A souvenir. From a big box he had.

"No. Ken Kennedy."

"Oh."

"Well, I mean I'm not sure. It was before I was born."

Obviously. Otherwise how could I be His child? Whoever exactly He was. I wasn't too good at American history. Even though it was turning out to be the story of my life.

"You want coffee?"

Horace was fiddling with beans and a filter. There was no place to sit. Except the bed, and if I plopped down there I'd be shorter than she was. That was my one advantage. It was like a duel. We were about to choose our weapons.

"You have anything to drink?"

"You mean alcohol? I don't think so."

"Sure you do," Marron said. "You have that scotch I gave you. Remember?"

"Oh. Right."

We looked at each other.

"Here," he said, bringing out this really fancy bottle.

So, you're pretty, I thought. And talented, apparently. But there's one thing I can do that you can't.

It was the kind that came in a blue velvet bag. Rich people's liquor. It wasn't even opened.

Drink like a fish, I smiled triumphantly.

"Of course it was a dream. It was an External Dramatization of the Female Psyche."

"She actually went to the police," he pointed out.

"I know. That's what's so great. She acted on it. She wasn't passive. You must be so in touch with your subconscious self that it *becomes* your real world, Eve."

"I just haven't been sleeping enough," I said. "My biological clock is all screwed up from working nights."

Wait. Was biological clock about having babies? Had I said the wrong thing? Gee, that would be a surprise. Of course, it didn't really matter since neither of them was listening.

"Not just her own subconscious but the Universal Subconscious." Marron was getting excited. I couldn't tell if she was making fun of me or not. "I mean, that dream is probably what the female side of every person in America was seeing at that moment."

"The female side of every person? But you said we all look at the world through a man's eyes. The Male Gaze," I remembered, shocked at seeing the words themselves, the words she had used that night at the gallery, come out of my mouth and glow in the air. I was plowed.

"When we're awake, we're men. When we dream, we're women."

"Everybody? Him, too?"

I nodded to Horace.

"I don't believe there's any difference between male and female," she said. "I mean, they're useful distinctions, for bathrooms in restaurants and stuff like that. But they're artificial. They're imposed on us by society. Really we're this complex mixture of both. Take me, for instance. Supposedly, I'm female."

"Supposedly?"

"But there's plenty about me that's male, too."

"Like what?"

"Well, I like to be on top, for one thing."

I choked. He'd given me a glass, but it was this clunky jam-jar type, with a thick rim. The ice cubes that came from his tiny freezer compartment were the size of aspirins. Which you're going to need, I thought, noticing how low the level in the bottle had sunk.

"Eve's from Iowa," Horace explained.

"You have a vagina," I managed to cough.

I'd seen it. Blown up. Poster-size.

"The vagina and penis are really the same thing. Anatomically. A penis is just a vagina that's been pulled inside out."

She was leaning forward, completely serious. She was her own best listener. You got drawn in because she believed her own act. I could see how guys would think she was beautiful. It was a question of confidence, really. It was just so unfair that she had breasts, too.

Horace kept trying to move the conversation along. Like I couldn't speak for myself.

"She wants to know how she got invited to your Opening."

"You must be on my list."

"But how?"

"I don't know. I get names from all over. I trade with other artists, with galleries, with photographers. Maybe it was from some modeling job you were on."

"I told you, I do *not* model."

"Are you sure? I thought that's why you were just 'Eve.' That it was a professional name."

"That's just about the stupidest thing I ever heard."

"Why does it bother you so much?"

"It's just irritating that you keep saying I model when I've never even let anyone take my picture!"

They both looked. I knew I'd made a mistake—by being born, for starters—but there was no going back. A monumental blunder was coming, and all I could do was get out of the way and watch with the rest of them.

"You've never let anyone take your picture?" Horace asked.

"Where I grew up, we didn't have cameras."

"They don't have cameras in Iowa?"

"Cameras are bad."

"Because they steal your soul?"

"It takes more than a camera to steal my soul," I snapped, getting mad, for no reason, at the wrong person, as usual.

"Then why?"

"Because they're the work of the Devil, all right? They're instead of seeing. They're a crutch. Instead of remembering what a person really looks like, or what kind of time you had, or how you felt, you get this crude little arrangement of colors and shapes. A camera tempts you to be less than human. Part of your brain shuts down. All pictures are Satanic. All images. That's why what you guys do, with your paintings and photographs and stuff, is such bullshit."

I sighed. That hadn't come out right. They didn't seem to mind, though. But "they," that was the problem. I had lumped them together and made me the outsider.

Good work, Eve.

"Excuse me," I said.

In the bathroom, sitting there, I saw a square in the tiles

where the soap dish must have been. Where she had taken that little bit of him, without his even noticing. It made me feel so hopeless. It was voodoo. She wasn't an artist, she was a witch! But maybe that's what a woman artist really was. Maybe that's what they had all been, before they came out of hiding, before they'd been allowed to make boring, blah-blah paintings, just like the men, and now they were trying to get back to what made them special to begin with. Black magic.

What are you doing here? a voice sneered. You are so totally out of place.

But that's what he likes about me, I argued. That I am not her.

But the more you try and fit in, the more like her you'll be, and the less he'll like you. So you'll never be anything but uncomfortable. And he'll always be disappointed. It's a lose-lose situation.

Which is why I'm so suddenly desperately in love.

Are you? In love?

I don't know. Maybe.

Well, if you are, if this isn't just you playing a game with yourself, then what are you going to do about it?

Oh, that's easy. Screw it up.

When I came out, Horace was waiting.

"Sure you don't want to come with us?" He nodded to Marron, who was across the room. "I forgot we were going to meet up. Otherwise, I wouldn't have brought you."

"Forget it."

I walked away, not looking back. If I could just apply the Rules of Cocktail Waitressing to my private life. Treat him like a customer. And then, to compensate, at work maybe I could date all the guys who came down the stairs. Maybe that was the way to have fun.

"I'm sorry," he said.

Like an idiot, I turned.

We were in front of his painting. We both looked at it. It was further along than before, still with lots of empty space but full of scribbles and signs. He started to explain that it was all formulas, from physics and chemistry and math, jammed together to make patterns, very thought out and geometrical, but also based on color, these muted shades and bright patterns. There were passages of books he had copied out, too, but so small, and in different shapes and type, that they became stretches of texture, part of something bigger. Everything was part of something bigger, he said, but itself, too. And there were pictures, pictures inside the picture. It was only now, when I was right up against it, that I saw how meticulous it was, like the teeth of a million tiny gears. I locked into them and for a minute felt my own million tiny gears, the bent, sticky gears of my drunken brain, grinding slowly to life. I didn't really understand. Mostly what I took away was that he cared about it more than he cared about anything else in the world. He'd channeled his feelings into it. Which was what made him so tantalizing. That you couldn't have that part of him. I put my palm flat against the canvas. He jumped, like I'd touched his skin. I pushed. It looked solid but it wasn't, really. It gave.

"She's better for you," I decided.

"Who? What are you talking about?"

"She probably sees what you're trying to do. More than me, anyway. Thanks for today, though. For coming back to that corner. You saved my life."

"Eve, wait a minute."

"I have to go now."

"I'll call you."

"No. Don't call me, please."

"Why not?"

"Good-bye."

We're breaking up! I thought, as I walked, for several miles, over the glossy white floor. We're breaking up and we were never even together! It was thrilling. Don't look back. Remember the rules. I got to the door. Don't look back, and then, when you turn, when you finally get to where you're going, he'll be right behind you, following. Remember, it's your Air of Mystery.

I kept walking.

This is a Great Love, I repeated to myself. Any minute now he's going to put his hand on your shoulder and spin you around and a whole new period of your life is going to begin. Any minute now.

I got outside. The door closed behind me. I didn't even bother to look. I knew I was alone. Still, I kept sensing something momentous was going to happen.

Any minute now . . .

I hadn't talked to Jesus in a long time. It was nobody's fault. We were both busy. I felt like praying, but didn't know where to go. Not a church. I had checked them out when I first got here, the big stone castles with organs and marble, where the ladies wore stockings and all the men had titles, Deacon, Reverend, Doctor. They were traps. Traps for God where you were the bait. You really think you're going to lure Him in with stained glass and pretty music? I felt like asking. I mean, look at your altar, it's a Plexiglas donations box, for crying out loud. All those bills, presidents' heads, jammed together like the inside of a cannibal's belly. This is where you *worship*? After a while someone came over and explained I was in the Gift Shop again, but even when I stood where I was supposed to, I felt the same thing. It was a Christ-Free Zone, the last place on earth to be surprised by grace. Instead, I'd been making my own spiritual map of Manhattan, finding spots that called to me, some of them because things had already happened there, but most because they had a feeling of promise, a sense that something was *going* to happen, if I was patient and stayed alert.

Like the coffee shop. It was still and quiet, no matter how crowded. People kept their voices down. It was clean. There were tables you could sit at and a counter with round stools that rose out of the floor on columns. It was open twenty-four hours. You could get any meal you wanted, breakfast, lunch, or dinner, at any time. I came before work. The waiter knew me, not by name, but he said hello in a certain way, a salute. I was a fellow anonymous citizen.

If there is a religion of the city, I decided, then this is one of its holy places.

I got coffee and stared out the window. My pale reflection was sanded away to nothingness, eyes, nose, mouth, so insubstantial compared to the bodies that pushed their way past on the sidewalk. What just happened? I couldn't even tell. Did I love him? What did that even mean? Maybe I needed Horace the way, when your body needs a certain vitamin or mineral, you crave a certain food. But love? I felt like telling the waiter, just to get sympathy, how I had discovered that my boyfriend (Was he? My boyfriend? No) turned out to be (Wait a minute. I hadn't even thought of this. She did have a key, though. Was it possible?) living with another girl! But he already knew. Everyone in Manhattan probably knew, and was laughing at me. Or would be, soon, because I would tell them all. I would blurt it out. I would turn it into a funny story. I smiled. Actually, it was kind of funny.

Eve?

I spun slowly on my stool to discover no one, just the diner's air of sanctuary, its even light and padded plastic booths. A wind blew down the street. The door banged. I kept spinning, pushing with my feet. But when I completed my revolution, returning to where I never left, a second face had joined me in the mirror.

It was her, the woman I'd seen. She superimposed her face right on my own. We kept moving, both of us, to see how we were the same and how we were different, staring deep into each other's eyes. Finally, our mouths lined up perfectly.

Where did you come from? I asked.

Nowhere. I've been here the whole time. Waiting.

Waiting for what?

For you.

The knife was at her throat again. She couldn't swallow. He had found her, tracked her down. She was cornered now, alone. She couldn't breathe. She felt this awful force. Not strength, but the crushing force of habit, the sense that this was how things were and nothing she could do would change them. She almost gave up. But then something happened. The feeling wavered, boundaries blurred. She became strong to the exact same degree that he became weak. She plucked the glowing metal, turned it around, and pushed him away. He responded so easily. It was a dance. He swayed back, then forward again. She pushed, using his own force against him, the mirror image of what he had been doing to her. He fell. She floated free, a balloon, and at the last minute, not even thinking, cut the string that held her down.

"Coffee?"

I jerked awake. I didn't fit the outlines of my body. Things didn't match their shapes. I was a thing among things. Slowly, the world came back into focus. My cup was cold. So was I. We were both shivering.

"I didn't want to wake you," he said. "You looked like you could use the rest."

"I was asleep? For how long?"

"Just five minutes or so."

I wanted to go home. It broke on me like a wave. It was time. My adventure was over. I would go back to being who I was, but enriched with this knowledge, this warning, of what the world outside held. I was scared straight. I had learned my lesson. I would go back to Iowa and never leave again. I felt this resolve freshening my spirit, making me sit up. It was all in my head. My head was the temple I had to scourge. My own imagination. I had this picture of me lashing the interior of my skull. Driving out all the sick, sex-soaked nightmares.

"Thank you, Jesus," I whispered, leaving a big tip.

"No problem," he called.

On the street, even though it was uphill, I felt myself gaining strength, becoming healthier with each step. I walked so fast it was almost a run, except I kept both feet on the ground at all times. That was the definition of Olympic Walking. I had read a book about it. This whole time, I had been secretly training for some event. And now it had come. In fact, it was almost over. This was the home stretch. A man was ahead of me. I came up behind. I didn't slow down. I climbed right up his back, then over his head, and down his front. He didn't even realize what had happened, that he'd been passed. He didn't even know it was a race! That was the key to my success. People cheered from windows. Cars honked. Lights changed as I approached. I was at one with the grid.

"I quit!" I practiced saying.

It sounded so positive. I quit everything. My job. Drinking. Love. Suddenly, the idea of giving things up really appealed to me. Was there still time to be a nun? I skipped down the steps to the bar, determined to keep this momentum.

I quit, I reminded myself. I'll give them a few days to find a replacement, check bus times, do my laundry, and then—

"So I said to him, Do you love me? And he said, What a question. And I said, What an answer. And he said, Of course I love you. And I said, Prove it. And he said, How? And I said . . ."

Everything had changed so much that it was weird to see them act like nothing had happened. Except, of course, nothing had. Not on the outside. I was still me.

"Hi, Eve."

"That's some dress," Viktor commented.

I kept walking, a little self-consciously, right past everyone, to the room in back. I locked the door and started changing. Through my newly virginal eyes, the bar seemed sinister. Scary, even. How come I'd never noticed?

"Hello, Eve."

I screamed. Nora was sitting in the dark. She had dragged in a chair. Crates of beer towered over her. The tip of her cigarette glowed.

"Can I have some of that?" I asked.

"You don't smoke."

"I used to. I mean I tried it, once."

She reached into her bag, but I said, "No, could I just have a puff of yours?"

She handed it to me. I tasted her lipstick. I was trembling, from excitement. I thought it would calm me. And maybe I wanted to commune with her. But all I did was cough.

"You're pretty tonight," she said.

I looked down. I had one leg of my pantyhose on. There was a stain, a huge one, like a birthmark, on my sleeve. I had no idea what it was or how it got there.

"No I'm not."

I handed the cigarette back to her. Our thumbs rolled against each other. We'd never actually talked.

"So what are you doing here, Nora?"

My eyes, getting used to the dark, saw she had a drink on the floor.

"Pretty, not beautiful," she went on. "Just like you can be smart without being wise."

"I'm not smart, either."

"No. You're not smart. You're actually kind of stupid."

"Hey!"

It was all right for me to say that, but not her. She was very drunk. I guess she always was, but usually she handled it better. She functioned. Now it looked like she couldn't even get up.

"You remind me of someone."

"You? A younger you?" I added quickly.

She laughed. She'd been lighting another cigarette (I noticed she hadn't taken another drag of the one I used) and put both down, the cigarette and the lighter, she was laughing so hard. This silent heaving. I smiled at first, along with her, but then it seemed more like a nasty laugh, the way it was soundless and directed at me.

"All right," I said. "So I'm not like you."

She stopped as quickly as she'd started, then finished her drink.

"How come you picked 'Eve' when you started working here?"

"I didn't pick Eve. That's my name."

"Mine's Eunice."

"Eunice?"

"I was going to be an actress." She picked the cigarette off the floor and lit it. So dirt was all right. Just not my germs. "They told me to change it. I took Nora from this play we were rehearsing."

"It's a nice name."

She nodded.

"I mean Eunice is, too."

"I think it's great what you're doing."

"Oh. Thanks."

"I think it's really *smart*."

I nodded. How did she know? I guess it showed on my face, that I was gone, in spirit. She was looking at me with this weird intensity, like she hated me. I had no idea why.

"Well, I've got to get dressed," I said.

She did that slow yawn, that shaking out of dreams. Except this time she almost fell. It was sad. Nora was so sure-footed, usually. She never dropped a glass or spilled a drink. I had thought she was a professional, if there was such a thing. A professional barmaid. It surprised me she'd wanted to act. She didn't seem perky or anything. Especially now. She looked all discombobulated and tired. Somehow, I had done it, was the implication. It was my fault. She found my dress, lying there, and mechanically began to fold it.

"I didn't know what I was doing. You never do."

"When?"

"When I changed my name. I hated my old one. I love it now."

"So why don't you go back?"

She shook her head.

"It's my mom's." I nodded at the dress. "I'm going to go see her. In a couple of days."

I was hopping around on one leg, trying to get ready and look up at her at the same time, trying to win back this friendship which I'd never had but now, somehow, I'd managed to lose.

"The thing is, I wasn't even playing Nora in that production. I just had a bit part. I wasn't any good."

"Oh, I'm sure you were good."

"You're such a little bitch, Eve. Or whatever your real name is."

"What?"

I stopped, still on one leg. You could have knocked me over. She had knocked me over. With a word. And then she did it again, kicked me when I was down, just to make sure:

"You have no idea what a little bitch you are, do you?"

It was a wild night. There were all these sailors, not the navy guys or merchant seamen who sometimes wandered in, but amateur, hobbyist types.

"It is the Tall Ships," Viktor explained, although at the time, over the noise, I thought he said "Tall Shits," because they were so obnoxious, acting like they'd been at sea for six months, asking for all sorts of drinks we didn't have, like grog or glogg, and actually saying, "Yo-ho-ho."

"Why are they all dressed like pimps?"

"They are reenactors. It is historical."

"It sure is."

"That guy says he's from a slave ship," Brandy complained,

as if it was a personal insult. "I mean, I didn't even know they had those anymore."

I am not taking money for this, I thought, as I squeezed my way between tables. It helped to know I had quit, in my mind, that this was actually charity work. I was just helping out Brandy, Crystal, and, yes, even that psycho Nora, on a busy night. I would explain to them all later how I was leaving, evolving really, to a higher plane of emotional maturity. How I was going home to live with Mother.

"So how are you doing?" Brandy asked, while we both waited for Viktor to fill our orders.

"What?"

"I said, how are you doing?"

"Great, actually."

"No. Really."

She looked at me. Her eyes were such a clear blue. She actually seemed to be concerned for my well-being, for once. I began to describe what happened in the back room.

"Nora's crazy," she cut me off. "Do what you want to do. Don't listen to anybody else."

It got so crowded people actually lined up on the stairs, waiting for a table. We were rushed off our feet. I saw Crystal standing talking to a customer, which was unusual even when the place was empty. It was good to keep moving. You were less of a target that way. But whatever he said must have really been getting to her, because the next time I passed, she was still there, talking back and forth with him. Then her voice rose above the crowd:

"Go to hell!"

Viktor vaulted over the bar. He must have been watching, getting ready, because he had the baseball bat he kept next to the cash box. The guys left. They even paid. New people took their place. Crystal was still standing there, solid, but quivering. Brandy and I got her to come back with us and sit. I caught Nora gazing from across the room, like it was a memory she was seeing.

"There are still customers," Viktor pointed out.

"What did he say?"

"It's OK, honey," Brandy was cooing. She hugged Crystal's shoulders, rocked them in her arms.

"I know," she said, trying to sound tough, staring in that sullen way, straight ahead.

Everyone's crazy tonight, I thought. Good thing I'm here.

I tried smiling at Nora a few times, but she ignored me. She was flirting, laughing, not her typical dreamy, spaced-out self. Everything was backwards. Brandy was being nice to me. Nora, not. Crystal was having a nervous breakdown. Viktor didn't mind my being late. Maybe they'd all had visions, too. Seen their past. Seen their future. Maybe this was The Night Jesus Did Manhattan.

"So what are you going to wear?" Brandy continued, passing by.

"What?"

"To get married in."

I got orders, filled them, got more orders, took money, then came back to the bar while she was just loading up.

"What did you say?"

"You going to wear a wedding dress?"

"I told them," Viktor said.

"Told them what?"

"Congratulations." Crystal was still sitting there.

"Thanks," I said automatically. "Do you mind if I ask what you're all talking about?"

Brandy was gone by then. We were working hard. Viktor

put out my drinks and touched my hand. Not his usual way, like he was leaving his mark, demonstrating his ownership, but this tender squeeze. It was much more obscene than when he acted like a jerk. I looked up at him.

"It was better they know. About us."

"What about us?"

"Eve."

"I didn't say yes."

"You didn't say no."

"I said I'd think about it."

"Ah yes, you and your thinking. I would never have asked had I not decided you were ready."

"Are those for the guys with the parrots?" Brandy came back, almost panting. "Because they want them. Now."

"Just a minute."

"Better go," Viktor said.

"I am not getting married," I told anyone who cared to listen. Which seemed like mostly Nora, who looked at me, hate still smoldering in her eyes. My God, did *she* want him? She was the last person I would have suspected.

"Ever?" Crystal asked.

"Well, no, not ever. But I mean *we* are not getting married. Viktor and me."

"Of course we are. What a question. These go to the buccaneers, Eve. Please."

He'd put the glasses on my tray, which he didn't do for anyone. You had to lift them yourself and try not to spill. He had been making all these little gestures, I realized now, starting with not yelling at me when I came in late. And everyone else had been watching, because he'd told them, before I came. But I had just been oblivious, as usual, with my head in the clouds, or in the cornfields, dreaming about going home, while they schemed and stewed all around me.

"The buccaneers?"

"The pirates," Brandy translated. "Over there."

I lifted the tray. It was heavy. My wrists strained, like they were in handcuffs.

"It came up."

"How did it come up?"

"I wanted them all to know. I thought it would make you happy. Proud, even."

We were alone. It was five-thirty. Almost light outside, I could tell, even though there were no windows. Just a feeling. The girls were waiting between the doors for him to drive us home. I stayed, pretending to finish cleaning. They knew we had to talk. For the last three hours I hadn't said anything to him but the names of drinks.

"You act as if it is a shameful thing. Marrying me."

"You said it was for legal reasons."

"Mostly. Yes."

Mostly. See, it was those little hints he threw in. I didn't even know if they were intentional. Little hooks, trying to drag me back. But it wouldn't work.

"When we kissed, I thought we were sealing some kind of compact."

"It was just a kiss," I said, numb.

"Not to me."

He was concentrating, counting money.

The bus was leaving for Iowa. I could hear them announcing it. All the stops. The big cities and little towns. Change here.

Change there. Then finally it slows down on the highway. You get up, grab your bags, move swaying down the aisle, bouncing off seatbacks, and jolt down those extra-steep steps. Then there's the steepest step of all, the drop down onto the ground. The bus roars off and you're not moving anymore. You're part of the landscape, again. Fixed. Was that what I wanted?

"By the way," he asked casually. "Are you still seeing the boy?"

"What boy?"

"The one who came here. Pointdexter."

"Horace. And he's not a boy."

"I agree. He is a veal calf. He has no muscle. He was raised in a box."

"What are you talking about?"

"You should never eat veal. It is a sin."

"I'm not seeing Horace."

"I thought maybe that was the reason you changed your mind."

"I did *not* change my mind!" I shouted.

"Shh. Please."

His lips moved. Every once in a while he pulled a bill taut so it made that snapping sound. He was a kid, delighted how it didn't tear, how American money was made of something stronger than paper.

"I'm going to wait upstairs. With the girls."

I don't even know if he heard, he was so engrossed. Or pretending to be.

"It was for immigration purposes. To get a green card. And I said no. Well, I didn't say no. But I definitely didn't say yes. I didn't say anything. Except that he was crazy."

"They ask you things," Crystal warned. "Things about him. To make sure you really love each other."

"Like what?"

"Like what kind of toothpaste he uses."

"So how long have you two been fucking?"

"Nora!"

"It's none of our business," Brandy scolded. "At least two months, right? Ever since that time he drove you home?"

"I did not say yes!" I wailed.

"That's what makes her such a little bitch."

Crystal turned and made Nora shut up with just a look. Of course, then there was this really embarrassing silence. We all stood there, waiting for someone to change the subject.

"I think I had an orgasm this afternoon," I announced, remembering my time with Horace. It seemed so long ago. "On the number six train. Going downtown."

"You haven't changed," Brandy said.

"Yes, I have. Actually, that's what I just realized. I've changed a lot. As a matter of fact, on the way over here, I decided I was going to—"

"No, I mean you haven't *changed*. Your clothes. You were wearing a dress when you came in. I remember because it was kind of a strange one. Even for you. It had writing on it?"

"Oh no."

I went back downstairs, to rescue my heirloom. Viktor had passed out. His head was down on the bar.

"Viktor?"

I went closer. He was crying. It wasn't that dignified-little-manly-tears-brushed-out-the-corner-of-the-eye type of thing. He was weeping. These sobs, into the money that was scattered around him like wet leaves.

Please, I thought. Not this.

"If," he said. His face was a wreck.

"If what?"

"If!"

Then I realized he was saying my name. In another language.

CHAPTER FOUR

"Start from the beginning."

"There is no beginning. It's more like I finally noticed."

"Noticed what?"

"Well, I got home from work and I was sitting here."

"Sitting where?"

"On the floor."

He looked around. He had that pad out again. The place was a complete mess. Even the cushions were scattered. How could I have not seen? That's what I couldn't understand. Was I so blind? He undid his jacket and sat where I had been. He looked funny, trying to squeeze himself into the small space, bending over and sniffing a glass, careful not to touch, like it was evidence.

"That's mine," I said, embarrassed. "The glass."

"Then what happened?"

"Nothing. I just realized everything was out of place. I mean I'm not exactly a neat freak or anything, but I don't leave every drawer open, and all my clothes on the floor."

He picked up the composition book by its edges.

"You said you were writing a letter."

"I said I was *trying* to write a letter."

"Who to?"

"No one."

What I hadn't told him was that I had taken off my clothes. I was just sitting, cross-legged in my underwear, when I finally realized that the apartment wasn't a mess, it was ransacked! Someone had gone through everything. It was this horrible sensation. My privacy, the only place I had never let anyone else contaminate with their presence, was gone.

"How much do you drink?"

"Huh?"

"I said—"

"I heard. How is that any of your business?"

"It's not. I was just wondering."

"I'm the one who got robbed here. I don't see what my personal habits have to do with it."

"Robbed how?"

He put the pad away and got up. He had this kind of authority to him. Because he's a policeman, I told myself. But it was more than that. He was very physical, the way his arms swung, like he could grab the whole room and shake it. The way he looked around, investigating me, how I lived.

"I mean, yes, your apartment's been broken into. That's clear. But what exactly was taken?"

"Nothing, I guess."

"Any idea how they got in?"

"Over here."

I went to the bathroom and pointed. The medicine cabinet door was open, all the boxes and jars dumped in the tub. Towels were on the floor. The window that looked out on the roof, that had prison bars, didn't anymore. Instead, there was a big open square mouth with air pouring in. He came up next to me. I smelled leather. It was enveloping, the scent. Very protective. He was careful not to bump into me, not to touch. I was evidence, too.

"Maybe I scared them off." My words sounded wooden and forced. "I mean, if they didn't take anything."

"Why do you think that? Did you hear them when you entered? Footsteps? Things being knocked over?"

"No, but it's what I'm good at. Scaring people off."

He looked at me. The same way he had before. This mix of curiosity and something else that I couldn't quite pin down.

"Maybe they did it because they could." I smiled to myself.

At work we had this joke: Why does a dog lick its balls? Because it can. Why do men act like jerks? Because they can.

"You mean to send you a message?"

"I don't know."

"So you got home," he summarized. "You sat down to write a letter. After a while, you looked up, saw you had been the victim of an attempted burglary, and then you called me."

He made that sound like the most interesting part. Calling him.

"Well, I had your card. You gave it to me that morning. In case I remembered something new."

"And have you? Remembered something new?"

"About what?"

"You know what. About that night."

"This has nothing to do with before. I mean, how could it?"

We were still standing in the doorway. I tried to walk away. I had to pass right next to him because he wasn't moving. I caught a glimpse of a strap over his shoulder. At first I thought it was suspenders, then realized what I had been smelling this whole time was the holster that held his gun.

"I was thinking about going home," I confessed. "That's what I was doing on the floor. Writing a letter to my mother. Asking if I could come back."

"Is that what you want to do? Go home?"

"I don't know."

He took out his pad again.

"So you're saying that maybe someone is trying to frighten you because of what you saw that night."

"I didn't say that. What are you talking about?"

"I understand you're a runaway, Eve," he said carefully. "I understand you not wanting to give me your last name and all. Not wanting to get involved with the authorities."

"I am not a runaway." I was shocked he had used that word. I never thought of myself that way. "I'm just someone who came to New York City. There's millions of people who do that every year. I'm not running away from anything. I am running *to* something."

And what's that? I wanted him to ask. What are you running to, Eve? Because I was curious to hear how I'd answer. Because I didn't know myself. If he asked, maybe I would find out, be forced to say. Also, I wanted him to act interested in me, not in what I had seen or hadn't seen, but in me as a person. Why? I wondered. You want him to fall in love with you?

"The problem is, what you told us just doesn't add up," he was saying. "Now, my aim is not to get you in trouble. My aim is to help you. But I can't help unless you tell me what happened that night. What really happened."

All right, I decided. I'll make up something else. Something new. To please him. To make this all go away, for real, this time.

But once I started, I forgot to lie. It wasn't out of any kind of moral sense. I just didn't have the energy. Or the imagination. And then I couldn't stop. I actually got excited, enthusiastic, as more details of that night came back. Her face. The sounds they made together. My seeing one thing and then realizing it was maybe another. Our eyes meeting. That moment of wordless communication. Her walking off. The man falling to the ground. Thc blood. For a while I didn't even notice that he had stopped writing things down, that he was staring at me. And even then, I figured he just didn't understand. That I was explaining it badly.

"I thought they were making love."

"You call . . ." He flipped over his pages. "You call being on the street at 5 A.M. 'out for a walk'? And you call what you said just now, you call that, 'making love'? Where are you *from*, anyway?"

"Iowa."

He took out a folded piece of paper.

"It says here a squad car was told to swing by the corner where you reported witnessing the incident."

"Seventy-third and Madison."

"Right. They found nothing."

"I thought it was a dream!" I looked at the remains of my apartment, at my attempt to live a normal life, be a normal person. "I thought it would be better if it was a dream. It would make more sense that way, if it was just . . . an External Dramatization of the Female Psyche."

He snapped his pad shut. He was really annoyed.

"Come on," he said, and grabbed me by the wrist.

"Let's start with the eyes."

There were twenty. Well, forty, really. Twenty pairs of scratched plastic souls, staring up at me from Hell.

"She only turned her head for a minute."

"You said you got a good look at her."

"Did I?"

"Yes, you did."

The man who was laying out the eyes waited a minute, then swept them away, a card dealer, and laid out twenty more. They were all different, from pop-eyed to slits, from wide apart to almost touching.

"Shouldn't this be on a computer?"

They didn't answer. I could hear, outside the room, the sound of phones ringing and not being picked up, just ringing and ringing. Muffled, friendly shouting. Teasing someone about something. But loud. I wondered what it would be like to work here. Oh, right. Officer Eve. That was definitely my calling. You have the right to remain silent. So I better shut up. Inside, I better shut up. I knew I was in trouble. All my competing selves had to line up so I could present a united front. So I could pass. Pass for sane.

"You said she saw you. That's when she ran away."

"She didn't run. She walked. Fast. And I'm not sure it was because she saw me. Maybe she just—"

"If you saw her, if you looked into her eyes, then she saw you. It's a two-way street."

He said something to the sketch artist. I couldn't hear what.

Not a street, a road. A secret road that took you in a new

direction, not uptown or down, not East Side or West. All you had to do, she seemed to be saying, was take this road, this hidden turn, and you could slip into a world where you would be alive in a different way. We looked at each other.

The man's hand reached out to take away the set of eyes. I stopped him.

"Wait."

I was in two places. You always are, I realized. There's this other drama going on, all the time, this force that makes everything that happens in your daily existence meaningful, this power that makes your conscious life what it is, not the jumble of random events it would look like otherwise. It was the magnet slid under things that organized them into a pattern, made them stand up. She was the magnet. That's why I had to find her, that's why I felt, somehow, that she was looking for me, too. Pulling me toward her.

"Is she there?" Detective Jourdain's voice asked, far away.

"Maybe."

"Then point her out. Point her out and you can go home."

But I didn't want to go home.

Growing up, I was always clutching the wrong thing. When everyone else had a doll or a toy, I would fix on some object, a spoon or a pincushion, and hold that instead. People would laugh at first, then try and drag it away. The harder they pulled, the more determined I got to keep it, like their saying how wrong it was gave it this significance, this power.

"Eve, if this woman did assault a man, possibly kill him—"

"Maybe she was getting raped."

"*Was* she getting raped?"

"I told you, I don't know."

"You'd know a rape if you saw one."

"Would I?"

"Just give us her description and let us sort this whole mess out. It has nothing to do with you."

I nodded. He was absolutely right. It had nothing to do with me. He had my best interests at heart. He was such a nice man. I liked his skin. There was so much of it, with that shaved head. I would invite him to the wedding. Maybe when they asked that question about anyone knowing why this marriage should not take place, he would object.

My hand moved. I followed its progress, a spectator. The world was a Ouija board.

"This one."

"You mean she's Asian?" he asked sharply. "You never mentioned that before."

But the sketch artist believed me. He fit it on a board with a blank oval that was supposed to be a face and said, "Let's move on to noses."

She should have gone away with the others, the other eyes that got stuffed back into the worn yellow envelope. She didn't. She smiled, grateful, but mocking, too, like she had fooled me, conned me, then turned, slowly, with all the time in the world. Had I done the right thing? I picked the rest of the fake face, faster now, wanting to go. She walked away and part of me followed. After a year of wandering, I had finally found my first clue. But now that I'd got it, I wasn't sure I wanted it. Clue to what? Some secret I was better off not knowing.

"Why did you not tell me?" Viktor complained.

"I don't know."

But I did. Because I knew telling him would bring us closer together, which is just what it was doing.

"I am coming right over."

"Don't. I like it better on the phone."

"So I have noticed," he said bitterly.

Instead of the couch, I was lying on the floor. He was in that same mystery space, with its deep sounds in the background, that welling up. It intrigued me.

"Are you mad?"

"That you did not come to work? You do not have to come to work ever again, Eve. But I want to *see* you."

He made it sound more than just sight. See me naked. See me whole. A threat. But maybe that's just how I interpreted it. I always felt that my place, no matter what position he took, was to be against him. That's why I knew that if we ever did it, it would be this struggle, like wrestling. And also that it might be great, that it might be what I really wanted, which was of course the scariest thought of all.

"Where are you?"

"It is what you always ask when you wish to change the subject."

It is *the subject*, I answered silently. Where you are.

Because at the same time I could feel him on top of me, lying on my back, pressing my bones into the threadbare carpet. I don't mean a fantasy. I could feel his weight, his body stretched out to cover mine, make it disappear. Not a daydream, a case of demonic possession.

"I could be there in forty minutes." He was reading my mind. Well, not my mind. "Honestly and truly. Maybe fifty."

His hands were circling my chest. I could even feel that ugly ring of his pushing up under my ribs, spreading them apart. His mustache burrowing into my neck. I sighed and shifted to more completely accommodate him.

"Eve—"

"No."

I was lonely and wanted to stay that way. Alone. Part of me. The part I liked.

"This is crazy. You go for a walk and see something you are not supposed to see. Instead of ignoring it, as any rational person would, you file a report with the police. Weeks later, your apartment is burgled. And now, around these two unrelated incidents, you weave a whole paranoid conspiracy theory. Don't you see what is happening?"

"That's just it," I said. "I see what is happening. For the first time."

"Wiolent attacks are part of life in this city. People are robbed every day. It would be more suspicious if you passed your time here completely unscathed."

"I saw—"

"You saw a whore. With her customer. And then something went amiss."

"I'll say."

"But it has nothing to do with you."

"She wasn't a whore."

Guys might call her one, but they called you a whore no matter what, if you did it with them or if you didn't. You were a whore the minute they decided they wanted you.

"And I wasn't robbed. They didn't take anything."

"Except perhaps your critical faculties."

"What?"

"Your brain."

"I saw something!" I insisted. I wasn't going to let him snatch that away from me. I held it tight.

"If you are truly concerned for your safety, then come stay with me."

My heart beat faster. The exact opposite of the sinking feeling when he had proposed. He was offering me his place. His secret place. That appealed to me in a whole different way than the empty gesture of some stupid marriage ceremony. I wanted to immediately say, "Come pick me up," before he changed his mind, then just lie back, let nature take its course. I had been swimming against the current for so long now. And for what? It wasn't getting me anywhere. I was using all my energy just to stay in place, to keep my lower lip above water. I was this close to giving up. The saving grace was his not knowing. He didn't see what moved me and what didn't. He didn't know me, except in this very general way, these ideas he had about women, which were right, some of them, but applied to us all equally, not as individuals, so even when he could have had me, could have pressed his advantage, he didn't realize it. My silence, which was me holding my breath, tempted like I had never been tempted before, he heard as just another refusal.

"I am arranging for your birth certificate to be made," he went on, changing topics.

Ask again, part of me begged. Ask one more time.

"Birth certificate?"

"For the marriage license. You must have documentation."

"Viktor, doesn't it bother you that you're going ahead with all this and I haven't said yes?"

"A woman says yes with her body, not with words."

"That's the stupidest thing I ever heard. Besides, it isn't even true. We haven't had sex, remember?"

"Had sex. As if it were something you could possess."

"Well, don't you think it's important?"

"Who now is denying the spiritual nature of love?"

I was confused. Because he is *trying* to confuse you, I told myself. Trying to keep you off balance, which is just the evil version of sweeping you off your feet.

"In any event, you need proof of your existence."

"I don't have any!"

"My friend will produce it. He can make anything. Birth certificates. Social Security. I gave him information about you, about your mother, your birth date, the approximate location of the hospital. He says that should be enough."

"How did you know all that stuff?"

"Things you said in conversation."

"So you've been planning this? You've been getting me to talk about myself and then writing it down, after?"

"I have been listening to what you say, yes. Is that a point against me as well? Would you like it better if I treated you like some 'dumb broad'? If I possessed your body and ignored your words altogether?"

"Yes."

"Why do you always make the proof that I care sound like a bad thing?"

"Sorry." I always ended up apologizing to him. He got everything he ever wanted from me, and I still apologized. "But if your friend can make a birth certificate, then why can't he just make us a marriage license?"

"Don't be absurd."

"What's so absurd about that?"

"Because then we would be living in sin."

I looked down at the phone.

"He needs to know your last name. I think it should be something simple, so as not to draw attention. What is the most common American name?"

"Probably Smith," I yawned. "But there's no way this is going to work."

"Yes, it doesn't matter what we put," he went on hurriedly. "After all, soon you will have to concentrate on getting used to your new name."

"My new what?"

It was easier talking back to him this way, too. Directing my voice into the receiver. It gave me the distance I could never get on him in real life.

"Your new name." He waited. He was surprised I couldn't figure it out. "You know. Eve Kholmov."

If the coffee shop was my neighborhood church, then Grand Central was the cathedral. There was a balcony overlooking the main floor. It was a bar, but didn't feel like one. That's why I liked it. You were outside, part of the bustle and flow, but separated from it too, sitting on a stool, sipping club soda, watching people go to the ticket windows, meet each other at the information booth, shop at the stores. It was past rush hour. There was still the clacking of the old-fashioned board, the kind that had millions of cards being flipped around until, by pure chance, a place, time, and platform number appeared, sending people off, just a few at first, a trickle, but then becoming more, more than just themselves, a crowd within a crowd.

"Eve? Is that you?"

I didn't recognize Marron at first. She wasn't dressed the same as the other times. She was wearing a denim jacket and had a bag hanging off her shoulder. Her hair was even blonder than before. She must have just colored it again. It made her face look dark, by contrast.

"What are you doing here?" she asked.

"Nothing. When I have to go to work, I come here first, sometimes. What about you?"

"Catching a train."

We stared at each other. She could have just said good-bye and walked on. But she didn't. I felt this deep urge for company, even though a minute ago I had been perfectly happy sitting by myself.

"Where are you going?" I asked.

"Connecticut. I have to buy a ticket. Want to stand in line with me?"

"Sure."

She smiled. She had perfect teeth.

"Where in Connecticut?" I called, as we went down the stone steps.

"Greenwich. That's where my mom is." Her bag kept bumping against her. It made her look clumsy. "But I never get a schedule, so I'm always waiting. I like killing time here."

"Me too."

"It's sexy."

I rolled my eyes. Everything was sexy to Marron. Except sex, I bet.

While we stood, she crouched and unzipped her bag. She was excited, wanting to interest me. It's almost like she wants to be friends, I thought, even though we were enemies, right? But why were we enemies? I had forgotten.

"So you live at home?"

"Not really. She's remarried. But there's a room for me. Look at this. Isn't it beautiful?"

She took out a bottle. It was shaped like wine, but clear, so you could see inside, to this peach, a whole round perfect blushing peach, somehow squeezed past the neck, preserved in thick liquid. If you tilted the glass you could see soft fuzz, swaying.

"It's Westphalian. That's what they told me. I just saw it today, in the window of a liquor store."

"Is it her birthday?"

"No. I just like giving people things. I like finding the perfect gift. The thing you never even knew you wanted. I do it with everyone I know, eventually."

"That's nice, I guess." I remembered she had bought Horace that scotch I got so drunk on. So what everyone needed was more alcohol? "Where's Westphalia?"

"Germany."

"Oh."

"Have you ever been to Europe?"

"Are you kidding?"

"You should go. Horace is going, this winter. He got a travel grant. You should go with him."

She put the bottle away and zipped up her bag.

I didn't know what to say. I didn't understand what she meant. You're sleeping with him, right? That's what I felt like asking. That's why we're enemies. It all came back to me now. Why I was supposed to hate her.

"What's your mom like?"

"She's great. She's more like a sister to me. And still a total babe."

"A what?"

She laughed.

"It's the truth. We make other mother-daughters look like shit."

Women who thought they were pretty. They amazed me, the ones who took it in stride, like it was a quality they had, a virtue, something they deserved. I couldn't get over that. Do you really think you're pretty? I wanted to ask. I mean, in your heart of hearts, when you look in the mirror, do you like what you see? I guess Brandy did. But she was incredibly insecure. She clung to her prettiness because she sensed it was all she had. Which it wasn't, I reflected. But it got in the way of everything else, whatever else was there. That's why she kept emphasizing her looks. With Marron it was different. She probably felt about her face the same way a guy did about his muscles.

After she got her ticket, we walked through the station.

"I may have to get married," I sighed.

"Have to?"

"To stay here."

"Are you an alien?"

"Kind of. He is, too. Apparently two aliens make one citizen. You know, like two wrongs make a right? Although they don't, do they?" There I went. I didn't know what it was about Marron, but with her in particular I would just let go and say whatever was on my mind and sound like a complete idiot. It was the Real Me. "Anyway, we're kind of made for each other. Still, it's scary. The idea. Even if it's not real."

"If you're doing it, then it's real. Right?"

"I guess."

"Do you love him?"

"Of course not!"

"So what's in it for you?"

"That's just what I asked. And he looked so outraged! He says he can get me a birth certificate. And I'll have a real last name. His last name, but still, that'll be nice, I guess."

"So he's going to make you legitimate."

"He's going to try."

We both began to giggle.

"Good luck," she got out.

I should leave, I thought. I was already late. Viktor would be getting worried. At the platform, there was a train, but it wasn't ready to take passengers. It was waiting there, all sealed up. Empty.

I liked it that she hadn't said, Congratulations.

"How come you invited me to your Opening? I mean how did I get on your mailing list?"

"Are you still hung up on that? What does it matter?"

"Because I want to know. I want to know why things happen to me."

"I don't know who half the people on my list are," she said. "And I certainly don't know why things happen to me. Do you?"

"I guess because I deserve to have them happen."

"You mean they're a punishment?"

"Or a reward."

"Which is getting married?"

I shrugged. I hadn't thought about that. Marriage seemed like the ultimate combination of the two.

"How do you meet *anyone* in your life?" Marron went on. "You really think you have any control?"

"Don't you?"

"No! I think there are these forces that sweep you along. That bring you together. And then for a while you can't get away from each other even if you try. And then the same forces rip you apart."

"What forces?"

"Just . . . forces. Like the wind. Or gravity. Invisible powers. The city's got a mind of its own. You can't figure out where things come from. You can't trace things back to their source. The population's reached some critical mass and begun to think for itself."

How do I even know this lunatic? I wondered.

"So, you don't live with him?"

She didn't get it at first. Or pretended not to.

"I thought maybe—"

"Nobody lives with Horace. I don't think even Horace lives with Horace."

"Then how do you know him?"

"We went to art school together. He lets me have a key so I can crash sometimes. If I'm out late. Or if I have somewhere to be in the morning. And there's a drawer where I keep clothes."

"Well, when you stay over, where do you sleep?"

She blushed. I don't think she was used to being asked such questions. It was different from being asked how she photographed her vagina.

"You don't get it. I'm like . . . this person Horace keeps around to keep other people away. At least, that's what I think I am, to him."

"Are you kidding?"

"It worked, didn't it? I mean, that last time you were at the studio, I was there, too. You think that was an accident? And you're the one who ended up storming out, right?"

"Right."

"Well, have you seen him since?"

"No. But I thought that was because you were his girlfriend."

She shook her head.

"He's going to Europe."

"I know. You just told me."

"You should go with him. He likes you. I mean he really likes you. I can tell."

What do you mean? I wanted to scream. Did he tell you? Does he like me the same way he likes you? Or is there a different way?

"You're crazy," I said. "It's not like he's called me or anything."

"You told him not to call."

"Yeah, but—"

"Then he won't. With Horace you have to do all the work. He thinks he's doing what you want, but of course really he's making you do what he wants. He's kind of annoying, that way."

She loves him, I thought. Not like me. I want to love him, maybe. But she wants to be rescued from her love, from her one-sided love. That's why she's telling me this. So I'll step in and save her.

They opened the doors.

"You'd be good for him," she went on, in this dreamy voice, talking to herself, maybe regretting what she had told me. "But I don't know if he'd be good for you."

"You know, when I first met you, I thought you were a real bitch."

She opened her eyes wide.

"Oh, I am way beyond bitch, Eve."

I nodded to the bottle in her bag.

"What are you going to get me? I work in a bar, so it can't be liquor. What do I need that I don't even know I need?"

She smiled.

"I'll think of something."

I followed her along the train, waved to her when she sat. She was surprised. She waved back. She looked happy, setting off on this journey, as if by telling all this stuff about Horace she had escaped her situation, dumped it all on me.

It was too late to go to work. I would have to miss another night. Back out on the main floor, I pretended I had just arrived. People were tired, leaning against walls, looking past me. Maybe I wasn't a crank. Maybe I was a reverse commuter. I'd read about me. I came to things when everyone else had gone. I came to dreams wide awake. At the balcony bar, someone else was sitting in my seat. Another me. A guy. A businessman, waiting for his train. My eyes kept going. They couldn't stop. They were floating to the surface. They found stars painted onto the ceiling. A real live bird that had gotten lost, trapped in the building, flew past. My eyes followed it. You always follow something living over something dead. When they refocused, I realized that's what *he* saw, the man who fell. That's what he had been staring at, stabbed, when I came over: the night sky, constellations, patterns that imposed their will on our lives.

I hadn't cleaned up. I couldn't face the prospect of putting things back the way they were before the break-in. I didn't even remember what the room looked like, how it had gone. I took out a big black plastic garbage bag and started dumping. Even if objects weren't damaged, the spell that made them special was broken. I never realized what a refuge my apartment had been. Out there, on the street, we kept our tight little distance, arms at our sides, trying not to touch, swaying like schools of fish. Up here, I had been able to expand, mingle with the molecules, spread out to the walls. That was all gone. I threw books into the bag, too. It didn't matter anymore, my cute little ways of dealing with the world, the dollar paperbacks, the games I played with food, the games I played with my own desires. I looked around and saw what the apartment actually was, a bare, smelly attic room.

At first, I thought throwing out all the ratty thrift shop cushions was what made the outside sound of traffic and air conditioners, that endless exhale, so much louder. Then I realized it had a source. I went looking, and ended up in the bathroom, staring out the window. Usually it was closed, except for a crack to let out steam, but after the burglars knocked out the bars they jammed the wood up high to get in. I tried shutting it. My hands strained. I pulled so hard I could feel my feet leaving the ground. Cool air fanned my face. I closed my eyes, like when the sun is bright you want to bathe in it, except it was nighttime now, so I rolled my head in this blast of meaty pollution and thought, Since they got in, why can't I go out? I climbed up on the lip of the tub and managed to get one leg through. It poked around until it felt something solid, then planted itself. I drew in my shoulders, slid past the narrow opening, and landed, panting, on tar paper.

So this is what it was like, being high up. I went to the edge and looked out. I could see across the Park, to the fancy buildings on Fifth Avenue. They shimmered. One had white walls. After a certain height, it began going back, a few feet every floor. There were balconies with railings and dripping vines. Then, as it got higher still, the spaces became deeper. There were deck chairs, tables with parasols, I imagined, squinting, creating what I saw. There were sliding doors so you could come out and feel like you owned as far as you could see. Closer to the top, it all broke up into individual houses that had architectures of their own, their own sections of miniature roof. I could sense their apartness and luxury, until finally, at the very top, lights along the whole outer square of the tower melted into sky, so you were living right up there in the real Plan, not its imperfect earthly representation.

That's where I belong, I thought. Not on this sagging, sticky rooftop, not in an attic room where everything is in someone else's name. Where is my name? Who am I going to be? Here it was, the famous skyline, this beautiful dangerous twinkling jagged row of teeth, and I had failed, so far. I hadn't gotten where I wanted. But I was here, higher than before, five and a half floors, almost six. And I was ready to take on more. I jutted out my chin. The trick was to fail at increasingly higher levels. To fall *up*.

"It's got a rubber handle. Black. With little holes. To soak up the sweat, I guess."

"And what does the blade look like? Serrated or smooth?"

"Oh, I don't know. But it was really sharp. I can tell you that."

The store was listed in the yellow pages under Hunting Supplies. It looked fancy from the outside, with a window full of tweedy jackets and funny hats. Inside, it was more serious. There were racks of rifles bolted to green felt. Each had a little telescope on top. There was a big photograph of guys hunting elk in a Jeep. A passageway led to the back, where the entrance to the dressing rooms would be in a department store, except here there was a private policeman stopping anyone from entering without a sales clerk. I found the case of knives. A whole display, under locked glass, all in a circle with blades pointing so their shiny tips met in a starburst. I stared at the gleaming sharpness. It was a religious symbol. I couldn't see what was holding them in place. Then I looked more closely and saw little bands of nylon thread.

"What you're describing sounds more like a switchblade,"

the man said. “Not a hunting knife. A switchblade is more in the area of personal protection.”

“Oh, well, that’s what I want. Personal protection.”

He looked me over. I guess I didn’t look like the killer type.

“I could offer you Mace. A spray jar. Like perfume.”

Yes, I thought. That would certainly be good on a date. Mace, by Eve.

“No. I really want the knife.”

“I’m curious. Why that knife? With that handle?”

“It goes with an outfit.”

He looked puzzled.

“Switchblades are mostly for men.”

Don’t I know it, I thought, trying to erase the bloody picture from my mind.

I couldn’t think of any other clue. Any other way to track her down except to become her, a little. Enough to figure out who she was and what she had done. He led me back past the security guard, past a mannequin of a guy in a black leather mask, holding a rope, then past a rack of handcuffs.

“Hey, where are we, anyway?”

It looked like a sex shop, all of a sudden.

“Personal protection,” he repeated automatically.

I was stopped at the whips.

“Protection from what? Vampires?”

“I told you, it’s mostly for men, this part of the store. Here are the knives.”

I couldn’t take my eyes off the fetish wear. Studded collars, latex bodysuits. It was this glimpse into the male mind. If you could even call it a mind. Everything was so simple. So spelled out. There was no maybe. No shades of do-I-want-this-or-don’t-I? which, for me, were the whole essence of sex. That tension. This wasn't even black and white. It was just black. I guess the white was the outer world. Your beautiful bride's white wedding dress. And meanwhile in your head you were whipping her with this flimsy-looking leather. I fingered it like I was at a sale. It was such bad quality, the workmanship.

"Where was this made?" I asked, looking for a label. "I mean you couldn't really use this, could you? It would fall apart. Or the person would die laughing."

"Miss?"

"Is that a dildo?"

He cleared his throat.

"It's not very realistic," I said.

"I wouldn't know."

"Of course you would. Look, it's like a leg of lamb."

"I thought you wanted to see the knives."

"I do, but—"

"Women don't usually come back here."

"They should."

That's what you need, I thought. A consultant. Maybe I could get them to hire me. Men really needed help. They were so ignorant.

"Here."

The switchblades weren't displayed as lovingly as the ones out front. But I saw mine instantly. The soft handle, the pinholes. For some reason it had stayed with me more than her face. Or instead of. You concentrate on things instead of people, I complained. It's a form of avoidance, really. Things and sounds and smells. A sliver of soap. A foreign accent. A knife handle. Those you remember. But faces you shy away from. Your own most of all.

"So you wouldn't happen to have a list of every person who bought this one, would you?"

"What?"

"I'm looking for a woman who had a knife like that."

"I thought you said you wanted it for personal protection."

"Well, I do. For personal protection against the kind of guy who attacks the kind of woman who would buy a knife like this. That makes sense, doesn't it? See, at first I thought, well, I just assumed, it was his knife. But I've been going over it in my head and now I realize it was hers. It was hers all along. I saw it in her hand. I never saw it in his. So I'd like to know a little bit about who she is."

"Listen, are you really interested in buying this item or not? Because if you're just wasting my time here—"

"Of course I'm going to buy it."

And I'll take two of those dildos, I felt like adding.

They were so big they were like furniture. They could be part of my new decorating scheme. On either side of a roaring fireplace. Yes, in my penthouse apartment. Just wrap them up. Do you deliver?

But the knife was enough. It fit in my hand. This surge of power went through me. Back on the street, I held it, hidden, walking slowly, meeting everyone's look. Practicing.

CHAPTER FIVE

When fall finally came, it was more to people's faces than the trees. The summer sameness left them. I began to see different colors and shapes: small dark wrinkled purple, veiny red, big bland yellow. They weren't just tossing manes of greenery anymore. They were all different, clattering past me, this human forest of hope and fear and a million other feelings that didn't have names but found some matching part inside me. We're so naked up there, I thought. Our face. The one part of our body we never cover.

"I accept your apology."

I had climbed the tilting steps, knocked, held my breath, and was relieved when Horace, alone, opened the door. He wore old smeared pants and paint-spattered shoes. He didn't look formal, for once. His expression was blank and confused. I tried picking up the conversation as if nothing had happened.

"You said you were sorry about her being here when we got back. Remember? And I'm sorry I got so mad at you."

He looked at me.

My problem, I finally realized, wasn't deep or mysterious at all. My problem was that I wanted sex in the morning, because it was my night, so it got twisted into ridiculous social encounters, while at night, their night, when everyone else was horny, I was just waking up and wanted to talk, wanted to do stuff, so other people's lust came across as this incredibly rude behavior.

"You came from work?"

"Yes," I lied.

I hadn't been in a week, but I was wearing the outfit, stockings, hot pants, the leotard. I pretended I was just off work as my excuse for coming so early. The truth was, I couldn't stand being alone anymore. I was afraid to go out, afraid people were watching me, which I knew wasn't true, but couldn't help feeling. Horace had been the answer before, when I panicked. He had a calming influence on me. So I got dressed up, as if I had been at the bar, and walked down. But also, part of me admitted, feeling stares from the occasional dog walker and early morning construction crew, I made myself look this way because apparently it was what men liked, and if I wanted a man I might as well try to be what he wants.

The room smelled of coffee. It was arranged differently. The big canvas was propped against the bookshelves. There were open jars on the floor, and brushes lying next to each, on an upturned lid.

"You're working."

He nodded.

The one chair was surrounded by equipment. He went back and slumped there. The overhead lights were on. The rays they gave out were thin in the sun. He had been working all night.

"It's morning." I went and turned them off. "Look."

"I don't know what I'm doing," he complained.

"What do you mean?"

"I'm stuck."

He nodded at the painting. I saw his eyes start to focus on it again. To stop him, to save him from himself, I went over and sat on his lap, blocking his vision, the way he had done for me, that time on the sidewalk. His clothes were soft. Paint drops made stiff circles. All around them the fabric just fell away. They were play clothes. I remembered how on Sundays, after Service, we were allowed to change into something meant for getting dirty in, and run over the fields, run not as part of a game but just for the feel of it, in clothes like that, clothes our bodies shaped, instead of the other way around. I faced him, looking into his eyes. His hands automatically came up to hold me. Everything had this predestined quality to it, like it was meant to be. That's how it felt, whenever we touched.

"What's this?"

"Oh."

I took out the knife. Since I didn't have a pocket, I had just stuffed it in the waistband of my skimpy shorts. I had a bag, but if someone came up and grabbed your bag, that's when you'd want your knife, right? It wasn't at all uncomfortable, the rubber handle. It made me feel like a gunslinger, walking down some dusty Main Street in a small town in the Wild West.

"Look. It's really cool."

I flicked out the blade.

His eyes got big. He reared up and almost dumped me on the floor.

"Horace! Be careful. What's wrong?" I looked down at the blade. It was so shiny. "Oh, did you think I was going to . . . ?"

He was standing ten feet away from me. With his hands up. And then down. He couldn't decide where to put them.

"It's for personal protection," I said. "I'm not going to use it. Look." I pushed the point back in. "Isn't that amazing?"

"What exactly is so amazing about it?"

"Well, the fact that it got you out of your blocked-artist-zombie-funk, for starters. Why didn't you call? It's been a long time. Didn't you want to see me?"

"You told me not to."

"If I told you to jump off a bridge would you do that, too?"

He stopped being scared and got puzzled.

"But you didn't tell me to jump off a bridge."

"Well, not calling me"—I tried working it out—"is like jumping off a bridge, for you."

I had forgotten his being so serious. It was flattering, but I had to watch what I said. Worse, I had to listen to what I said.

"So my not calling you is like committing suicide?" He frowned.

"It's just something my mother used to say. About jumping off bridges. Which was funny, because in Iowa there were no bridges. So actually it sounded kind of exciting. Not jumping off a bridge, but just being on a bridge that you *could* jump off, if you weren't careful. Where there was even the possibility."

The good thing was it forced you to be honest. To be bold, even. To say what you meant.

He was still staring at the knife.

"You know what I mean?"

"Not really."

"You're my bridge," I said, putting it away.

He approached me slowly, as if I was some kind of dangerous animal, which I liked, and steadied me, the way he had done before, outside the train. I moved closer. He was looking for the bottom of my leotard. He kept digging deeper.

"Wait, there's a snap."

I wanted to do it myself, but he stopped me.

His hand rested between my legs. I swear I felt the subway start up again. We had been at a station this whole time, stuck, and now the train was slowly coming to life. I couldn't breathe. His fingers found the snap and undid it. There was this release of tension, revealing about a million times more and different tension underneath. I managed to swallow. Once. He gathered the sides and pulled them up. I raised my arms. Everything went black. Oh my God, I'm passing out, I thought, then realized it was the fabric, this scratchy synthetic, pausing, bunching, until finally it gathered enough energy to pop over my head and tomorrow came. He took off the rest of my clothes. My knife fell to the floor. I heard it bounce, gently, and saw where it landed. I didn't want to forget it. I wasn't lost in some romantic mist. I was thinking. I was thinking fifty times faster than normal, more brilliantly than I had ever thought before, about everything in the world, everything I normally didn't have time to think about, because what was happening now didn't need thought. His shirt smelled of sweat. I fell against it, found one of the buttons, and ripped it out with my teeth.

"Let me just put away the paints."

"Sure," I mumbled.

I had this button in my mouth. I got it out and held it in

my hand. Marron had his soap, but I had this. It was more of a talisman. It came from closer to his heart. My voodoo was stronger than hers. He started screwing each lid back onto its jar. I could see he liked even this, the cleaning-up part of painting. He did it so carefully. I didn't mind waiting. Not when I knew what was going to happen. I could ask him anything now.

"Where did you grow up?"

"Japan, mostly."

"Japan!"

"My father worked for an aid agency. He was based in Tokyo. He used to fly around Asia a lot."

"What was that like?"

"We lived in a house for Americans. It was very big. It had a yard, which was unusual. They don't have any room at all, most of them."

I looked at him again. There *was* something Japanese about him. How he held back. His inner quiet. He was gathering up the brushes now.

"Did you like it there?"

"I loved it. I really got into the culture. How it all fit. There's this answer for everything. The right way to do something. Of course, you never question what it is you have to do. That's determined for you. You just have to learn how to do it. So even though it's complicated, it's easy. It's all technique."

He stopped, on his way to the sink, and looked at the painting again. I was getting cold. But he kept talking.

"The first girlfriend I had was Japanese. She was the daughter of my calligraphy teacher. That's like handwriting, but different. It's more of an art form."

"I know what calligraphy is."

"You do?"

"I read a book about it."

"I never know what you know and what you don't."

I know everything, I wanted to tell him, except what's in your head. And soon I'll know that, too.

"Anyway, when we made love, I actually saw it as this character we were forming together. Our bodies. This word picture. Brushstrokes. Do you think you could wait just one minute?"

He didn't listen for my answer. He knelt back down to open up some paint.

"What happened?"

"When?"

"To you and that girl."

"Nothing. That's it."

"Did you break her heart?"

"I didn't break anyone's heart." He sounded sad about it, like he wished he had. "It's when I decided to go to art school."

"Marron says you won some prize. That you're going to Europe, next."

His face had this unguarded quality, like a sleeper's, but with his eyes open instead of shut. Oh, bring it over here, I tried sending by mental telepathy. I have a place for your beautiful face. Several places, actually. I even knew what order I wanted him to visit them in. It shocked me. He made me feel so sexually alive. He crystallized my desires. Made them achingly real. I'd never thought about exactly what I'd wanted until now. I just thought I'd like a guy, or to make love. Horace was the first man who seemed created especially for me, for my needs. Every part of him answered some urge of mine. Urges I didn't even know I had until I met him.

"She says you got a travel grant. Where are you going?"

"Tuscany."

Tuscany? That wasn't a country either, was it? Like Mingrelia. Like Westphalia. Why couldn't these people talk about normal places, the kind you found on maps?

"When do you start?"

"Sometime after my show."

"So you're leaving the city."

"I guess. I hadn't really thought of it that way." He put down one brush and picked up another. "Talking to you just now, I think I figured out a way to get going on this again."

"Great."

"It's really a kind of American ideogram."

"Uh-huh."

"You help me out, Eve. You always do. I don't know what it is about you."

There was this poster that was really popular then. It was of a girl lying naked on her side with this snake on top of her, coiling along the curves of her hips and shoulders. I decided to take matters into my own hands, to *be* that snake. Because that's what Eve did, basically, if you thought about it. She accepted the snake-in-her. Adam didn't. He just ate fruit and got fat and watched TV. Besides, I was freezing.

"Hey," he said.

I reached around his waist. My hands were icy. He jumped. My fingers met at the small of his back. I had this fantasy I could lift him, but I couldn't. Still it was thrilling to try, to feel my muscles test themselves against this resistance.

"You're like a boa constrictor." He smiled, condescending, still holding his brush, not taking me seriously. That was the push I needed.

"Want me to swallow you?" I asked.

The way to a man's heart is through his stomach. That's what it said in *The Fannie Farmer Cookbook*. I had bought an old, cracked copy for a dollar. The trifle recipe was from there, the faded cover and crumbling pages. I was past all that now. Anyway, what could a lady named "Fannie Farmer" possibly know about the way to a man's heart? I undid his belt. The soft fabric fell. I didn't need a cookbook anymore.

Dear Mother,

I just gave a man a blow job and now I'm pretending to be asleep instead of letting him make love to me. Why? I don't know. I guess because I'm not as "liberated" as you. I wonder just exactly how much sex you really had. You talked about it so much, or referred to it, at least. Maybe I was just picking up on all these comments because they were what I wanted to hear, although at the time I remember how much I didn't *want to hear. How I wanted to hold my hands flat over my ears and scream, "Shut up!" You were always dropping these hints, like there was this central mystery you were dying to let me in on. And I'm still resisting, even though you're not here and I am. Even though the mystery, whatever it is, is inside me, now. But I still don't want to know. Part of me. I want . . . What do I want, Mother?*

"You can do it to me while I'm asleep," I murmured.
"Why would I want to do that?"
"I don't know. Maybe it would be nice."
"Nice for who?"

I didn't answer. I found this cave between his arm and side, and burrowed.

"I'll wait," he whispered gently, stroking my hair.

Yeah, you'll wait, I answered silently, disapproving, like his being nice was a character flaw, which it was. He should have shaken my eyes open, spread me out on the thin mattress, and taken me. I meant to tell him that, but I had done such a good job of pretending to be asleep that I almost was. My mouth was the mouth of a cat, with that false, curved animal smile. I wanted claws, so I could scratch, really scratch him and leave marks. Make an *impression*. He was so hard to reach. Of course, it was my fault, not his. He didn't realize what a bad person I was. I had already gotten what I wanted. I had had my way with him. That's how it felt. I didn't want to make love, yet. I wanted to stretch everything out, because when we got to the end, I didn't know where that was. Maybe no place. I didn't know if there was anything to us besides the buildup. That's what was so terrifying. I ran my hand along his flat, smooth side with this feeling of ownership. He was mine. He was money in the bank.

But the sleep I finally fell into left me groggy. It went on too long. I kept struggling with nightmares, trying to untangle myself, sinking deeper, until finally I sank so deep I came out the other side, fell out the bottom of a hole, and was sitting, shivering, on a mattress, on the floor of a bare studio, in Manhattan, in the dark.

I lay back down. It was a relief to know everything that had gone before wasn't real. I felt it fade, and waited to make out what really was, the facts that didn't disappear with the dream, dim outlines at first, that got stronger and more distinct, that kept growing. Facts like Horace. His smile, his smell. The way his long endless body had fallen so slowly. Where was he? It occurred to me he wasn't here, where he should be, next to me. In the bathroom? I waited, strained my ears, but heard nothing. I got up and walked around. It was two in the morning. On the counter, next to the little refrigerator, was a note. I didn't want to turn on a light, so I held it up to the windows, which were lit by the highway. It said he had to go out, to an Opening. I squinted, looking for another sentence, one that told me to wait, that he'd be back. My eyes went down to that space between the last word and his name, looking where he should have written "love," but hadn't.

He was gone.

I couldn't believe it. It seemed like the most basic etiquette to stay, to work, or read, or eat dinner while I was lying there passed out, but not to let me wake up alone, feeling for his beautiful warmth, having my hand reach farther and farther, still not finding him, until I was caressing hopefully, pathetically, the cold paint of the floor. Well, I could wait him out. What did he think, that I was just going to disappear? He had turned his painting to the wall so I wouldn't see. Like I cared. I cared about him, not what he did. I was infatuated. I could still feel him, feel his absence. It was like those drug ads, warning you'd be hooked "after just one puff." And he hadn't even bothered to stay with me, to wake me up, to kiss me good-bye.

My attention strayed past the window, to the night. It was strange to see so far. The two places I spent time in, the bar and my apartment, didn't have real windows. Not the kind you could look out of. They showed a brick wall or travel posters. Here, there were cars. It never stopped, the buzz saw of traffic. Past a fence topped with barbed wire, in the river itself, people walked on water. I squinted, rubbing the sleep from my eyes, and looked again. People. Walking on water. A crowd. A Scene, at 2 A.M. If I turned on the light, they would vanish. Everything out there would turn black. It's what I was going to do, turn on the lights and wait for Horace. How much longer could he be? He was probably on his way right now. Then I realized his coming back scared me more than his being away. What if he didn't want me here? What if he had left because he was hoping I would go? Of course! He thought I was still working. He assumed I was at the bar by now. The certainty I felt a few hours before flipped over into doubt.

No, I thought. He loves me. Maybe he doesn't know he loves me, yet, but once I explain it to him . . .

Who were these figures moving, dancing it looked like, in space, their feet not touching the ground? It was only because I was letting the night seep in this way that my consciousness was getting swept back out with it. It's just leftover dream, I told myself, and kept waiting for it to fade, catch up with its fellow hallucinations and disappear, but instead what I saw overtook plain depressing reality until I couldn't look at anything else. It was a spit of paved-over landfill in the middle of the Hudson River. People walked hand in hand, stopping to socialize, to chat, then moving on. Others rode bicycles; one, a unicycle. This gorgeously dressed woman stood perfectly still. I saw a man pause, exchange a few words with her, then the two turned and disappeared down the steep bank, past a crumbling layer of blacktop to what must have been the rubbly shore, out of sight. I stared after them for a moment, then watched another woman dance. She writhed, arms up, feet stamping. In appreciation? Celebration? Or the desperate urge to escape? People walked by, unnoticing. She was as much a feature of the landscape as a tree, except there were no trees. This spot, this one stretched-out block, existed beyond some urban timberline. It was pure community, with no buildings or cars, no landscape other than the city dwellers themselves. Nature had been banished and this was what remained: a man, stripped to the waist, wearing tiny shorts, gleaming even in the weak light. Muscles had taken him over, popping twisting ropes, mounds like tumors. They walked him in a clumsy, roly-poly stroll, pressing limbs that had lost any will of their own. A bodybuilder. I was so repulsed I wondered if I was secretly attracted. I couldn't take my eyes off him. Couldn't, that is, until I saw a beautiful girl go by on Roller Blades. She sped past everyone, winking in and out of the crowd, this ripple on the surface, people stepping back to where they had been, closing in behind. She was in a white tank top, heading uptown, pushing against the ground, digging to go even faster. I followed her until my head knocked against the window frame.

I want to go down there, I realized. I wanted to *be* there.

I wheeled around and with this burst of energy looked for my clothes. But they were pathetic. The hot pants and the leotard and the stockings. They were so high school. I couldn't believe I actually wore them in broad daylight. No wonder Horace took them off. It wasn't that he was attracted to me, he was just offended by my incredibly poor fashion sense. Undressing me was really this *criticism*. What could I wear instead? I wasn't home, and even if I was, what I had there wasn't much better. Something led me to the bottom drawer of his dresser. I don't know if it was instinct or if I saw stuff peeking out. It didn't want to open at first, but that just made me try harder.

"Come on, give up your secrets," I grunted, while another

part of me said, Eve, you're talking to furniture. With a final yank, I fell back and saw piles of clothes spring up.

Marron's clothes, I confirmed, touching the material. This was her special drawer. I could barely make out, in the dark, what they looked like, but I knew they were expensive. I reached deeper. She had underwear and socks. Everything. I put on slacks and a silk blouse. There were even shoes and, amazingly, they fit. I ran across the floor, still not knowing what I was doing, not consciously, then stopped at the door. My knife. I went back, squatted on the floor, feeling with both hands, and found it. I found the button, too. The one I'd ripped off his shirt. The pants were crushed velvet.

Why didn't I buy comfortable shoes? I asked myself, walking, clicking smartly along. Why didn't I buy clothes like this? Why did I always go to thrift shops or take what was handed down to me like that's what I deserved? Why didn't I have tastes of my own? They had tastes, the people on the river. Maybe not ones I shared, but they had tastes and a style and they were alive in a way I wanted to be, in the way I pictured myself being when I came here. Instead, I had gotten sidetracked, gotten involved with these types who weren't worth my attention. I was quaking with excitement. I had to get across. To that magical place. It was the answer to my search, the distilled essence of city life.

From Horace's windows it looked so close, but down on the street the very shape of things curved me from my goal again and again. I kept walking. There had to be a way. I wanted to be cool, for once. I wanted to promenade up and down this narrow strip, an island off an island, live a weightless, frictionless life. The eagerness stayed with me long after the impossibility began to sink in. My momentum was carrying me past where it could possibly be. I should go back, but back to what? Horace's empty studio? Press my nose against the glass again? I couldn't. I was locked out. Try crossing the highway and get run over, flattened by some drunken clubgoer on his way back to New Jersey? Plunge into the polluted water of the Hudson and die of some horrible disease?

Where are you? I felt like shouting.

I had seen Paradise, but there was no way to get there, no bridge, no tunnel, no magic carpet. I kept walking. It's all I was good at. I was always walking and never getting anywhere. I could feel the sadness and terror of my daily existence itching to return. If only I could marry Viktor and go on the honeymoon with Horace. Yes! That was perfect. It answered each of my problems with the other. It made it clear that, even though we were getting married, I wasn't going to be Viktor's wife, and it was a way of reassuring Horace that whatever we did wasn't serious, wouldn't lead to anything, because I was already taken, spoken for, in the eyes of the world. So it made me safe, not a threat. I could get a husband and a lover and still stay me, not lose myself in either one of them. If I couldn't get to Paradise, I would make my own Paradise, right here, with what I had.

All I needed to do now was come up with a plan. To think. I walked faster.

"Male sexuality is binary. It is either on or off. Mostly on. A switch. Women operate along a spectrum, like the tuner on a radio. So for you, love is different. It is perhaps harder to determine. Like finding an obscure transmission. Searching along the dial."

"How do you know? Have you ever been in love?"

"I have loved every woman I ever sleeped with."

"So it doesn't mean much, your love."

"It means everything, at the time. But as I said, it is on, then off."

He made a gesture in the air. Flicking a switch.

"That's not love, Viktor."

"Who are you to tell me what I feel is not love? When I feel it, it is the most intense sensation known. Maybe stronger, more pure, than what you feel."

I was lying in his lap, looking up while he drove.

"Then, if you'll pardon me for asking, how come we've never done it? I mean, if supposedly you've wanted to so much?"

" 'Done it,' " he mocked. " 'Make love.' 'Have sex.' American is a child's language. You are like primitive peoples, not wanting to say out loud the name of your deity."

"How do you say it? Where you come from?"

"We don't. We do not talk about such matters. We are beyond such sentimentality."

I waited. I was beginning to learn that the best argument against bullshit is just to let it sit there and start to stink.

"Maybe because I was afraid," he admitted.

"Afraid of what?"

"Of the switch"—he made the same gesture—"going off. I was perhaps afraid of not loving you. After."

"Why would you be afraid of *not* loving me?"

"Because that would be a fate worse than death."

We went over a pothole, both bounced, then fell back against each other, even more united.

I didn't understand men at all. And somehow I sensed it wasn't going to get any better. I bet the more you knew them, the less you understood. I had called the bar as soon as I got home. They would just be closing up. I figured I could leave a message and wait for him to call me back. Instead he came to the phone right away, which he had never done for anyone, in all my time there.

"Where have you been?"

"Nowhere. Walking."

"I have been trying you for hours."

"Why?"

"I was concerned. You said there might be people watching."

"And you said I was paranoid."

"Yes, well, just because you are paranoid does not mean a bad thing could not happen. It is many nights since you came to work. We are all worried sick for you here. Are you all right, Eve?"

I took a deep breath.

"Actually, there is something on my mind. Maybe you could come over and we could talk."

He didn't understand, at first. There was this sound. He was changing the phone from one ear to the other. I could hear voices in the background.

"Viktor?"

"Yes, why not? But I don't like your stairs. Wait outside and I will pick you up."

"And go where?"

"A place I know."

It wasn't part of my plan, but I did have to get Viktor to do something for me. Maybe this was the best way. I hesitated.

"Be down in twenty minutes."

"Wait," I said. "This doesn't mean I'm going to—"

He hung up without saying good-bye, like the time he drove off while I was still talking. He left me standing there, holding the phone.

And now I was in his clutches, where I'd been heading all along. Was that good or bad?

"Where are we going?"

"You will see."

As soon as I got in the car, he had taken my head and pressed it down. Did I need to hide? I wondered. Were people really after me? I blinked through the top of the windshield. Bits of building and sky were chopped up as we spurted ahead, then screeched, turned. There were all these poles and wires, connecting things. I was seeing the city from underneath, the back of an embroidery. The stitching.

"How's that birth certificate coming? The one your friend is making for me?"

"I only just called him. These things take time. There is a huge demand."

"I was wondering, do you think he could make me a passport, too?"

"A passport!"

"Well, if I'm going to become a person, I might as well go all the way. You know what I mean? Maybe I'll want to go abroad someday."

We drove in silence.

"So you are just oozing me," he concluded.

I lay back and felt guilty, for about one half second.

"You're oozing me, too," I remembered. "You're just doing all this because you want to be a U.S. citizen."

"It is true. At times I confuse you with Lady Liberty."

"I mean, you're not even attracted to me."

"Attraction is a disaster. It contains the seeds of its own destruction. When I am attracted to a woman, part of me resents her."

"Why?"

"Because it is always for some superficial reason. Her hair. Her eyes. Her ass."

"Hips," I corrected.

"No, in this case you say ass. And the attraction is based on what? An extra layer of fat. The way dead cells are extruded from her scalp. I resent myself, too, for being such a slave to illogic. It makes sex an act of exorcism. Laying the dream to rest."

"So it's true?" I hadn't really meant it. I was expecting him to say, No, of course he was attracted to me. "You don't even want me?"

"I am not attracted to you at all," he said proudly, as if it was this great compliment. "And you, I think, feel the same. It is why we make such a perfect couple."

He hit the brakes and grabbed me, to stop me from rolling forward, off his lap. His hand held my breast. I don't think it was intentional. He was very concentrated on his driving. This chill, this prickliness, spread out from his fingers. It was this instant skin rash. And then, whether it was an accident or not, he didn't let go.

"So what about the passport?"

"OK, OK. Why not?"

"Thanks, Viktor."

"I can refuse you nothing."

His hand controlled me. Not with force, but pressure. He'd found the wavelength of my nervous system. I watched his face as it searched for a parking space. We were going slow, circling. Where was this? From the sky and buildingtops I couldn't tell. A block like any other. His hideaway, in the middle of the city. I was glad it wasn't on some desolate stretch of outer borough.

He was so foreign, with his mustache and his hairy chest and his ferocious eyes. Sex to him is like the English language, I thought. Something that's not natural, that's learned, so he uses it differently, like it's not part of him. Something he uses to get what he wants. But maybe I was the same way. Maybe we all were, and he just recognized it, faced the truth. I got that sense again that he had something to teach me, about how to live, although it all got mixed up now with something to teach me in bed, because I realized he'd been taking his hand off, every few seconds, to shift, then putting it back, casually, like I was this place to rest, and the more he did it, the more my breast ached for his return, even though each time his fingers did come back my spine arched, like in the dentist's chair when the drill starts up.

"Why can't I look up? You think there really might be people following me?"

"Girls your age always imagine they are watched by strange men. And more often than not they are correct. Enjoy it while you can."

"You don't understand. After the break-in, and what that detective said, I got scared. But I didn't expect you to take it seriously. I thought you'd tell me I was crazy. Then everything would be back to normal."

"As I said, it is not uncommon. You put out some sort of scent. Not a perfume, but a secretion, from a gland. In insects it is pheromones. I do not know what in humans it is called."

"Viktor, I'm worried about people thinking I'm mixed up in a murder, not asking me out on dates!"

"But it is the same thing, really. You choose to look at it a certain way, that is all. You would rather imagine you are the object of insidious designs than romantic intentions."

"Why would I want to think that?"

"Because it scares you."

"Being attacked?"

"Being loved."

"Will you take your hand off me?"

He pressed down even harder, like a bolt. I squirmed, then thrashed, trying to get out from under him. The car stopped.

"And here we are," he announced.

I went limp. What had I been thinking, saying I would go home with him? This was just what I had feared. But it's not like I had any other place to go. If there really were people after me, if I had seen something I wasn't supposed to see, then my best chance was to disappear, to go down Viktor's little rabbit hole and hide out. At least until the wedding, the wedding to my husband and the honeymoon with my lover.

"Where is this?"

He finally allowed me to get up.

"Hurry. Don't look around. Just come."

He took my hand and dragged me out his side, hustling me to the curb before I could find any street signs or get my bearings.

"You're parked next to a hydrant."

He was pulling me up the steps. It was just an ordinary brownstone. Not what I associated with the deep, soul-stirring sounds that came through the phone. I thought it would be under the ocean.

"Is this where you've been calling me from?"

"What?"

Maybe there was a secret passageway or a trapdoor. He buzzed once, long. I noticed he held his hand over the name.

"You don't have a key?"

"I have to park," he said. "You go on in."

"I don't understand. There's other people? I thought we were going to be alone."

The doors clicked open. He shoved me in ahead of him.

"It is on the second floor."

"What is?"

He was marching me up the steps. This wasn't making sense. Suddenly, I was cold.

"Eve." For the first time he sounded nervous. "You must understand. Not everything I do is what I want to do. There are forces I must answer to. As must we all."

"What are you talking about?"

I'm dressed so well, I thought, smoothing my silk blouse, feeling the velvet of my pants. Nothing really bad can happen to me.

"Just remember, after, that this was not a choice I had. I was instructed. I was powerless."

He was close behind. I couldn't turn. Couldn't spin and push him aside and run away. And even if I could, where would I go? He reached around to knock on the door. I was being kidnapped! Except I had gone so willingly. I was so stupid. I had let it all happen to me without thinking. And now it was too late.

"I have to leave you."

"Wait. Aren't you going to at least come in with me?"

"I have to go. The car."

"Oh. Your car. Excuse me."

My hand was in my pocket. He was right. Words weren't really the best way to say yes or no. He never believed what I said, anyway. He never took me seriously. It was all lies. This whole time I thought he was listening to me, and really he was selling me out! I was hysterical inside, but calm and determined in my movements. I knew exactly what I was going to do. If I couldn't refuse him in words, how else could I refuse him? What kind of no would he understand? My fingers curled around the switchblade's soft rubber handle. All I had to do was take it out, push the button, and—

"Surprise!"

Brandy, Crystal, and Nora were crowded into the doorway, trying to open a bottle of champagne. I stared at them. Viktor was gone. I could hear him taking the steps, two at a time, down to his precious, illegally parked car. Running away from my anger.

"It's your bridal shower," Brandy explained, seeing how totally clueless I was. "We got the idea from Nora. Remember? A surprise shower?"

They were still dressed from work. They had been waiting every night to throw me this party, they said. But I never came. So that morning, when I finally called, they frantically motioned for Viktor to make me come with him, to drive me around in circles, basically, with my head down, so I wouldn't recognize where we were going, while they got back here, to this apartment Brandy and Crystal shared. It was only a few blocks from the bar, a sunny room in the back of a building. It had two kittens, both white with a big brown spot, chasing each other. The furniture was cheap, used, but went together, a couch and two chairs, this tropical living room set. A chain of letters, from a card store, hung between the two windows, spelling C-O-N-G-R-A-T-U-L-A-T-I-O-N-S. There were flowers, and champagne with orange juice.

"But we're not really getting married." I was confused, secretly trying to unglue my fingers, which were still wrapped around the knife. "I didn't say yes."

"Where have you been?" Nora complained. "Every night we've been ready and every night you haven't showed."

"I've been sick. I didn't know you were planning this the whole time."

"Sick how?"

Crystal looked at me. I followed her eyes to my belly.

"Oh no, not *that* way," I said with such emphasis we all laughed.

For one terrible moment I actually thought it was possible, that I was pregnant, carrying Viktor's child, that he had managed to put it in there, somehow, with one of his looks. It was just the sort of sneaky trick he'd be good at.

"Is he coming back?"

"Girls only."

Nora poured. Very professionally. She was back to her old self.

"I wasn't really sick. I was crazy."

"Crazy how?"

"I thought . . ." What had I thought? My fears seemed so silly, in the light of day. "I thought there were these guys who were after me."

"Not anymore. You are *taken*."

"What?" I didn't get it at first. "Oh. You know it's not real, right? I mean it's just this mutual use job."

"What is?"

"Marriage." I looked around wildly. "What are we even doing here?"

Brandy giggled.

"You are so funny, Eve."

Crystal raised her glass. I thought she was going to make a toast. And she did, kind of. She said, "There's cookies."

* * *

We talked. In a way it was just what I'd wanted before, this bonding time with all of us, and no Viktor. But for some reason I found myself arguing with them, defending things I was usually the first to make fun of.

"All families are cults. You grow up in this closed-off world, with its special rules and rituals. You even have private family names for each other. And you think it's normal, that the same rules and rituals are followed in every house, up and down the street. Then you get older, you go out, see people doing things differently, and you think they're the ones who are weird. At first."

"So you're saying the place you grew up in wasn't strange?"

"I'm saying it was just a family for people who didn't have families. So yes, in a way it was less strange than what it was based on, from where you guys all came from, it sounds like."

We had been drinking, except for Crystal, who was more into the hostessing part of it, filling up everyone's glass, bringing out more food. All I ate was the cookies. They were so soft. Sugar and alcohol, my ideal diet.

"You had to wear a uniform?"

"Didn't you have rules about what you could and couldn't wear?"

"Sure."

"Well, so did we. They were just narrower, the rules. So we looked more alike. But didn't you dress pretty much the same as your friends? I mean now that you look back on it?"

"It certainly explains a lot," Brandy said.

"About what?"

"About you and clothes."

What was funny was how *they* were all still in their uniforms, the outfit from the bar, even though it looked different on each of them. Brandy wore hers so well. She was the model it was based on. It showed her off, made her body look long and slim. It didn't break her up into segments. Crystal managed to desex the whole thing. She canceled out the slinkiness, acted like she was in overalls. Nora *was* the outfit. You couldn't see where it ended and she began. She was worn in places, threadbare, but completely comfortable, moving inside it like the material was a second skin.

"What else have you got?" she asked, holding the champagne bottle upside down, squeezing out the last few drops.

Crystal went to show her. Brandy and I stared at each other. We weren't usually alone together.

"I tried your trick," she said.

"What trick?"

"Going on that train. The number six. Downtown."

I blinked. I didn't know what she was talking about.

"You said you were on that train and . . ."

"Oh."

Then I remembered.

"But I was with someone."

She nodded like, "I knew that," except obviously she didn't. I couldn't figure out if it was a joke or if I'd discovered a new depth to her innocence.

"I should have made myself more clear. I didn't mean the train made me feel that way. Although maybe it was the train, now that I think about it."

"No. It wasn't." She tapped her glass, trying to make it ring. "Sometimes I think there's something wrong with me."

I struggled to get out of the chair. It was this cage of peeling bamboo. I gripped the skinny arms and pulled.

"When I was little," she went on, "someone told me what touching was. Like a stranger touching you. Know what I said?"

"Listen," I whispered, kneeling in front of her. Crystal and Nora were still over by the sink. "I don't really want to get married."

"I said, You mean there's a *word* for that?"

She was always staring at things, getting lost in them, like her empty glass now, running her finger along the rim.

"Is that from the bar?"

"What isn't?"

I looked around. Everything was. Glasses. Ashtrays. The liquor we were drinking. How had they gotten them away, with Viktor watching all the time? Unless he was only watching me.

"It's a little late, Eve. I mean you've been trying to get him ever since you started working."

"I have not!"

"And now that he wants you, you act like it's not even happening. Well, it is. You're marrying Viktor. There's nothing you can do to stop it."

"Of course I can stop it. I can just say no."

"You know what he told me?"

"What?"

"That when he loved someone, it was like a trap snapping shut. And that the only way the person could escape his love was to gnaw off their own foot."

"He never said that."

"You think I made it up?"

She had a point. She was too unimaginative to come up with something so disgusting and twisted on her own. No, that definitely sounded like my husband-to-be.

"So it was with a guy," she murmured. "The way you said it, I thought it was just the train."

"Why would I feel that way about a train?"

"You're so normal, Eve."

"I am not."

"Yes, you are. That's what you can't admit. You're the most normal of all of us. I mean look at you, you're getting married."

"Nora's been married."

"Yeah, to a serial killer."

"He was just a murderer," Nora said. "And that was after we split up."

It turned out they hadn't been looking for something to drink. They'd been getting my present. It was this big box done up in white tissue paper and frilly white ribbons. White on white.

"What is it?" I asked suspiciously.

"Open it."

I didn't know how. I sat back down and put it on my lap. I didn't want to tell them that I had never gotten a present before. That we didn't do that, growing up, for birthdays or holidays or anything. No presents in the Bible. You were never supposed to admit you needed anything. You already had what you needed, if you were blessed, if you were graced with His love. I didn't want to tell them anything about that, it sounded either too stupid or too right, I couldn't decide which, so I looked for a way in, but all the ribbons and wrapping looked so perfect.

"Just rip it," Crystal said.

"Thank you," I remembered to say. I thought it was better to say it before. Before I saw what it was. "Thank you so much."

"Do you still see him?" Brandy was asking Nora.

"Once a month. I go upstate. Because we're still married,

technically. So they let us be together. There's this trailer, right next to the prison."

"You're kidding."

"No."

It was a box, thin cardboard with pleats at each corner, taped shut. I had to start opening it all over again, running my finger under the edges.

"So what's in the trailer?"

"They think a camera. But nobody knows where."

"Gross."

"It's not so bad. It's very basic, but it's clean. It's stripped down. I mean, you know why you're there."

I got the lid off. Next, there were these white blankets of thick tissue paper. Is this ever going to end, I wondered. I parted them and then almost dug past the present itself, it was so flimsy, a lacy black bra and panties.

"What's this for?"

"Eve!"

"The trailer," Brandy said.

Everyone laughed. I was beet-red.

"There's a book, too," Crystal said. "Keep going."

It was a dictionary. English to Russian, Russian to English. I liked it that they didn't really know what country he came from, what language he spoke. It made me feel like Viktor and I did have a special knowledge of each other. Even if it was sick knowledge. Nora leaned over and kissed me on the cheek. I could feel the invisible shape her lipstick left. Then Brandy and Crystal came over and hugged me, too. The cats thought it was a game. They jumped on my lap, and bounded away again. I was making these horrible sniffling sounds, not knowing what to say, how to act.

"It's just not what I expected," I finally got out.

Immediately I wanted to say I didn't mean the presents, but the emotion, that it was so sad the only way we could feel close was by banding ourselves together against men. Because that's how it felt, like I was being armed for battle.

Nora was the first to go. She was almost as mysterious as Viktor. I couldn't imagine her heading home to some ordinary little studio apartment. But I also couldn't imagine where else she had to be, so drunk now, at noon. The rest of us could barely get up to say good-bye.

"I should go, too," I said, instead of actually moving, as if expressing the wish could transport me there magically.

"You could stay here, tonight," Crystal offered.

I looked around. Where did they sleep? I wondered. There was only one other room.

"How do you two know each other, anyway? From the bar?"

"School," Crystal said.

"School?"

"Cris wanted to come to New York." Brandy got up and began walking a tightrope, holding her arms out, putting one foot after another. It was a good imitation. You could see her almost falling, the way her body would go over its center of gravity, that point of no return, and then jerk back. She was concentrating hard. She really believed it, that she was high up. "I came along, to make sure she didn't get in trouble."

"Her mom." Crystal gave this other explanation. "There was this guy she let live with them. But he was a real jerk. That's why we left."

"I miss my mom."

"I miss mine, too," I answered suddenly.

Brandy looked up, just for a second, then went back to balancing. She was making her way someplace, along this imaginary line, walking heel to toe. I remembered how she drank at the bar, all night, so she was even more wasted than me. Crystal watched, making sure she got wherever it was she was going, taking care of her, every minute.

"Eve's in love," Brandy said.

She walked right by me, on her way to the bedroom. She raised one arm high, sticking this imaginary parasol up in the air. The fabric of her uniform stretched and her hip flared out. She really did have hips, not an ass. I was drunk enough to see the difference. To see things not from a male point of view. I frowned as she made her way by, oblivious not just to me but to everything. She was sleepwalking. But her course was off. Crystal saw it before I did. She was up instantly. I'd never seen her move so fast. She got there just as Brandy was about to walk into the wall. She was careful not to grab her, just touched her lightly, held her by each hip, where I had been staring—Wait, I thought, was I looking there, seeing her body that new way, before or after what just happened? Time got jumbled—and steered her gently through the open doorway.

"Hey," I suddenly remembered to object. "I am not. In love."

At least I didn't think so. And if I was, who with? Maybe she knew and I didn't. Maybe it was this secret everyone knew but me. Who I loved. Maybe it was obvious.

The door closed. My last glimpse was of Crystal's heel, kicking backwards, making it shut, while the rest of her was settling Brandy down onto the bed. That's where they slept. Their private universe.

I cleaned up as much as I could. Everything was already so neat. The mess rested lightly on top, just the opposite of my place, where there was this deep chaos I always struggled to mask. I washed the glasses and lined them up, then looked around for anything more to do so I wouldn't have to face the fact that I had nothing, no clothes to sleep in, not even my toothbrush. I decided to take a bath.

"Eve?"

Crystal poked her head in about a half hour later. There were bubbles. I had dumped in way more than I meant to. She stared at this mountain of foam rising over the sides of the tub.

"Sorry," I said.

"I have to pee."

I had been luxuriating. The floor was covered with fluffy white carpet. All the other surfaces had baskets or glass trays with little soaps and creams. The only thing I dared use was the bubble bath and that had turned out so hilariously I just looked at the rest, reading the backs of the jars, the Instructions for Use. They were all about *you*, your skin, your eyes, your hair. I stretched out. The water was slippery. It slid off my arms and legs. I lifted my whole body and saw myself emerging from the white perfumy ocean. I wanted to be beautiful, for a change. I was tired of feeling ugly. It was so boring.

Crystal was wearing a big white bathrobe. Her hair was back. I sank down in the hot water, protected by suds.

"She's asleep," she said solemnly.

I nodded. She sat and looked at me.

"I love it here," I said. "Here, I mean. The bathroom."

"I did it myself. I did the whole apartment."

"It's great."

"She gets that way, late. Usually we're alone by then, so no one sees."

"It's all right."

"She doesn't remember what she says. When she wakes up."

"It's all right," I repeated. "It was nice of you both to do this for me. The shower, and everything."

"The dictionary was from me."

"I figured. Is that true, what she was saying? That it was you who wanted to come here? Originally?"

She smiled.

"Her mother's boyfriend was after her all the time. She didn't have anyplace else to go."

"Why didn't she tell somebody?"

"She did. That's how we ended up leaving. Jane's mother kicked her out, basically. She didn't want to hear this guy was a pervert."

"Jane?"

"Oh. Don't ever tell her I told you that."

"Brandy's real name is Jane?"

"It's Brandy."

"But what about you? Why did you come? Your family didn't kick you out, did they?"

"I had to come. I wanted to rescue her. I mean, she rescued me, so—"

"Rescued you from what?"

"I don't know." She was so solid, her look just blasted through everything. She never blinked. "Remember that guy at the bar? The one who freaked me out so much?"

"The one you yelled at? What did he say?"

"Nothing, really. He just called me a dyke bitch."

There were kids upstairs. Little feet pounding over the floor. Put those children to bed, I thought, and then remembered it was the middle of the day. But for us there was this exhausted silence of 3 A.M.

"If I'd stayed in Menominee, I would have just gone

along, done what was expected of me. That's my nature. It's hard for me to stand up for myself."

"You seem to do a pretty good job of standing up for yourself. Most of the time."

"No. I can't do anything for me. I have to do it for someone else. Someone like Jane."

I shook my head.

"But does she know? I mean, about how you feel?"

"She does and she doesn't. Sometimes she says things that are so right-on you can't believe it. She's the one who told me about myself. What I was. I know that sounds stupid, but I'm not sure I would ever have figured it out on my own. Not until it was too late. I mean, we're from Michigan. But on the other hand, she keeps complaining that she never really wanted to come, that I bullied her into it, that she would have gone back. She would have begged her mom to take her in, with that guy still there. So she blames me. She says I use people. She calls me names."

"Like what?"

"Sick. Which I guess I am."

I slid deeper into the tub. The water came up to my chin. I was looking at these castles, all bubbles, popping gently, releasing scented steam.

Crystal got up.

"I know what will happen. Eventually. She'll meet someone. Someone just like Roy, probably. And that'll be that."

"Who?"

"Roy. He was the guy her mother found. Her mom's just like her. Or she's just like her mom. I'm not even sure she didn't *want* something to happen with Roy. At first, anyway. Then it got ridiculous." She shook her head. "But by the time it happens again, I'll be here, instead of Menominee. So maybe she was right. Maybe I was just using her, like she says. Using her to get away."

She very quietly lowered the lid. It had a little cloth cover.

"I'm going to make a sandwich. Do you want anything? You want a candle? There's a candle that smells like lavender."

"Do you have a razor?" I asked.

"Sure."

After she left, I soaped up my legs and shaved them. It was no big deal. Then I started poking around all the tubes and jars again. It was time to get beautiful.

CHAPTER SIX

"Name?"

"Eve Smith."

"Age?"

"Twenty-one."

I kept waiting for some buzzer to go off, for armed guards to invade the little cubicle and arrest me. But the machine kept up its steady beep. Graph paper came out. It looked damp. He made a mark after each answer, then let it collect in a wet curl on the floor.

"I'm just going over obvious stuff. Setting the parameters."

"The what?"

"The baseline. So we get a sense of what normal is, for you."

The only reason I thought this might work was because it was all happening by accident. I had started out with a big resolution: to buy clothes. Not used, not borrowed, not hand-me-downs, but brand-new clothes that I alone wanted. Instead of a uniform for work or an outfit for a date, I was going to design a whole new look for a whole new me. I mean, if someone like Crystal, who was at least as confused as I was, could make a bathroom, an entire apartment, that looked and felt so right, then why couldn't I make myself over into an entirely new Young Woman? Every magazine cover and bus ad seemed determined to offer me these options of what to look like, how to act, who to be. It was only a question of making the right choices.

So I went to Bloomingdale's.

Now, this is a house of worship, I thought approvingly. Everyone was charged with excitement, looking wildly around, on the hunt, elbowing, jostling aside, like they didn't want to let the other person get there first, even though they didn't know what it was they were trying to get to themselves. There were no windows, just like in a church. Because what you call stained glass windows you can't really see out of. It's a trick. You think you're seeing reality because it's where the window should be, but it's not real at all, it's a picture of, say, Jesus, or some words from the Bible, and since you're used to seeing the world out a window you think Jesus or the Bible is in the world. But they're not. They're just pictures. Bloomingdale's had mannequins where the windows should be. They were the stained glass of Shopping. You looked at them and took them in the way you would the Savior or a verse of Scripture. At least, I did. The dummies and the clothes they wore gave me this clue as to what kind of attitude I should assume. In life.

"All right, I'm going to ask you a series of questions. Answer yes or no. Were you previously employed as a salesperson by the Paris Boutique in Chicago, Illinois?"

"Yes."

"And before that, did you receive a degree from"—he looked at my application—"the Des Moines Institute of Fashion?"

"Yes."

I fell in love with a mannequin and decided I wanted to be her. She was reaching out, offering to help, ministering to someone, but at the same time her hip was slouched. She was tall and absolutely unblemished. She wore a white dress with all this detail at the throat and wrists. It was simple but so beautiful. It was my dress. It belonged to me. I belonged to it. We were made for each other.

"Excuse me. How much is this?"

"Are you interested?" the lady asked.

I circled the pedestal until I was dizzy.

"Is there anyone with you?"

I looked. Maybe some guardian angel was by my side. The dress spoke to me. Not that I knew what it said, but I would, when I put it on.

"Most girls come with their mothers," she said gently. "Or a friend."

"Right." I blushed. Because I saw now this was the bridal shop. It was a wedding dress I was drooling over. "Of course."

I couldn't even tell what the material was. It had all this pattern worked into it. It was different textures in different places, a shiny blinding wall of white, but also soft and inviting, almost cuddly. It wasn't a gown. It ended above the knee.

I really liked that feature, that you could move, down the aisle, and then break free, run away, right at the altar. Before or after the ceremony, though? Avoid the commitment, the "I do"? Or just the honeymoon, the sex? Because despite all the patterning it was still white. It was the kind of dress that would turn you back into a virgin each time you put it on. It was so formal and ornamental and gorgeous. You'd really feel like a bride. And why shouldn't I feel like a bride? I wanted that glow, of specialness, of triumph, and I wanted it every day, not just once with a guy and his obnoxious relatives and bad catered food and six screaming babies to follow.

"I am interested," I tried saying casually.

If I really pushed, I sensed I could try it on. But I didn't need that. For now, I only wanted to look. I would save that sensation, wait until I'd earned it. But how? Very quietly, and just for a second, I practiced the pose the mannequin was making, extending one arm, looking straight ahead, deep into the eyes of the invisible groom. The sounds of the store, of the shoppers all around me, didn't fall away exactly, it's more like they came together, the way music does sometimes when you don't realize it's there, when you're not listening for it. All the buzz of conversation, the click of hangers, the chatter of cash registers pumping out receipts, even the hum of the hidden lights, matched up and canceled out the chaos to make this mystical harmony. And out of that harmony came a revelation.

"Is there an employee discount?"

I don't know what barrier I had crossed. I didn't even stop to think if it was good or bad. I went to the eighth floor (Staff Only) and asked to fill out a job application. My pen flew over the blanks, making up everything, a past, a future, whatever I needed to get hired. I wouldn't have to work here long. I wanted that dress. I could visit it during breaks, like you visit a chapel, when I wasn't busy stocking the shelves with packets of panty hose or refolding tried-on outfits from the Junior Department. Whatever mindless, menial, entry-level chores they found for me. I wanted it so much that, for the first time, I was willing to lie.

"Just a few more questions."

I felt this unshakable confidence. Things were going my way. They had looked at my application and said there might be a position available. A man came down to talk to me. Then a woman. I was dressed right, I was acting right. They were impressed by my experience. I was, too. I talked about the kind of clothes we sold at the Chicago store. How the owners, this elderly couple, trusted me so much I was left to close up some nights. I let them in on my dream of designing a line of evening wear. I thought that was good, considering I didn't know what evening wear was. They looked at each other. Where did it all come from? It sounded more real than my so-called real life, certainly more plausible. That's what I liked about it. I was coming across as this fresh-faced, slightly clothes-crazy girl from the Midwest. This person who maybe I was, but didn't feel like, most of the time. And who would work for practically nothing. "To learn," I said eagerly. They smiled again. And, oh yes, I managed to find out there was an employee discount. Forty percent! I was smiling so hard my face hurt.

"Have you ever been arrested?"

Then, as a kind of afterthought, they sent me back to this dingy bunch of rooms (it was weird how dirty everything was behind the scenes, like they had to make up for how clean and light they kept the store itself, the part the customers saw) and had this guy attach black rubber leeches to my wrists and temples. The same places I had dabbed Brandy and Crystal's perfume. Pressure points. Where my pulse pounded. At first I thought it was all over. A lie detector, blowing to smithereens the innocent Eve I had created. But my momentum was so strong it rode over the machine's objections. I watched the needle nod drowsily in time with the man behind it. Of course, I considered more sensibly, it's because I lied from the start, about the things people don't usually try to conceal. My name. My age. My history. So he never got to establish what was a regular rhythm for me. What "normal" was. Now the problem was, did I have to keep on lying? If I suddenly started telling the truth, would that screw things up in the other direction, start registering just as wildly as a lie?

"Arrested? No," I tried experimentally.

The needle jumped. The beeps the machine made, it was like those heart monitors in hospitals, came faster, almost double. I glimpsed the graph paper, on its way down to the floor, and saw he had made a small "x," not a check like before.

It wasn't fair! I wanted to say. I never *had* been arrested. That was the truth. It was those other things that were lies. My name and who I was and where I'd been.

"Have you ever been convicted of a felony?"

"A felony? Well, how could I be convicted of a felony if I was never arrested? I mean, is that a trick question?"

Maybe this was really an intelligence test, in disguise.

He didn't make any mark next to that.

"Answer the question yes or no, please. Have you ever been convicted of a felony?"

I was back on the street. I saw her eyes, this look of complicity, like we were in this together. But that didn't count, did it? He meant convicted in a court of law, not by some guilty conscience.

"No."

His whole manner changed. Before, he had been bored. Now he was puzzled. It didn't make sense. It's almost like he knew I was telling the truth and couldn't figure out why it was coming out on his machine as lies.

"Have you ever committed a crime?" he tried again.

"What crime?"

"Just answer the question."

I had to find a way to lie and tell the truth at the same time. We were both staring at the machine. Slowly I said, "Yes," and watched as the needle resumed its nice even course, listened to the beeps fall soothingly back into their evenly spaced intervals.

"Yes," I repeated, for the pleasure of telling the truth, of having what I knew, what I sensed, all along, confirmed, finally, the guilty pleasure of admitting that we had conspired, the mystery girl and I. That we had something in common. "Of course I've committed a crime. Who hasn't?"

"Well," he said, not knowing what to ask next.

That was the end of my dream. The man and woman who interviewed me said there was nothing available now, but that I should keep in touch. Yeah, right. I slunk out of the store. It was still light. For some reason I expected it to be dark. Well, it would be dark soon enough, or just had been, moments ago. I was all turned around. I couldn't remember if it was sunrise or sunset, if the day or the night was behind or before me. What difference did it make? Everything was its own opposite.

Stop it, I scolded. Get a grip. Now, exactly what have you just been doing?

Shopping for clothes. Applying for a job. On the surface, they seemed like such rational activities. I always thought I was being bold and crazy and then discovered later I was doing exactly what was expected of me. The most conventional things in the world.

A breeze sliced through me. The sun left a purple stain. I read off a man's watch 6:15. He caught me looking and smiled. I smiled back, but that was it. I was standing still, up against the department store window, and he was being carried away by this river of people. I stared at the back of his head. I couldn't have said what he looked like, only what time he had. The way men sized you up, sized you down. Did I ever do that? When I looked at a man, I searched for his watch, because I didn't have one of my own. I didn't like the idea of a watch, the weight, the ticking. But I always wanted to know what time it was. As if I had to be somewhere. Men had time. I had something else. What? Someplace to be. A magical destination. Maybe men could tell me where. Maybe that was their appeal, if there was one. Or maybe they were just roadblocks. Obstacles. Sunset. I got my bearings, took on the responsibility of being me again. I wasn't crazy. Like Brandy said, I was normal. I was the most normal girl on earth. That's what made me so crazy. Evening. I slipped back into the flood, let it carry me along.

"What do you mean, you might have committed a crime? You don't know?"

"Well, it all depends."

"Depends on what?

"On what she was doing. I mean if it was self-defense, if

she was getting raped, that's one thing. But if she wasn't, then maybe I'm an accessory after the fact."

"What fact?"

"I don't know. You're the one who gave me the idea."

"Me!"

He didn't like it here, Detective Jourdain. I hadn't picked very carefully. It was the scummiest, least cushiony, least fancy place around. There were wooden booths and wobbly stools. The smell of cigarettes was overpowering. Still, it was packed with people just off work, shouting with relief. We leaned forward to hear each other. His breath smelled of mint.

"All I did was ask you questions."

"Yeah, well, you made me think."

"My apologies."

He looked at my glass. It was empty. I could tell he was wondering what to do, if he should ask did I want another? He couldn't know this was already my second. Although maybe he did. After all, he was a detective. What did he think I'd been doing in the time it took him to get here?

I had called (his card was furry around the edges, I had been holding it, clutching it so long, without even realizing what it was) and asked him to meet me.

"Where are you?"

I found out from the bartender.

"What are you doing there?"

"I have no idea." I took a deep breath of stinky air. It wasn't just smoke. It was the history of ground-out butts, billions of them, fifty years' worth. "That's why I'm calling, I guess. Because I don't know where I am or what I'm doing."

It felt good to ask for help. He didn't ask for details. He

just came, dropped everything because he heard I was in trouble. But by the time he got there I wasn't so desperate anymore, because I knew he was coming and because I was just starting my second martini, which I hoped he would assume was my first. I don't know why I ordered a martini to begin with. I guess I wanted to be sophisticated. Maybe I wanted to turn this into a date. I was still looking for my first one, although calling a policeman and telling him you might have committed a crime probably wasn't the best way to go about it. But you have to talk about something, right? You have to be interesting. That's always the problem.

I even found the courage to tell guys I was waiting for someone, which was actually true, though I could only say it by pretending it was a lie. I raised my hands to rub my aching skull and swear I heard the technician warn, "The electrodes!" like I was still hooked up to the machine.

"Do you want another?"

He nodded to my glass.

"Yes, please."

At first he had ordered a Coke, then saw the look on my face and changed his mind, made it a beer. But he didn't drink it. I watched him take a sip from the bottle and put it down. The level was unchanged.

"Aren't you off-duty?"

He smiled.

"The line between off-duty and on- isn't so clear."

"I didn't think you'd still be at work."

"I had things to do."

"Don't you have someone to go home to?"

He stopped smiling.

"What's wrong, Eve?"

I took a deep breath and told him everything. Because I

wanted to keep him here. Because I wanted to keep myself here, not go to an empty apartment that would be even more empty when I brought with me the ache that was expanding out of control inside my chest. I told him about making up the picture of the girl I had seen, sending him off on a wild-goose chase, about going to the hunting supply store and buying the switchblade, about telling the lie detector man I had committed a crime and the needle nodding in agreement. I confessed, made him the priest of my private church, and he listened, almost in spite of himself, not taking notes, for a change, raising the bottle to his lips, putting it back down, making that sound when rounded glass breaks its seal with soft lips, that quiet *oh!* I somehow heard through all the din. And when he ordered a second (but really a third) martini for me, he got himself another beer, too. That's when I started feeling we were getting closer. We had been calling to each other from opposite mountains and now we were sliding downhill, toward each other.

"We knew you gave us a fake description, that other time."

"You did? But how could you?"

"Look, why are you telling me all this?" He frowned. "It puts me in an awkward position. Should I try and force you to give us another statement, now that you admit you lied? You don't want to do that, do you? I mean, clearly you're trying to run away from whatever it was you saw."

"I am. But the more I run away from it, the more it comes forward to meet me. It pops up. Like it did just now with that stupid lie detector test. I could have been a salesgirl at Bloomingdale's! I could have gotten a 40 percent employee discount! I could have bought that dress I wanted! But instead—"

"Calm down. What kind of dress was it, anyway?"

"Never mind," I muttered.

Our drinks came. He paid. I saw the bartender look him over, then shoot me this quick, inquisitive glance as if to say, So this is the guy? And I thought, Why not? He was a grownup, which meant I would always be young. He knew right from wrong, which meant I didn't have to. He had a gun, which beat my knife. And most important of all, he listened. He didn't treat what I said as if it was just girlish chitchat, like Viktor, or make this big show of listening, but then go off and be totally deaf to my feelings, like Horace. I couldn't stop telling him things, and he couldn't stop listening to what I said. Was that the basis of a good relationship? Or was it a meeting of weaknesses? I raised my glass and he held up his beer bottle.

If I have sex with you, will you protect me forever? I toasted silently, through the icy gin.

"I have a daughter," he began. Then he corrected himself. "Had a daughter. She and her mother left. A year ago."

I didn't know what to say. It never occurred to me he had a life. I'd been so concerned with my problems I hadn't even thought about what he really did go home to. Or didn't.

"She's almost your age."

"Where did they go?"

"Seattle, Washington. I went and saw them last May."

"Seattle," I echoed. "That's a long way."

"Her mother remarried. This man she'd met, he took a job with Boeing."

"Oh."

We both drank. It seemed to have gotten even louder. Or the noise around us was more harsh, because of what we were discussing.

"That's why I'm here. Because when I see someone making the same mistake, I take an interest. More than I would have, before."

"Wait. I don't get it. You think I'm screwing up? Like your daughter? Or like your wife?"

"Like me."

"Like you!"

"Not accepting what's right before your very eyes."

He drank the rest of his beer, gulp after gulp. I watched his Adam's apple. He was forcing it past this valve.

"All right. I give up. What's right before my very eyes?" I squinted. "All I see is you."

"I saw things happening, in my life. I saw them with my eyes, but I didn't let what I saw travel back into my brain. Not consciously. I was in trouble, but I wouldn't admit it. So all this anxiety came out in other ways. Made everything around me look strange. Unnatural. Kind of like what you're describing. In the end, it turned me into a bad person."

"Well, I'm not bad." I was getting angry. I didn't need to be lectured to. I needed to be comforted. Couldn't he see that? "I'm good. That's my problem. Sometimes I wish I wasn't. All it does is mess things up. And I'm not blind. I'm intensely aware. Too aware. I see all kinds of things that other people don't, that get me in trouble. So I'm nothing like you at all and I wish you wouldn't say I was."

I got off my stool. It was supposed to be this grand gesture, except the floor was much farther down than when I had climbed up to sit. Some tide had gone out. My feet landed all wrong. He reached out and caught me, not by the hand or forearm, but by that part between your elbow and shoulder that doesn't have a name, where policemen must be taught to hold you, because it instantly held me captive.

"I'm concerned about your drinking," he said.

"Me too. The martinis here really suck."

"Eve—"

"I have to go to work now."

"Work?"

"Yes, work. Some of us work for a living," I announced with great dignity, as if I was the one being hassled. Why are you ruining this? another part of me asked. "And if I'm late, my boss will be furious."

"You mean that greaseball I caught trying to hump you against the hood of his car?"

"We were not 'humping.' What a word! That was a very tender, intimate moment. He had just proposed. And you didn't *catch* us. We weren't hiding. You're the one who was lurking in front of my building like, I don't know what. Like a mugger."

Oh God, I thought, seeing this incredible look of hurt flicker over his face. Why did I say that? Why did I even think that? And why was I drinking a third martini?

"I'd been waiting for you there all morning," he said softly.

"But how come? That's what I don't understand."

"Don't understand what?"

"Why you take such an *interest*."

His eyes were red. He was still holding me. People looked at us. My arm was going to have bruises, he was pressing so hard. His fingerprints would be part of my flesh.

"I still keep her room like it was. I'm hoping she'll visit."

"Couldn't she have come for summer vacation?"

"She could have." We walked a little more. "Like you said, Seattle's a long way."

We were going up the side of the park. Streetlamps lit trees from underneath. The leaves were "peaking," that's what everyone said. I didn't get it at first. I thought they meant peeking out at you, the way they were beginning to get dry, rustling and talking to each other in the wind. I looked at his reddish-brown face in the electric light. Remembering made him come alive. I saw how handsome he must have been, this hungry, fierce, lean young guy, with his life in front of him.

"She didn't approve of my work."

"Your wife? What's wrong with being a policeman?"

"I'm a detective."

"I know, but—"

"That's a different thing altogether. Anyone can be a policeman. Detective is much more difficult."

The trees made this sweeping, rippling sound, starting behind us and then whooshing past.

"It's hard enough to make detective, but almost impossible if you're black. I had to do things, things I'm not proud of, to get where I am. Which I *am* proud of. Where I am." He looked over. "You understand?"

I nodded. I felt the same way. I was disgusted with what I'd done, how I'd acted. It all felt so less-than-perfect. I was leaving this trail of Error behind me. But I wasn't ashamed of where I'd gotten to. I was proud to still be here, when so many others had given up at the first sign of trouble, paired off or gone home. Settled for less.

"And you think that's why she fell in love with another man? Because she didn't like what you'd done?"

"She didn't like what I'd become. At least that's what she

said. But the point is, I saw nothing. I thought all the sickness in my life was outside, the stuff I dealt with every day, professionally. Not coming from within, from my own home. Within my own self, maybe."

"I still don't see what this has to do with me."

He stopped us under a lamp. Leaves floated on thin stems. The light itself was buoying them up. They winked at us, yellow, red, pink, this nighttime heaven sky. One let go and came spinning slowly down. The air was full of spiral passageways.

"You say you're a good girl, but you're not."

"I am," I said stubbornly.

"How can you be a good girl and do what you do? See what you see? How can you be a good girl and hang out with those people, like that character I caught you with?"

"I told you, you didn't *catch* us together."

"How can you be a good girl and be here, now, with me?"

His eyes just tore into me. I wasn't ready for whatever it was he had in mind. That's what went through my head. But then I thought, maybe I was. After all, I had called him. What did I think was going to happen?

"Look, could we just forget about all that for now?"

"Then why did you want to see me?"

"I don't know. I wanted to talk."

"Talk about what?"

I let my mind go free.

"Tell me about her room."

He opened his mouth to say something else, then stopped.

"Whose? Vonetta's?"

Why not his house? Why not her bed? It's not like I'm his daughter, and he's definitely not my father, so why couldn't we lie and tell the truth at the same time? We could lay the dream to rest. I mean, that's what you need, isn't it? Someone whose dreams match your own? My whole body changed, went through this transformation. I made a mental note to tell Viktor, You're wrong, there is a switch, an off-on to a woman's sexuality, but you'll never find it because it's not a place, it's not a part of her or a part of you. It's a *thought.*

"There's a rug," he said. "It's the damnedest thing, because you can't really cross it. It's matted like a dog's coat gets if you don't brush him out. I must have walked through that room fifty times since she left, to open a window or water a plant, and every time I catch my toe, almost go sprawling."

"What color is it?"

"Gray. Off-white, I guess. It's impossible to keep clean. I vacuum on Sundays. Do some dusting. I told her not to get it." He shrugged. "You know how kids are."

We started walking again. I put my hand in his.

I could see the future. I could make the future. That's how it felt. I could control my destiny, or maybe I was just in tune with it, accepting the inevitable and pretending it was my idea. Either way, I saw what was going to happen next. I created his house, this miniaturized suburban two-story box in Queens, with a tiny lawn and a porch and maybe a garage. I heard the screen door whine, saw him fumble with the keys. Her room became real to me as he described it. The thick bedspread. He had left it on all summer, not wanting to change anything, then decided he should, but now it was too late. The nights were getting cold again. Posters on the walls, pop stars he didn't know, couldn't even pronounce the names of. She was a mystery to him, his own daughter. He hadn't *been there*, the last few years. So now he was there all the time, in his mind. And more, I knew, though he didn't say. I knew he had slept there, in her bed. His hand told me that, as he held on.

"What about her clothes? Did she take anything?"

He shook his head.

"It's all just like she left it."

So there it was, waiting for me. We weren't just wandering aimlessly. Had we ever? I felt the tension between us mounting, and wondered, has everything that's happened to me until now been leading up to this one moment? Is this love, some twisted form of sacrifice where you get rid of your craziness by heading right into it and then emerge as what? A sane person? An adult? With normal longings? I was still waiting for some guy my own age to ask me to the movies. Was that a totally unrealistic fantasy? Was that even really what I wanted, or just what everything and everyone around me told me I wanted? Why did I feel, instead, this delicious scary sexy feeling of being sucked out to sea?

I had to go. I knew I would either go now or sleep with him that night, and even though part of me, almost all of me, wanted to, that alone was enough of a reason to slow things down. He understood. I think he was relieved. His car was parked back near the precinct, but I wanted to walk. I wanted to be alone so I could live over these very moments that were happening right now. I pressed my legs tight against each other.

"Well, you can't walk home." He read my mind. "It's late."

"I'll take the bus."

It was great to lie again, to get back a little of my self-respect, my defenses. We went to a deserted stop and then he just stood there.

"You don't have to stay."

He was planted, standing guard. If I made a big deal, he would figure out what I was planning and wait, protecting me. But I really wanted to be alone, so I did something outrageous. I reached up with one hand and touched the side of his face. The way you reach up to a low branch of a tree and feel the leaves tickle against your palm. Even though his head was smooth, there was this stubble on his cheek. I cupped my hand, just slightly, so I was drawing him, almost magnetically, down. I took one tiny step forward and the night closed over me, this utterly perfect, wet, bottomless kiss. He tasted of mint, beer, cinnamon, and this animal taste that wasn't a taste at all. This essence. It was just one kiss, but when he lifted his head again, I was on tiptoe, not wanting it to end, actually thinking my body would leave the ground to follow, to levitate.

"I think you should go," I said.

He nodded like he understood, which was more than I did. Every cell in my body strained toward him as he turned and headed back downtown.

I was finally by myself again.

Well? I demanded.

For once, all the voices, the choir of suspicion, insult, and fear, were silent. They were so used to saying nasty things, but now they were stunned, overwhelmed by the same feelings as the rest of me.

Good kisser, one of them finally mumbled.

I walked.

Before, I never looked up. That was for tourists. You saw them with their guidebooks, gawking at buildings, standing in dog shit, getting their pockets picked. They were so vulnerable, not just their bodies, but their minds, vulnerable because they were admitting they were in awe of something, admitting that they weren't in control. I didn't want to be that way. I couldn't afford to. I *live* here, I tried to show, keeping my head down, charging straight ahead. But now I looked for the spot where it all began, the bloody cement, and when I got there, I tilted my neck straight back. I was determined to stop seeing it, in my mind, once and for all. Now that I had so much else to think about, it was silly to be obsessed by something that didn't even have anything to do with me, really. I stood where I stood before, in the middle of the street. In my private Manhattan this was the black hole, the kink where reality rippled and I glimpsed another universe. The building rose up out of where he had fallen, what he had been looking at, his eyes filled with terror, when I walked over. I had knelt down, but hadn't really seen anything, even though my eyes were staring, because at the same time I was listening to her footsteps. The way her heels met the pavement so cleanly. I remembered being impressed, because I never felt right in heels, I always shuffled, so there was a scrape, like I was dragging my own body. But her feet banged down, precise, and the sounds passed through me. I felt them, registered them in my mind, while I watched the man. I was charting where she went. That was the thing about the city. It could be a graph, too, with its blocks and corners, so laid out. I knew where she was, or thought I did, without looking up, just hearing her heels hammer away and placing them on this invisible map. Then, from one footfall to the next, they stopped. She had taken this turn into another dimension. I swept my gaze around, but of course there was nothing, the same as now. I saw her absence, all around me, what I had been seeing ever since that night, just streets and buildings, the same as before, but different, this place she had dissolved into, leaving no trace, except she had dissolved into me, too.

* * *

"Is like cancer."

"Love is like cancer? How?"

It was a slow night. Viktor had gotten it into his head to make this drink with many layers of liqueur, each a different color. They were supposed to lie on top of each other. A book was propped open on the bar. There was a picture.

"Each has a different specific gravity."

"What's specific gravity?"

"I have no idea."

He had bought all these bottles, not the kind we usually stocked, and spread them out. He used a spoon to pour. If they mixed, no matter what the colors were, the whole drink turned brown. A few times he had gotten as far as three, but after that it was harder.

"Cancer is the bogeyman. The death sentence. The Big C. All science worships it, tries to solve its mysteries. People throw billions of dollar bills at it. For research, they say, but really because they hope it will go away, go murder someone else." He let the liquid, a bright green, crème de menthe, seep gently over the side. It unrolled on top of what came before, some evil-looking cherry red. "So you would think, by now, with all that, they at least know what cancer is. But no, it is not clearly defined at all. 'Cancer' turns out to be a catch-all term for a number of different conditions. We give it a name to provide ourselves a false sense of certainty about what we are dealing with, to make it seem less what it actually is."

"Which is what?"

"A random, all-devouring maw."

"Maw?"

"That is so cool," Brandy said.

"Don't come too close."

"Can I drink it yet?"

"It is not for drinking."

"Maw?" I asked again.

"Mouth."

He took his hands away, slowly. All his motions were careful. We weren't allowed to lean on the bar. When the occasional order came, he made us come around to get it. He was obsessed.

"Similarly, with love. The whole culture acts as if it is a universal goal, the aim of every young life. And more. The word is stretched to include ridiculous things. Love yourself. Love life. Love a sparrow. But even in its narrowest, simplest sense, loving another, there exist so many kinds, so many arrangements, that it is a joke, lumping them all under one heading. Again, it is to give us a feeling of comfort, that we are united in this great pursuit, that there is at least one common good upon which we can all agree. Love. Instead of the truth."

"Well, of course I can drink it. Otherwise, why is it in a glass?"

"And what truth is that?" I yawned.

"That we are merely seeking shelter in each other's body."

"Shelter from what?"

"Ah," he said, like that was the big question.

"Cancer is the Crab," Crystal corrected.

He shook one more drop of hideous yellow on top, stood back, and bared his teeth like the winning tiger in some showdown. They were white. You wouldn't think they would be, the rest of him was so stained and crooked.

It was two weeks since I came back. Nothing had changed. Nothing and everything. We all slipped into our old routine. Nobody mentioned my being away. Our engagement, if that's what it was, had been added to the menu, a new item for conversation. It was referred to casually, almost as a joke. It didn't bother me anymore. That was the weirdest part of all. The whole marriage issue. A big bumpy scar had grown over it, with the foreign object still buried inside. Instead of getting rid of it, my body had surrounded the idea with tough tissue. I guess that's the way I felt about Viktor, too, that he was still inside me, but I had neutralized him, at this cost to my own feeling. The whole atmosphere was different, though. It was more self-conscious. Everything was about what went before, as if there had been this Golden Age of getting along and now we were just remembering, trying to reenact it. At least, that's how it seemed to me. I could feel the bar turning into one of those places, a memory, a spot on my private map, a street I would find myself walking past and shiver. I looked around to see if everyone felt the same, but if they did, they didn't give it away. It was business as usual, except business was off. The last of the summer tourists, who had trickled in all through the first part of the fall, were finally gone.

"To drink it would be impossible," he explained to Brandy. "The slightest movement would disturb the layers."

I saw her looking at the colors, one magically suspended above the other. I could see her mind working, see that little furrow form in the middle of her brow.

"Well, I'd be really careful."

"Eve."

Nora nodded to the bottom of the stairs. Horace was standing there. I was surprised I didn't feel more. I went over, not to lead him in. To bar the way.

He was the same. His smile. His clothes. That space, somehow, between the waistband of his pants and his shirt, that made him look even thinner than he was. He was lovable, but dry. This Powder of Love you had to add water to, but once you did, watch out. That's why I was being very careful. Protecting myself, looking right at him, straight, so he couldn't get underneath me. I didn't know what I was doing, but I felt, like I always did with Horace, how important it was, every move I made. How significant. Except maybe that was the phoniest feeling of all.

"One?" I asked.

"What?"

I turned and led him to the farthest table. I knew enough by now not to look back. Instead, I looked at my friends, how they were not watching us, pretending to be spectators at Viktor's mixology show, taking care of the few other customers, or just staring into space. But when I got to there and turned, he wasn't behind me. He had veered off and was standing a small distance from the barstool, where I had been perched when he arrived. He looked back at me questioningly, as if to ask, Could he join us?

Hey, you let me down, I complained, while the other part of me, the instant echo to everything I said and did, warned, Eve, you're talking to your ass.

I walked over, smiling.

"What's so funny?" Brandy asked.

"Nothing." It was true. I didn't know what was funny. I was mad at him. The grin didn't seem part of my face. "Everyone, this is Horace."

"Do not cause any disturbances," Viktor warned.

The next color was purple. It was good he was making the drink, because I could tell he didn't want to look up, didn't want to make eye contact.

"Hi," Brandy said.

Crystal grunted. Nora examined him once, her gaze traveling from head to toe, like he was hanging off a meat hook, then went back to her cigarette.

"Is that a pousse-café?"

Viktor glared. I caught him glance over to the book and make sure, not wanting to reveal his ignorance, or, better yet, hoping Horace was wrong. Which he wasn't. I could have told you that, I smiled. He is never wrong. That's his only flaw.

"Yah," he said. With certain people he became more foreign, not just his speech but his whole manner. "Pousse-café."

I'm proud of him, I realized. Even though I'm mad at him, and mad at myself for liking him, still I want him to make a good impression. Why? To raise my status in the group?

"Horace is an artist."

"Really?" Brandy straightened her shoulders and grew three inches. Her chest got bigger, too. I never understood how she did that. I mean, I saw she was just sitting up, but the way she gave her hair this little flick like she was blurry before and now she was bringing herself into focus, that still intrigued me. "What kind of artist?"

"I paint."

"Paint what?"

"Pictures," Horace said. "Well, paintings, not pictures. When they're good, they're paintings. When they work."

"Oh."

And he speaks gibberish, I boasted silently, which I alone understand. Kind of.

"I used to draw. In school. Remember, Cris?"

Crystal frowned.

"In high school."

"I did people. Do you do people?"

"People are hard."

"Not really. I did Viktor. Remember, Viktor?"

"It is true," Viktor said. "Our Brandy is quite talented."

Horace took something out of his pocket.

"I wanted to give you this."

I tried handling it casually, but found myself holding it by the edges as if it was precious. An invitation to his show. A postcard.

"You could have just sent it."

"I guess."

"I mean, I'm on your mailing list, aren't I?"

"I don't have a mailing list."

"You told me everyone had a mailing list."

"Let's see."

Brandy took it.

"Horace Dean," she read. "Recent Paintings. The Panko Gallery, 41 . . ."

His eyes were turquoise. Had I noticed that before? I must have, but didn't remember. If I had a mailing list, they seemed to be saying, you would be the only name on it. The rest of him was silver. That's what he reminded me of, that kind of jewelry from the Southwest, glowing and shiny, turquoise and silver. A belt buckle.

"Lispenard Street," he supplied, staring at me.

". . . Lispenard Street, November 13, 6 to 8 P.M. Wow," she concluded, fanning herself with the card.

"How come there's no picture?" Nora asked.

She seemed more knowledgeable, less impressed.

"I finished too late for them to take photos. I just finished," he added, as if he had thrown down his brush and come here.

This tremor went through me. I put my hand on the bar.

"Shit!"

Viktor had been trying to pour the purple on top. For a

second, there was this swirl, all the colors mixing, then it turned the color of water in a mop bucket.

"Eve!"

"I'm sorry. I slipped."

"We used to paint those in Color Theory," Horace said. "The instructor had one."

"What do you mean 'had one'?" Viktor asked irritably. "You mean he kept it on a shelf?"

"Most of the time. They're in display glasses. The layers are separated by clear disks." He turned the book around. "That's what this is a picture of. You can see. Look at the borders. There's always this buffer of white. What you're trying to do, make one from scratch, is almost impossible."

"Let me see."

Brandy held her hair back with both hands and leaned forward. She was pretending to be interested. It was so phony. Then she let her hair go and it tumbled against him.

Hey, I thought.

"Oh, I get it," she exclaimed, in mock amazement.

"Now's your chance." Crystal nodded at the ruined cocktail. "If you want to taste one."

"Oh, no. I want to drink what's in the picture."

"But didn't you hear? That's not real."

Brandy had dropped the card on the bar. It was soaking in a wet spot. I got it back and tried drying it off without anyone seeing. Her stool was closer. She was practically on top of him. I guess I should have done something, but didn't know what. It's not like I had any rights. I wasn't even supposed to want him here. What should I say? Get your hands off him! But her hands weren't on him. Everything else was, instead.

A group came. I went. I didn't know if Horace counted as

my turn or not, but I couldn't stand this anymore. Nora came, too. She almost crashed into me.

"Are you about to get your period?"

"What?"

"You're acting like some kind of sex-starved kitten back there."

"How can a kitten be sex-starved? I mean, if it's still a kitten? Kittens don't have sex. No," I said wisely, "you're thinking of 'sex kitten' and 'sex-starved.' But together they don't make—"

"You're acting like a bitch in heat."

"Why do you keep calling me names?"

I smiled at the band of idiots, turning to lead them in. She walked alongside me, speaking in a normal voice. Both of us acted as if they weren't there.

"If you don't like what she's doing, then talk to him yourself. Don't just glare like you wish he would disappear."

"But that's what I do wish."

"It's got nothing to do with your friend. You know that, don't you? Viktor's just jealous, and she's picking up on that. She's trying to make trouble."

"Who is?"

"Brandy, you moron."

"I know that," I mumbled. "Of course. It's obvious. Stop being mean to me."

She shook her head and went off to the bathroom.

"What do you want?" I asked the new people, rudely, and took their orders, at the same time putting the question to myself. What did I want? To buy a wedding dress and skip the ceremony. To honeymoon every night, not with my husband. To be someone's little girl while staying fatherless.

I was more like Brandy than I was willing to admit.

That's what put me in such a bad mood. I wanted to drink the drink you couldn't touch, to be a hummingbird, hover over the surface, beat my wings, stay absolutely still, and sip each luminous layer of life, one at a time. Back at the bar, I gave Viktor my order and slammed the tray down right where he made the drinks, so he'd have to load them for me. Fiancée's privilege, I felt like announcing.

"Excuse me," Horace said, "but do you think I could talk to you for a minute?"

"Who? Me?"

Nora had said I should talk to him, but she didn't tell me what to say.

"I know you're mad."

"No, I'm not. And by the way, what are you doing here?"

"I came to explain."

"Explain what?"

Before he could answer, I was telling him everything that was on my mind, everything I'd been keeping inside all this time, keeping from myself, too. I was screaming, basically.

". . . and then, after all that, you leave me a *note*, saying you're going to some stupid Opening. You didn't even tell me to wait, or that you were going to call. Which you didn't. While I've been sitting around like a fool for the past—"

"Something happened that night."

"No kidding!"

"It's what I came to tell you. I couldn't explain, but now, if you'd just give me a chance. . . ."

I grabbed the last drink before Viktor finished gunning soda water into it and yanked the whole tray, spilling each glass. I didn't want to hear. I hated him, hated what he made me feel. I hated him for having control over my emotions. And the fact that he didn't even know he had control, acted like he was this victim, this calm guy, sitting in a bar, chatting with my friends, getting yelled at, that just made it worse. I made my way through the maze of chairs and tables more by memory than vision. I got to the table, gave everyone their order so fiercely they didn't even think about complaining the glasses were half-empty, then turned and smacked right into him. He had followed me, come up behind, invisibly, silently, like he had before, like he always did, materializing with no warning.

"Go away," I muttered. "Stop bothering me."

"Will you come to my Opening?"

"Why should I?"

"It would mean a lot. I have to know you're coming. I won't leave until you promise."

"Is everyone happy?" I shouted, turning away from him, to the table again, to my loyal customers. They were always my first concern. "Can I get anyone anything else? Are you sure?"

"Did you hear me?" he asked.

"Excuse me. I'm working. Do I ever bother you when you're working?"

"Yes. All the time. Not that I mind. Will you promise to come to the show?"

I still wanted him to go away, now more than ever. Part of me. The part that was drowning in the other part. I held my tray in front of me to ward him off. But he wouldn't go. He just stood there. He never seemed uncomfortable. Even when he had reason to be. Especially when he had reason to be. I mean, acting like he cared, there couldn't be anything more embarrassing, could there? But he didn't seem to think so.

"Actually, miss," a voice said, "this isn't what I asked for."

"I'll let you get back to work."

He nodded to the customer who was holding up his drink.

Oh, don't, I wanted to answer. It'll only take me a second to crack that beer stein over his head.

"But you are coming, aren't you?"

"Of course." I acted as if it was never an issue.

He's back! I thought happily, watching him go up the stairs now, his beautiful lean body. He's back and he's taking part of me with him, wherever he goes. He's wearing me around his neck, like a charm.

CHAPTER SEVEN

There was a statue, past where kids sailed their boats, of a girl sitting on a mushroom. It was bronze, rubbed bright in places. Creatures—a rabbit, a mouse, a dwarf with a hat—ran around her skirt. What I liked was how the children were allowed to play underneath and on top of her. There were all these spaces, tunnels and mountaintops, except they weren't closed in or high up. They weren't scary. Grownups sat on benches and watched. Black nannies with white children. It was 10 A.M. I'm seventeen, I told myself. What am I doing here? I should be going to happening places, "clubs," whatever they were, having wild times, not sitting in Central Park wishing I had children, a little girl I could dress just like me, so we would be twins, mother-daughter twins. Was there such a thing? Of course not. How could there be?

My mind drifted, thought poured out of it, didn't shimmer in layers like Viktor's drink, but was more like that thick smoke from the ice that melts but doesn't drip, dry ice. It wrapped itself around objects I never noticed before, the steel legs that held up this bench, the morning sky, these children. They played so seriously. Play was work, to them. I remembered doing that, bringing a sense of purpose to the smallest thing. Now it was the opposite. All this supposedly life-determining stuff was happening to me, but the more crucial it got, the more I decided to just wing it. I didn't even decide, that was the point. Nothing you decided really mattered. It was an excuse or an afterthought or a wish. Things just *were*, and you had to deal with them.

"So," I'd asked Nora, as we climbed the stairs after closing, "what do you think?"

For some reason, her opinion was the only one that mattered. Brandy and Crystal were ahead of us. Viktor was locking up.

"About what?"

"About Horace."

"He's good-looking."

"Yeah? And?"

"I don't know." She shrugged. "He's young."

"Not for me."

"No. Not for you."

Do you really think he's good-looking? I wanted to ask. I mean, I thought so, but hearing it confirmed by Nora, this woman who went upstate and slept with murderers in trailers, made me weirdly euphoric.

"But you're getting married," she reminded me.

"I thought maybe he could be my best man."

"Women don't have a best man."

That's what *you* think. My mind was on fire. I pretended I had forgotten something and went back down. Viktor was fitting the big padlock in place. I wanted to know how the passport was coming along, the one his friend was supposed to make me. He acted surprised I remembered.

"You did ask him, didn't you?"

"Yes. But he needs a photograph."

"That's no problem," I said recklessly.

"I thought perhaps it might, considering your religious convictions."

"A passport picture? I'll have it for you by tomorrow."

I was clipping away bits of my specialness, but only the unimportant stuff. I dug into my pocket and got out the tiny envelope with the photos inside. I hadn't looked at them yet. It was hard enough finding a place open early, then being sat on a stool against a blank wall. "Here," the man had said, pointing to a piece of black tape stuck on the camera. So that's what everyone's staring at, I thought, in all the pictures you see, with those dulled expressions. Black tape. "Just stay still and try not to blink." I panicked. He was taking something away from me. Caviar gets ripped from the pregnant fish's belly, then they throw her back in the water to die, I remembered reading. Reading where? Or was I making it up? I'd got rid of all my books but they were still in my head. Now I couldn't even check to see if what I knew was true or false. The flash went off. Was memory itself a creative act? Twice more. I didn't feel any different. That was the scariest part. Maybe I had already given in, long before, to everything, without even realizing, and this was just a long overdue confirmation.

How can you lose your soul? a voice asked. Anything you

lose so easily was never part of you to begin with. You can't lose your soul. You wouldn't be you, anymore, if you did.

Maybe I'm not me. After all, take a look. Who is she?

There were six, altogether. I eased the sheet out a little, keeping it in the envelope so I could slide it back quickly if anyone came by, as if it was shameful.

She is the future Eve Kholmov, I answered. Graduate of the Des Moines Institute of Fashion, a school that does not exist. After her marriage to a native of Mingrelia, wherever that is, the bride will be honeymooning in Tuscany, with another man, an artist, who reminds her of a giant belt buckle.

A girl fell off a mushroom and began to cry. Her baby-sitter got up to hold her. I couldn't decide who to be, watching, the hurt or the comforter. I was halfway between. The rest of the nannies were all talking in island accents, laughing, cackling sometimes. It took me a while to get used to the rhythm of their speech. It was English, but my understanding kept shying at the last minute, like when you're trying to jump a rope two girls are holding, how it slaps flat against the ground, and you wait and wait and then suddenly—

"I said, Are you married? And he said, You mean am I married now? You mean am I married *presently*?"

More laughter. Another was unwrapping a sandwich. It was mashed down so hard, the bread was so soft, that the filling had soaked through. She tore off a chunk with her fingers and put it in her mouth. I had never seen anyone eat a sandwich like that before. Did that make it not-a-sandwich? The city, in all its strangeness and all its even stranger familiarity, rose around me like that mist that comes up with the dew. Did I really want to leave? I mean, I just got here. But going was the only way to hold things, to capture them in your memory, the way I was finally getting some distance on my childhood now, realizing there *was* a past, where there had not been, before. A past I could push off from, that I could use to get somewhere else. But where? Here? Or away? I looked at the photos again and thought of Horace. Could I go away to some romantic landscape where I wandered over the man himself? My lover? But did that mean saying good-bye to all this? I stretched my arms out along the back of the bench, trying to hug tight the magic circle.

Now, as for Europe, I told him, very businesslike. Don't worry. You won't have to pay. Not financially. Yes, you'll pay emotionally. Yes, I'm difficult. But there's nothing wrong with that. You don't want one of those easy girls, like Brandy. Believe me, they turn out to be the craziest of all, once you get to know them.

And what are you? I made him ask.

I guess what I want to be is life-changing. I want that to be my appeal. That I am someone. Some one. Not one of many. To you.

But how *will* I pay for it? I wondered. I couldn't let him support me. I had savings, but not that much. Wait, will there be wedding presents? No, it was probably frowned on, selling wedding presents to go honeymooning with another guy. It was probably against some obscure rule of etiquette. And I hadn't even told Viktor yes, yet. He didn't even seem so interested anymore. That was another minor problem, actually living my life. But it was the least interesting part. What I liked best was this, snuggling down into this bench with my eyes closed and my ears full of kid sounds, bird sounds, traffic sounds, fantasizing so hard that the life I imagined was real, real-in-my-head.

Still, the semipractical part of me insisted, if you want to have any say in your so-called future, any power, if you want to do something, anything, besides sit on a park bench and dream, you need money. Serious money. And where are you going to get that?

Yes, Eve, I attacked myself some more. Where?

Drinks cost ten dollars at the bar. I didn't even make that much an hour. I depended on tips and what I could keep by sipping water and calling it vodka. Why did men pay so much? Because of how we looked? No, it was because of how we dressed. When you thought about it, it wasn't so much different from prostitution, except in degree. They paid their money and then they felt they had the right to stare at us, to talk to us in a certain way. Plenty of them would reach out and touch you as you went by. And the weird thing was how we thought it was OK, how we regarded it as natural. I had been trained since birth. Getting a pat on the ass for giving some friend of Mother's a smile, being bought a free meal in return for a kiss, having a job, a whole existence, based on parading around in front of total strangers. My God, tonight I had even talked to my ass, like it was a separate thing, apart from me, the way hookers must see their entire bodies. My whole life here, wandering the streets at five A.M., the bizarre relationships I already had with men, was it all a subconscious rehearsal? I mean, if I ever decided to become a prostitute, I wouldn't even need to buy a new outfit!

Don't be silly, I told myself. You could never be a whore. You can't make change.

It was true. I was really bad with cash. Especially when customers tried to help out by giving some odd total, like thirty-four dollars and seventeen cents. I had to take it to

Viktor and have him figure it out on the adding machine. Still, it was disturbing that I even thought about it, that for a minute I couldn't see the difference between selling drinks and selling myself.

I blinked, stopped my mind from going there, tried bringing things back into focus. There was still a blur, though, no matter how much I yawned and rubbed my eyes.

And then it all disappeared.

A week later, when I got to work, there was a sticker on the door: CLOSED BY ORDER OF THE OFFICE OF THE SHERIFF, CITY OF NEW YORK. It was half on the door itself, half on the frame, gluing the entrance shut more than any lock. I buzzed. No one answered. I tried the knob. I still didn't understand what the sticker meant, even though it was pretty clear. I banged on the glass. There was a deep silence. I went back up the steps and tried to look around, tried to see into the hidden garden of upended concrete chunks, the weeds that had flowered, unexpected and big, turning into pods that burst with feathery seeds that blew around the confined space, balling in corners, getting stuck on screens, a few managing to rise all the way up and out, beyond the building. Where would they go then that was any better? I saw it all so intensely, now that I couldn't get there anymore. I had always meant to go out, to ask Viktor for the key to the back door. I was on the street now, pawing at the front, where it became the next building. You could barely tell. There was no break. Viktor? I asked quietly, in my mind. Why hadn't he called? Suddenly I was nowhere, with no job. I looked around. I should wait for one of the girls to come. Maybe they knew something. But my feet kept carrying me. Mechanically, I wiped my hands, got rid of the mortar that held the bricks together, as if to say, well, at least that's done.

But now what? a voice asked.

I was already wearing the outfit. I had stopped bringing my own clothes a long time ago. I let my feet learn this new rhythm, block after block, the sudden drop off the curb, the strange, pillowy feel to the pavement, then the steep climb back up, crumbling asphalt pulling away from white curb like a section of diseased gum. Where was I going? The city doesn't give up its secrets so easily. That's what I had spent this past year discovering. You have to bargain with it, offer something in return. Through all the emptiness, I sensed what to do. I was walking not just downtown but downhill. A force was pulling me toward my fate. My steps had that halting motion, digging in. My vision jolted. I went faster, arms swinging, flapping like wings, gaining speed to take off. But take off where? Where was I going? Across the river?

Then I saw it, a break in the traffic. All the cars on the highway had stopped, revealing an invisible path. I went closer, straining to keep my eyes steady, stumbling but not slowing, and managed to see, just as it disappeared, how a small row of lights, stretching from lane to lane, let in a side street. It wasn't for pedestrians, there was no crosswalk, but that didn't mean you couldn't use it. On the other side, beyond a fence that had been pried up at one corner, instead of shore, a tip of land touched the edge and angled away, getting higher and wider. Once it was a little farther out, it began to be its own place, with pavement and people and life, not an island but a peninsula, a promenade. That vision of paradise I had, this is it, I recognized. Society with all its phoniness peeled away. It had looked so liberating, that night, from Horace's studio. Now that I was closer, now that I saw a way in, I wasn't so sure. A cold gust of air blew in off the river. There were all these women dressed just like me. I watched them walking up and down, moving with the grace of animals, all external, with nothing hidden, no complex emotions or histories, and a slow, druggy haze to it all, a distance, because of the cars whizzing by, so everything appeared in gaps you pieced together. The poisonous exhaust did something to the light, put a thickness between us and them. "Us," because there were others now, waiting at this signal that only turned green once every century.

What are you doing, Eve?

I am turning in the direction of the skid. See, that's the difference, when you know you're not a child anymore. When you recognize what you're up to. You see yourself repeating the same old mistakes. You see that it's not some accident, what happens, that lovers and friends may change, but they're all the same types, playing the same roles, in the same situation. You admit you're lost, wandering in the woods, fitting your feet into old footsteps. So instead of asking Where am I going? you ask Why? Why this shape to my life and not another? And that gives you the chance to stop being lost, realizing that there is a shape to it, the disasters you always find yourself in, that it's just habit, and a habit is something you can break.

The cars, the constant roar of the universe they made, slowed, then stopped. The sea parted. I started off, a little behind the others, so I could follow them, do what they did, whatever that might be. The road was hot from tires.

You're talking like a crazy woman.

Well, I'd rather talk like a crazy woman than go through my life without really seeing it, like some "normal" girl.

Oh, so you're a woman now?

Yes, I decided. Why not? Of course I'm a woman. You got a problem with that?

Then a car hit me.

I had never been hit. I was so terrified of it when I first got here. It seemed inevitable. The way they came at you, accelerating as you stepped off the curb. I couldn't believe how people nonchalantly walked into traffic just because the light had changed and faced down a city bus or a taxi that came careening around the corner, how they believed the WALK sign gave them some kind of moral authority. "I have the light!" I once heard somebody yell, as if they were one of the Chosen. Gradually, I must have become the same, because I didn't even notice anymore. I don't know how I managed to feel invincible, but it was like we were made of different matter. There was no way a car could touch me or I could touch a car. The laws of physics wouldn't allow it. So when this fender I hadn't even seen gently poked my hip my reaction was just, Hey! Like I'd been nudged, except I went flying. My feet left the ground. I saw my reflection in the chrome as I did a slow glide. It was herding me, bumping me. I was floating on my side. I relaxed. The quiet that lay between all noises expanded and blanketed my brain. It was almost pleasant, this airborne feeling. Gravity took a vacation.

Of course, being a woman doesn't necessarily mean getting run over by a car, I calmly continued the conversation in my head. But at the same time, I can't say I'm surprised.

Then it was over. Everything speeded up again and I had to make up for lost time, that stretched-out moment. I slammed into the pavement. The sounds that had been blocked out came back, too, all at once, the screech of tires trying to stop, the thud. All the air came out of me. My whole body grunted. I reached to bring in more, to refill my lungs, and for a long minute it didn't happen. My muscles were frozen. I lay there, gasping, or trying to gasp, my eyes getting bigger and bigger.

I heard a door slam and shoes scraping on pavement.

Oh God! my brain panted, bringing up the rear, late, as usual. I just got hit by a car!

"Are you all right?"

"I'm fine," I chirped.

I was, too. I felt great. Was I alive? Maybe I was dead. Maybe this was the afterlife, that little glow of awareness you have when the heat from your brain keeps everything functioning a split second after you cease to be.

Strong arms lifted me up. My heart was pounding. My eyes were emitting this light, these twin laser beams. It's adrenaline, I realized. My body was on high alert.

"What the hell were you doing?"

Whoever was carrying me did this little curtsy, dipping down to free one hand and open the passenger side door.

"Can you sit up?" he asked.

"Of course I can. I'm fine, really."

I saw the others, fading figures now, crouching to get under the fence. They were going on to Paradise, but I was left behind.

"I don't have any change," I warned. "I mean, I have a couple of twenties, but—"

"Stop talking, Eve. Just get in the car."

I looked at the man who was arranging me in the seat. It was Detective Jourdain.

"Oh," I said. "You go to prostitutes? That is so disgusting."

"Just sit in the goddamned car."

"There's no need to swear."

The seat had crumbs and cellophane wrappers on it. He slammed the door and went around to the other side.

"I do not go to prostitutes," he announced, very huffy,

like he really did, but how could I possibly know? Like it was a lucky guess, so it didn't count. "What were you doing back there? You practically dove into my fender."

"I didn't see you."

"Didn't look like you were seeing much of anything. Like you were in trance."

"I just wanted to see what was on the other side of the road. What about you? What were you doing down here?" I answered my own question, staring at him while he gripped the wheel. "Were you following me? Were you rescuing me? That is so romantic!"

"Put this on." He reached in back and grabbed something, without taking his eyes off the road.

"What is it?"

"Just put it on."

It was a heavy-knit wool sweater with a picture of a chipmunk.

"I hope you didn't buy this."

"It's Vonetta's."

"It's for a fourteen-year-old."

"I found it in her drawer."

"No wonder she left."

"It's cold," he said simply. "You were shivering."

"Where are we going?"

"Hospital. I'm getting you checked out."

"No," I said. "I'm not going to a hospital. I'm fine."

"Eve—"

"I am not going to the hospital!"

He sighed and shook his head.

"All right, then."

He speeded up. He was taking me somewhere else. He had made some decision. I could see it in the way his jaw was set. I didn't ask him where we were going. I didn't want to know. I was still getting used to the idea that he had done something for me, something so wild, and, the word came again, making me feel dumb for feeling thrilled, so romantic. Even the way he was pretending to be furious. I smiled. We were barreling up the side of Manhattan. Vonetta's room. I held the sweater in my lap. That's where we were going. What else would I find in those drawers? Knee socks? Culottes?

"You think you know things," he complained, "but you get everything wrong. You get everything so one hundred percent wrong that you almost get it right. By accident. You know what I mean?"

"You don't have to explain. I'm not mad at you."

"Mad?"

"For following me. I understand."

"You don't understand nothing. I have been trying to protect you this whole time. I have been putting myself between you and the powers that be. But I can't do that. Not anymore."

He started signaling. We got off at Seventy-ninth Street. The car turned and I fell against him, not entirely on purpose, but when he picked me up I had felt something, and I wanted to confirm it. My hand touched his side. He was hard. Like stone. He must have worked out constantly because it was unnatural, the muscles he had. You could get bruised just by bumping into him. I was surprised I hadn't noticed. I mean I guess I knew he was powerfully built, but this was different. Under his jacket and shirt and tie he was like some Mr. World.

"I'm taking you to see someone."

"Oh." We drove in silence for a minute. "Who?"

"A man I do work for."

"What kind of work? Police work?"

"Like I said, the line between off-duty and on- isn't so clear anymore. Maybe it never was, for me."

So we weren't going to his house. The inside of the car got darker. He had dimmed the lights in my heart. I looked around and saw everything without the excitement I had been feeling.

"Is that why you brought me the sweater? So I wouldn't look like a clown for your friend?"

"I gave it to you because you were shivering," he repeated. "And you do not look like a clown. You look beautiful."

I hated the way compliments, especially compliments about my appearance, made me feel like I owed the person. Oh, thank you, I'd be happy to do whatever you want me to do, be whoever you want me to be, now that you've told me I look nice.

Beautiful, a voice corrected. He said "beautiful."

Bite me, I shot back, and then wondered if I had said it out loud. No. Of course not. I pressed my lips together hard anyway, to make sure no other words leaked out.

We parked on Fifth Avenue. The buildings had fancy canopies held up by brass poles. There were streaks of polish where they hadn't been wiped completely clean. Long red carpets lay rolled out underneath, sticky frog tongues waiting to catch flies. He led me down one and motioned for the doorman to let us in. This fear began to grow in me.

"Maybe we should do this another time."

His hand gave mine a little squeeze, crushing my fingers.

We went through a gorgeous lobby with big mirrors and fresh flowers to an old-fashioned elevator run by a man sitting on a stool. We went by him, too.

"Stand here," he ordered.

I looked and saw this camera bolted to the ceiling. Then another elevator, it was more like a section of the wall, opened up right next to us.

"Listen," I began, "I think you have the wrong idea about me. I was just going for a walk back there. And these clothes, they're what I wear for work. You know that. The only reason I was wearing them on the street was because when I went to the bar tonight, it was closed. They shut it down. Normally, I dress very modestly."

He pushed me in. Gently. I was an obedient pony.

"I'm not a whore!" I said. "I'd like to make that clear. Before we get to wherever it is we're going."

I could see how, coming out of nowhere, it made me sound like a total idiot. He looked at me with his mouth open.

"You think that's why I brought you?"

"Well, isn't it?" I was already turning red. "I mean you follow me in your car, and then take me to this 'friend' of yours—"

"He's not a friend. I told you, he's a man I do work for."

"Yeah, right. Work."

"You think I'm a pimp?" He rolled his bloodshot eyes.

"Well, then what are we doing here?"

"Aren't you ever going to understand, Eve? We're here to talk about that night. About that girl you saw. That's what it's always been about."

We were going up and up. I had that feeling of leaving my stomach behind. The elevator was slow, but there were still no buttons. None had grown since the last time I looked. We were going all the way to the top.

"It's like I said back in the car, you refuse to get things. The more obvious they are, the more you turn them into something else entirely."

I began to laugh.

"This isn't funny."

"It *is*. You don't understand. I already had this happen to me, once before."

I explained about Viktor, driving me, to his secret hideout, I'd thought. To safety. And then our showing up at that brownstone, his shoving me ahead of him almost exactly the same way I had been shoved into this elevator. Both times, when I got in the car, I thought I had known where we were heading, that there was this oasis of security, Viktor's hidden room with the mysterious vibrations to it, Detective Jourdain's house where his daughter had slept, where there was a thick woolen bedspread we would pull back, together, and underneath find . . . I was babbling, but didn't care. As long as I kept talking, the elevator wouldn't stop, the door wouldn't open. I wouldn't be forced to face what was on the other side. And instead what I'd found was fear, a paranoid fear Viktor was selling me out, taking me to someone who meant me harm, because that's the kind of thing he would do, Viktor. Not the kind of thing you would do, I was implying, and I paused for a second, hoping he would say, Of course not, everything would be fine, don't be scared. But he didn't, so I went on, quickly, I went back to telling the story, trying to amuse him, telling how funny it all ended, that instead of some evil men waiting for me in a strange apartment it was just Brandy and Crystal and Nora throwing me a stupid bridal shower. Nothing sinister at all. The opposite. Like this, I was sure, even though I felt the same fear, wasn't as terrifying as I was making it out to be. I was just being crazy. He would never let anything bad happen to me, would he? There was nothing to worry about, right?

"So you're going through with it?" he asked. "You're going to marry that guy?"

"I guess." It seemed totally irrelevant. "But that doesn't

mean I can't sleep with your friend, too. I mean, if it'll stop him from asking questions about what I saw that night. I mean, in a way you *are* a pimp, aren't you?"

He slapped me.

I had never been hit. It stunned me into complete silence. Which I guess was what he wanted. I was "hysterical." Meaning I had been telling the truth. I put my hand to my cheek. It was burning. The blood was rushing back to the surface. There were tears in my eyes but they weren't falling, just clearing my vision, helping me see better. So this is what he did. This is why they left, his wife and daughter.

The elevator stopped.

"Mr. Van Arsdale is a very important man," he explained. "I can't have you going in there all out of control. He won't appreciate the kind of games you play. Just tell him what he wants to know and you'll be fine. I promise."

The door opened. He moved to leave. I stopped him. I reached out and held him back, just to see, really, if I could. What he would do. He waited. He was the one who seemed uncomfortable. Not me. My fear had passed into him. All I felt was cold, not the temperature, but this calm.

"You never told me your name." I looked at him. "Your real name. Even your card just says Detective A. Jourdain."

He cleared his throat.

"Arthur?" a voice called. "Don't just stand there. Show the young lady in."

The elevator led right to the apartment. There were no doors. We were in a little room with a scuffed pink marble floor, a ratty old chair, and a half-open closet for coats. It was empty, with two or three hangers and an umbrella. Then we walked down a short hall and everything changed. My feet sank. It was an enormous space done all in red, with thick red carpet and red walls. The walls weren't paper or paint, though, they were padded fabric, with what looked like water stains running down. The stains repeated. They were a pattern, an effect, one I'd never seen before. There were windows everywhere, big ones that started at the floor, and little islands of elegant furniture, low armchairs, a mahogany table, a bar, a desk, all these separate areas. I looked up and saw there was no ceiling. Instead, there was colored cloth, stitched loosely so it billowed around chandeliers that lit folds and cast shadows, making private clouds and sky. I didn't notice the man at first, even though he was standing right in the middle of it all. I was too knocked out by the room. He was old, holding himself very straight, with white hair that stuck up in tufts at each eyebrow. His eyes were blue. His skin had that papery, talcum powder look to it. He wore a blazer with some kind of patch over the breast pocket, and instead of a tie this piece of polka-dotted silk bunched in his open collar.

"Carl Van Arsdale," he introduced himself, holding out a hand.

Excuse me, but is that an ascot? I managed not to ask, although what did come out of my mouth was almost as bad.

"This is the coolest place!" I squealed. "You *live* here?"

"Not normally, no." He smiled. "I come here at night. When I can't sleep. Or when I have someone to meet."

"Wow."

"This is Eve," Detective Jourdain sighed.

"Eve . . . ?"

"Just Eve."

The bar wasn't like the one at work. It was small, for two, and topped with a thin sheet of metal.

"You like it here, Eve?"

"I love it! What floor are we on?"

"There is no floor. This is the penthouse. There's a bedroom upstairs."

The penthouse. So we had escaped numbers entirely.

"My apartment's on top, too," I said. "Only it's not as big."

I went over to the windows. They made me dizzy, the way they started at the floor.

"My family has always had an interest in New York real estate," his voice came from behind. "These towers were built by my grandfather."

"Uh-huh."

It wasn't what I expected, being this high and looking down. I thought it would be like getting above the stars, being able to read the constellations. The way people said, "That's Orion's Belt," and I would nod, pretending to see what they were pointing at, but really couldn't. I thought if I got up high enough, I could see it all the way it was meant to be seen, that everything would match up with its name. The city most of all. Chinatown, for example, would look like, I don't know, a place, separate and distinct, instead of when I was down in it, trying to find it, and noticed just as I was leaving that all the signs were in Chinese. I was always realizing things when I was past them, when it was too late. I had this dream of seeing the city whole, seeing things as they really were, and then making a plan for conquering it. But it wasn't like that, the view. I couldn't even tell which way I was looking. There were a million lights and they weren't fixed, they were all quivering, this pulse was running through them. At first I thought it was just me, that I wasn't used to taking in so much, from such a height, all at once. But then I realized it was actually moving. Instead of being a map of itself, Manhattan was this living breathing creature.

One of them coughed, waiting for me.

"Mr. Van Arsdale wants you to do him a favor," Detective Jourdain said.

I turned.

"What kind of favor?"

"He wants you to provide an accurate description of the woman you saw that night."

"She is a friend of mine," he began carefully. "Someone I care for, deeply. Unfortunately, she is also a very troubled girl."

"Wait, you mean you already know who it is? Then why do you need me to say what she looks like?"

"I'm trying to protect her."

"Protect her from what?"

"From me," Detective Jourdain said.

"From herself," he corrected. "She has gotten herself in a great deal of trouble. As you witnessed."

"Well, like I said before, I don't know what I saw."

"Of course you do, Eve."

The way he pronounced my name, the way he stared, was hypnotic, this gold watch swinging before my eyes. We both waited.

"She stabbed a man." Detective Jourdain took out his pad. "Almost killed him."

My knees were weak. I wanted to sit, but it was the usual problem. They would be taller than I was. Even taller than they were now.

"I got his name here. He's nobody you know. A stockbroker. Well, portfolio manager, whatever that means. Married. Father of three. Met her at a bar, he claims. Then they went out and partied some more. A little before dawn, they were engaged in consensual relations, on the street, when, for no reason at all, she produced a knife and attacked him."

"So you knew I was telling the truth the whole time? That I really did see something?"

"Of course I knew. Hell, I'm the one who cleaned up the mess. Which, believe me, was no picnic."

"But he's going to be all right?"

"He's going to be fine," Mr. Van Arsdale said. "He has no interest in pursuing the matter. He has been more than handsomely compensated."

Jourdain shot this annoyed look. I remembered his saying he wasn't proud of the things he'd done, but he was proud of where he'd gotten to. And this must be how he had gotten there, by doing favors for this big shot, by protecting—the rest of it finally came to me—this rich man's girlfriend.

"Unfortunately, having the victim withdraw his complaint isn't enough for Arthur, here."

"She could do it again," he said bluntly.

"My friend is an adult, legally. I can't force her to accept the kind of treatment she needs."

"Treatment?"

"Medication. Therapy. A controlled environment. Round-the-clock care." He looked at me. "You've seen what she's capable of."

"You mean keep her locked up someplace?"

"She's a danger to herself and to others."

"You want to make her a prisoner."

"She would already *be* a prisoner," Detective Jourdain said, "if she was anyone else. If I was allowed to do my job. But because Mr. V. here is a friend of the department, I'm trying to let him handle this problem in his own way."

"She was being raped!"

That didn't seem to impress either one of them. The old man ran a hand through his white hair.

"She's headstrong. She gets angry. As if she resented the very attention she had done her best to bring on."

"You mean she gets mad when some guy pushes her up against a wall."

"I'm saying there's a history. One that could be exploited at trial."

"Oh, so now you're saying she was asking for it? That is so typical."

"She needs to be taken care of, Eve. She needs to be watched."

"I don't understand. You both act like you want me to help her, by getting her into even more trouble."

"Are you sure Arthur can't bring you something? A soda, maybe?"

I didn't even have to answer. We watched Detective Jourdain trudge off to the bar. His heavy shoes and dark suit didn't go with the decorating scheme.

"She came back here," he whispered, in a different tone, urgent, like I was the only person in the world who could help him. "Right after. She told me what she'd done! How she'd led him to this very spot! I don't know why, to shame me, I suppose. Or because she knew I'd protect her. She told me everything. And then she left again. Left all this in my lap. Forcing me to get involved."

"What do you mean, 'came back'?"

"Don't you see what I'm afraid of? That I won't be able to save her. She could spend the rest of her life in an institution!"

"You mean this is where she was to begin with?"

"This is where she should always be. This is where I want to keep her. This is my private place. It's safe here."

I looked at the windows again. We had come in on Fifth Avenue, but it was the penthouse, it went all the way back to the next block. The city, wheeling like the night sky, locked into place now. There was Madison, behind me. Madison and Seventy-third Street. Yes, this was where it happened. This is where her footsteps had disappeared into. This soft carpet.

"The reason I finally had Arthur bring you here was because you've been so unwilling to give us what we need. I thought if I appealed to you personally, explained how important it is that you help me—"

"Help you how? By betraying her?"

"By saving her life."

He was desperate. It was awful to see the pain of rejected love on the face of someone who must have been at least seventy. It didn't go with his features, with his skin. I hadn't thought old people felt that way. But I didn't doubt him for a second. He was sincere. I was even embarrassed, that he felt the need to confess this passion of his to me, of all people, as if I could understand, as if I could sympathize.

"Diet Coke?"

"Oh, you didn't have to put it in a glass."

He went back to talking the same way as before, formal and polite.

"There was another reason I wanted to meet you. Arthur tells me you may need funds."

"Mr. Van Arsdale is prepared to offer a reward for your cooperation. Ten thousand dollars."

The ice rattled like a lie detector. Even the slightest shiver made a noise. I put it to my lips and drank. Then, buying time, I crunched down on a piece while they watched, the two men. I made my throat numb, so when the words finally came out, they didn't have any emotion to them. I refused to admit my fear. And if you refuse to admit it, I reasoned, then maybe you aren't really afraid. Even if you should be.

"So you want me to say it was her. Officially. And then you can blackmail her into coming back."

"Blackmail isn't the right term."

"Because otherwise she would go to jail, right?"

"I think of it more as leverage, so we can convince her to do what's best."

"You might have to pick her out of a lineup," Detective Jourdain warned.

"No." He shook his head. "It would never come to that. She's a very sensible girl, really. Except in certain areas."

"Yeah, certain areas like between a guy's legs." I giggled. "Oh come *on*. I was just kidding. And you're willing to give me ten thousand dollars for helping you put her away? That is so sick."

Van Arsdale held up his hand. He was married, I noticed. Or at least he wore a wedding ring. Big surprise.

"I'd be willing to go as high as twenty."

I wanted to put my glass down. Zinc. Was that a zinc bar over there? I'd read about zinc bars. It's funny what I knew. What stuck. The metal had a yellowish-green gleam.

"I mean, what if she was just defending herself? That's not a crime. She shouldn't have to pay for that."

"I already said, she has a history. She puts herself at risk, all the time. For all sorts of things. She needs to be monitored."

"No offense, but why should I believe you?" I turned to Arthur. "Maybe she just walked out on him. Did you ever think of that? Maybe this guy is just some horny control freak trying to turn his ex-girlfriend into becoming an all-night live-in concubine."

They stared. There was this silence.

"Concubine?" I asked, suddenly not sure. "Is that the right word?"

Detective Jourdain took a step forward, but Mr. Van Arsdale said, "Arthur," very mildly. He was looking at me, looking into me. He had this tender blue gaze. It trapped me. The way it did her? And then she escaped. Escaped into what? A nightmare. Which maybe now she wanted to wake up from. But doesn't part of us want to be trapped, to be taken care of? I knew part of me did.

"I'm sorry," I said, while this voice complained, Why are you always apologizing? "But I couldn't do a thing like that to her. No matter what she did. We had this moment back there. You wouldn't understand. It's a girl-type thing."

"If you two met, if you spoke with her, you would see why what I'm proposing is really for the best. Would you do that for me, Eve? Would you meet with her?"

His eyes held me. Maybe this was a mistake, but there was no way I could refuse. It was my destiny to meet her, to find out what happened.

"Sure," I said.

Detective Jourdain cleared his throat, loudly, the same as when he had seen Viktor kissing me in front of the building. Trying to express this deep disapproval.

"I'll arrange it, then. The next time she gets in touch with me."

"You mean you still talk?"

"Oh yes. Daily. Nothing's changed between us. Nothing important. In a way, this has just brought us closer together. Strengthened our bond. She's just a little flighty, that's all."

I would be, too, I thought, looking around at the penthouse one last time. It was so modern. So quiet and rich. You could fly in here a long time before realizing it was a cage.

* * *

Outside, I started walking. Detective Jourdain came trotting after me. I didn't look at him. I waited until he got close.

"You've been lying this whole time! About everything! All those conversations we had, you were testing me, to see how much I knew."

"You're the one who kept calling," he pointed out. "Because you had a guilty conscience."

"I did not. I was lonely. And scared. And you were leading me on."

"All I'm interested in is justice."

"Oh, right. You used me."

"I got you to see what you already saw. Got you to face things. Hell, you should be thanking me. I don't know why you're so mad. All along, I've been the one protecting you."

"Well, who asked you? I can do a pretty good job of protecting me all by myself."

"Are you serious? You can't deal with the Carl Van Arsdales of the world as if they're regular people. They're not."

"He seemed all right. I mean he's a creep, but I work in a bar. I know the type."

He caught me by the shoulders and spun me around. I flinched, but he wasn't violent. He was pleading.

"You should have told him what you saw and got out, like I said. I'd have taken care of you. Now he expects something."

"What can he do to me that's so bad?"

He wiped his face clean, like his hand was a wet sponge.

"Listen, I shouldn't be telling you this, but your bar tonight? It didn't just get shut down. The Sheriff's Office didn't just happen on by. You understand? He had it closed. He has that kind of pull."

"Why would he do that?"

"To cut down on your options, of course. So you'd be out of a job. To soften you up. Don't you see?"

I thought of Detective Jourdain trailing after me in his car, watching me about to cross the street, then trying to cut me off, block me from where I was going. I tried to see it from his point of view. My face looking brave? Scared? Lost? And then, after, how terrified he had been, how mad at me. Why? For making him feel? And that sad sweater he kept in the backseat.

"So you did rescue me."

"Rescued you from embarrassment, maybe. Do you even know where you were heading?"

"Just some special-looking place. A hangout."

"For drag queens."

I frowned.

"There were no cars there. There were only—"

"Drag *queens*. Not drag racers. Those were guys, Eve. All of them."

"Don't be ridiculous. There were these women with me. I saw them."

"It's what I've been trying to tell you all along. Between what you see and what you think you see, there's this space. More than with anyone else I've ever known. That's why I keep wanting to help. You are not equipped to deal with things on your own, here."

"Yes I am!"

I started moving away again.

"Where are you going now? To that boyfriend of yours? His place is all closed up, remember? What's he got to offer you?"

"He's treated me nicer than you," I said slowly. "He never lied to me."

"You think the truth is so great? Go see him, then. Go see what the truth gets you."

"I'm going home."

"Go visit your boyfriend, Eve," he mocked, and then announced to the world, like there was an audience: "Women! The choices you make."

They're not choices, I felt like answering. That's the problem. We never get to choose. It's an illusion. Choice.

I looked back once. He was standing, his arms curved, flexing their muscles, working out some rage. When men were in the wrong, they found a way to get mad. Anger was to them what love was to us, this thing they were good at, that they had a talent, a weakness, for. I turned away again. He wasn't going to come after me. He was too busy being pissed off. I went around a corner. Now you can lose it, I told myself, now that you're finally alone, now that the last man is gone. But I didn't. I touched my side, where the car hit me. It hurt, meaning I was here, in this world, with all its necessary pain. Give me more necessary pain, I thought, holding my hip, feeling the bruise. So I'll know I'm still alive.

CHAPTER EIGHT

"Port Authority Bus Terminal," he told me. "Second floor. At the top of the escalator."

I went expecting to find him waiting for me, but of course he wasn't. So I looked at the store windows. Now that I wasn't making any, I saw how everything was made of money. Not just items, but places (Boston $75, Phoenix $120), bodies ("Because I'm Worth It"), even thoughts, what you allowed yourself to think. I can have this. I can't have that. Money was the stuff of the universe. Ideas covered it, clung to its surface like lint or dirt, but the inside, the essence of anything, was how much it cost compared to how much you had. Which in my case was less and less. It kept leaking out.

I liked the bus station, though. It was different from Grand Central, more my speed. People's lives happened here.

It wasn't about commuters and tourists. Whole families camped out with suitcases held together by tape. Little girls were dressed up for trips. An old lady used a walker. I watched her set it down and heave herself forward, again and again. The ceilings were low. Whatever was for sale was cheap. And I wanted to buy. I wanted to spend. It was a bizarre urge, considering how careful I had to be now. Let's get it over with. That's what part of me felt. Let's throw away these last few fig-leaf bills and see what's underneath. Because if I'm right, if everything is money, then when I reach zero, what will happen? Will I magically merge with the chaos all around me and cease to be?

I tried lifting my brain firmly with both hands and setting it back down into some kind of groove, but there was none. I was skittering along, sleepless and staring. Someone had set up a shrine. It was strange to find religion between a magazine stand and a drugstore, but why not? A million Manhattans were arranged on shelves. They were all the same, some big, some small, but the same repeating skyline, each separate, kept in the beautiful clear crystal case of its own personality, row after row of them, as many cities as there were people in it, showing how, together, we were more than just the sum of ourselves, how we formed something beautiful and unique. I even saw one—maybe it was just the way the light was hitting it but how could that be? There was no direct light, no shaft of sun, I was as inside as I could get, at the very heart of things—lit up for me especially, my Manhattan, the one I had come for, the one my presence created. I reached out. I didn't know what to do, how you were supposed to worship here. I took it in my hand and spread my fingers wide over the Brooklyn Bridge, the Empire State Building, the Chrysler Building, but also over the little figures below, this microscopic crowd I hadn't noticed before, and at my touch they began to dance! I must have been shaking, because these angels, all in white, were swirling in the liquid air, level with the tops of the make-believe skyscrapers, greeting me, accepting me.

"Eve," a voice said, "you are in the Gift Shop."

"I know."

I did. I was perfectly aware. But a place can be two things at once. When you start your own religion, you don't go to church. There are none. You make a church. And how do you do it? By an act of will. A way of seeing. But the places don't stop being what they were before. They don't stop being what made them special to begin with. I looked up and saw a banner saying, WELCOME TO NEW YORK.

"I want to buy this."

"You want to buy a snow globe?" Viktor asked.

"Is that what it's called?"

He thought a minute.

"Snow globe. Yes, why not?"

It was a big one. I emptied my pockets, gave the lady more than I needed to. When she tried giving some back, I shook my head. I wanted to be absolutely free. Pure.

He stared at me.

"You look different."

He did, too. He wasn't wearing a colored undershirt. I guess that had been his uniform, as much as the leotard and hot pants had been ours. I had only seen him at work or right after, except the first time, in the coffee shop, when he chose me, and that's what this reminded me of. In an ordinary place he looked human. He was dressed in a white shirt and blue pants. His mustache was less threatening, more moody, something to chew on. Even his eyes weren't glaring. They were sad, philosophical. He actually looked attractive.

"So," he said.

I threw myself into his arms. We were the same size. It was such a relief after all these tall people.

"Hold me?" I asked, and he did, in the middle of everyone, in the middle of the announcements about arrivals and departures. He held me so unashamed. We knew so much about each other. Things no one else would ever guess. I breathed in his after-shave or cologne or whatever it was, that medicine smell I'd never known was his before, that was part of work, that stayed with me after, was part of my life, that I hated, but now, I realized, was gone, lost forever.

"They closed down the bar!" I wailed. "I went there and—"

"I know, I know."

Of course he knew. But I had to get it out, saying how I tried to pry apart the walls, how all the time I was there I was desperate to get to the garden in back, but never had and now I never would. How those greedy weeds always looked so dark green in the electric light.

"They were armed!" he complained. "Armed men! The sheriff of New York City. That's what he calls himself. I did not realize the national childishness here extended to the titles of your elected officials. They broke down the door and had a locksmith right behind them to put it back up again. You never saw such a waste of tax dollars."

"And, uh, did they say how they knew about the place?"

I kept my head buried, trying not to look up.

"One of those periodic crackdowns, no doubt. I disclaimed all knowledge. Said I was the janitor. A dumb émigré. That is the problem, though. Your sheriff turned my name over to the INS."

"What's that?"

"The Immigration and Naturalization Service. They have begun deportation proceedings."

I nodded slowly. So it was my fault.

"I have been watching you window-shop."

"From where? You live here?"

"Well, not on a bench."

I wouldn't have minded if he was homeless. It would have made me feel like we had even more in common. This place seemed very close to something. The true city I had come for.

"So where do you sleep?"

"In there. Come."

He led me through a set of heavy glass doors opposite where I had been standing, where I had been lingering, basking, without realizing, in his attention. Or had I seen him out the corner of my eye? Did I know what I was doing on some semiconscious level? Is this flirting? I asked, and a sound hit me, a light shattering, not of destruction, more like liberation, a breaking free. Where was I? It was all so familiar that for a minute I had no idea, just someplace I knew, intimately. A heavy ball bounced once, wobbled on oiled wood, then settled down and came rumbling toward us.

"A bowling alley?" I asked stupidly.

"Port Authority Lanes. Didn't you see the sign?"

"You live here?"

"I manage it. For a friend. The bar was always, what do you call it? A sideline. A place where I could dispose of leftover supplies."

"You mean you stole liquor from your friend and sold it there?"

"Yes, well it is more complicated than that, of course. I was compensating myself. It was a form of self-pay. There is an office in back. With a sofa. Since I work nights—since I *worked* nights," he corrected, "it was cheaper to take naps during the day."

"You live in a bowling alley?" I repeated.

"It is a bourgeois concept. Permanent housing."

"This is where you call me from."

It never occurred to me there was a bowling alley in the middle of New York City. Now I understood why his calls had that magic. He was talking about the raid, its aftermath, all the legal and money troubles he was having, but all I could do was look at the men in their loose colored shirts, the women with wide hips and high hair. It was so Midwest, right down to the counter with the hundreds of pairs of shoes, the snack bar, the pro shop.

"It's League Night!"

"Maybe you should sit."

"I never played. We weren't allowed. But I used to go and watch. I sneaked in. It was the coolest place in town, when I was a little girl."

"You were not allowed to bowl?"

"No bowling in the Bible."

I could see he was going over the four Gospels, all the books of the Old Testament, then the Apocrypha, looking for bowling references. Well, maybe he wasn't. Maybe I really didn't have a clue what went on in other people's heads. I just always assumed they were like me. He guided us past vending machines, through a passageway that turned, so we weren't in the public part of the lanes anymore.

"Where are we going?"

We went down a staircase, not a full staircase, not the

kind that takes you to another floor, only four or five steps, then we had to duck, so we were halfway between things, before turning and ending up in this windowless room, more like a closet, with shag carpeting, a desk with food on it, a lamp with a dirty shade, and a couch.

"*This* is where I call you from."

Just then another bowling ball started its journey. Several, actually. They hit the boards over our heads and slid for a moment—I thought of my brain back there, how I had tried to launch it that same way—before something took over, before they all straightened out and started racing for the pins. The vibrations echoed off each other in the little box of an office. We sat on the couch. He poured me a drink. There was no ice. We clinked our glasses and looked at each other, suddenly serious, swearing a suicide pact. More bowling balls were hitting the ceiling, at regular intervals. Not regular enough, though. You couldn't get used to them. At least, I couldn't.

"How can you sleep here?

"I have slept in much worse."

"Me too, I guess."

"You get used to things."

I nodded.

We drank.

It was so dependable, that first sip. The space inside me expanded. All my interior walls were knocked down. I was an empty room, ready to echo. Now that I knew where he called me from, now that the mystery was solved, I liked him more. He wasn't some sinister creature loaded down with all the scary clichés I had about the big bad city. He was just someone who came here from far away, trying to make it. Like me.

"I'm broke," I pronounced. I wanted to hear it out loud. I

wanted to get used to the fact in advance. The words were less scary once they hit the air. I had put the snow globe down on his desk. "I mean, I still have money. But I'll *be* broke, soon."

"What will you do?"

"Get a job."

"Doing what?"

"Waitressing, I guess."

"You will find it is not so easy. And won't pay. Not the way I did."

"You didn't pay so much."

"I let you steal."

"Taking money instead of pouring a free drink is not stealing."

"A wife of mine," he said carefully, "would not have to work."

"What?"

"A wife. There is something to be said for the old system. The husband goes off to work. The wife, who is not good at this thing, who does not meet with such attractive opportunities, provides the 'home' you are so shocked I have, so far, been able to do without."

"And what does she do there all day? Mop? Watch TV? Make dinner?" I listened to the crash of the alleys. "Reset the pins?"

He reached over and took my glass.

"She spends her day being my wife. The mother of my children."

"Oh." I laughed. "Children, right. Getting a little ahead of yourself there, aren't you?"

He didn't understand the expression. He had taken both my hands in one of his, and raised them together, high over my head.

"Ahead of yourself? How can you be ahead of where you already are? It makes no sense."

"Never mind. What are you doing?"

We had rotated, somehow, without getting up, so we were lengthwise on the couch.

"Wrists and ankles," he explained, letting me in on this big secret, instructing me. "Weak links in the body's chain of bones. Try to move."

"Viktor—"

"You can't, can you?" All his weight was on top, but he wasn't really pressing, just lying there. My arms were stretched out of their sockets. My feet were apart, nailed. And his one hand was still free. But he went on as if we were having a normal conversation. "So, you are broke. Broken."

His fingers found the top button of my jeans.

"Stop," I said, except it came out so small, so weak-sounding. A plea. I tried to move. "Viktor, let go."

He undid the top button, and all this panic flowed out.

"In a minute, I'm going to scream."

"What's that? I can't hear you."

On League Night, every lane was in use. I remembered the thunder in the old building on the edge of the cornfields. Arhat Bowlerama. I had wanted the sound, the smells, the deep vibrations in the pit of my stomach, all my senses, to overwhelm me, to take me someplace. I was thirteen. Take me where? I didn't know. His hand snaked inside my panties. I arched my back and as soon as I did I knew that was exactly what he wanted. All his muscles came to life. Before, he hadn't even been trying. Now I saw how much stronger he was than me. We struggled for a minute, then, once it was clear to both of us that I couldn't do anything, he let go, took my pants on either side, and yanked so hard they were down around my ankles, binding me. Then he took my shirt and did the same thing, pulling it over my head.

I was too scared to make a sound.

"I don't like it when you bring other men around. Not even men. Boys."

"I promise never to—"

"Think of how nice it would be. A proper marriage. Think of all the things you would never have to worry about again. How to get money. Where to live. Whom to love. I can give you all that. Far more than any pretty-boy painter. But first you have to give up your will, Eve."

"My what?"

"Think of sex as a game, a competition, where we stack up our resolve, our determination, against each other, and the winner takes all. Tonight, when I do to you what you have been begging me to do for months, all your will will pass over to me. And you will be happy. For the first time ever."

"I never said yes."

He leaned down and whispered, his tongue licking the sentences into my ear:

"I told you before, a woman agrees with her body, not with words. Now for God's sake give in to your desires. You won't regret it, I promise."

His knee was between my thighs. I was struggling to maintain boundaries, where I began and where he ended. His shirt was still on, but the hairs were crowding around his open collar, dying to get out, climbing over each other, eager to cover me, colonize my smooth skin. I was choking on his after-shave.

"Get off," I managed to say, one last time.

"Or what?"

His teeth had that taunting, I-win grin.

I laid the knife handle flat against where his stomach curved out and released the catch.

I don't know how I did it. My hand had worked free. He was leaning on a shirtsleeve instead of my wrist. And my pants, when he pulled them down, it had fallen out of the pocket and stayed on the couch. I squeezed the soft rubber the way I had a hundred times before, just a nervous tic, like checking for your keys, practicing, practicing for this very emergency, and the blade came shooting out. It might have actually cut him, just a little, because he gave this cry and was off me in a second.

"Jesus Fucking Christ!"

"Please don't swear."

My knife was the only clean, pointy thing in the whole room. It glittered.

"Where did you get that from?"

"A store," I said. It seemed like a funny question. "It's for personal protection."

"You are so unromantic," he complained. "Why do you always feel the need to ruin these tender moments?"

"Tender moments?"

"It is the last time I propose marriage to *you*."

"That wasn't a marriage proposal. You were trying to rape me!"

"Marriage. Rape. As I said before, you people make such arbitrary distinctions. And only when it is in your self-interest to do so. Why not say I was offering you a job? Just as I did before. I thought that was why you came here." He pulled up his pants. "Why not say I was taking pity on you?"

"Being someone's wife is not a job."

"It is the most likely one you are going to get. Believe me, your prospects were far brighter the first time we met than they are now."

"What's that supposed to mean?"

"You are not as innocent," he said sullenly.

I didn't know if that was an insult or not. I mean, what was the opposite of innocent? Guilty?

"How's my passport coming along?"

"Your passport? You think I am still going to get you a passport?"

"Why not?" I looked at the couch, the only witness. There wasn't even bedding to be mussed up. It was like it never happened. Except there was this hair stuck between my teeth. I tried pushing it with my tongue but it wouldn't budge. It was jammed in. "We can still get married, can't we?"

That made him mad all over again.

"You tried to mutilate me!"

"Yeah? Well, you tried to get me pregnant!"

"Listen to us," he muttered. "We are practically husband and wife already. In terms of argumentation."

"You need me."

He looked up.

"For that green card thing. I mean, especially if they're going to kick you out."

"But, correct me if I am wrong, you need me too, I think."

I tried holding on to my anger, but couldn't. It was always like this with Viktor.

"Crystal was right."

He got this alarmed expression.

"Crystal? What did she tell you?"

"It's all about past lives. You remind me of someone, of a time and a place. I can't separate it all out, but that's why it will never work with us. Why it shouldn't work. You're more about where I came from than where I want to be going."

"What on earth are you doing to your mouth?"

"There's this hair."

I was trying to pick it out with my knife. He came over.

"Stop. You could hurt yourself. Please."

He made me bare my teeth and then very gently reached in.

"It is not that way for me." He was concentrating. "You remind me of no one. Or rather of someone I desired before I had any notion she could exist. For me, you were, what is it called? A dream come true."

I felt him grasp the hair between two fingers and tug. He could be so delicate, when he wanted.

"I try explaining this to you a thousand times, but it always comes out wrong. I thought, perhaps"—he nodded, embarrassed, toward the couch—"if I demonstrated physically, since you laugh so much at my words, my poor English, it would make more sense."

No, not when he wanted. That was the problem. He could only be nice in spite of himself. I always ended up wanting him after he was finished wanting me. And he never sensed that. Even though we were standing as close as two people can stand without touching, he was deaf to what my body was saying now. He pulled the hair out and showed it to me.

"I don't laugh at your words," I said.

"Of course we should not marry. The whole idea is ludicrous. I am sorry I ever brought it up."

"Viktor—"

"No, it is for the best. It is my fault. I had the stupid notion it could be more."

"More than what?"

He turned away.

"I hoped you could save me."

Well, *this* certainly isn't love, I thought, looking at his back. It was more like a sickness. What I wanted to do now was what I had almost killed him for trying just a few minutes before. It was all my fault. That was the feeling I had, even though I knew it wasn't true. He had been so totally in the wrong. But he was the one hurt. He couldn't even look me in the eye. He sat back down at his desk and pretended he was busy, that I was dismissed. He was back to being a jerk, or trying to be. He nodded at my snow globe.

"Don't forget your Big Apple."

A cold wind came and blew everything down. I had never been in weather like that before. I was shot in one direction, spun around a corner, knocked sideways by another blast, not dead leaves but this city mix of grit, paper, cardboard cups, and out-of-control pigeons. Still, it was the same as trees being stripped: a bareness, revealed. The streets channeled and funneled it all. When I finally got to the gallery I was messed up, my hair and clothes, but my cheeks were glowing and my eyes were shining. I had been so worried, setting off, about what to say, how to act. By the end, all those fears were blown clean out of my head. I was just happy to be here. It was getting dark early. I remembered last time, lazily wandering up the street in what still felt like summer, looking at the invitation, not sure, even when I got there, that I was actually going in. Now, I tilted into this incredible resistance, full of purpose, even though I didn't know what exactly my purpose was.

"Eve!"

The building had a wide terrace of steps before you got

to each door. People were sitting along them like bleachers, passing bottles of beer, smoking cigarettes. They all seemed to know each other. An older woman sat apart. She was the one who had called. She patted the space next to her.

"Come sit with me first."

The wind was whipping her hair. It was Nora.

"What are you doing here?"

"Reliving my youth."

She passed me her cigarette. It wasn't the regular kind. It was hand-rolled, and pink.

"Don't let that go out."

I took a puff and coughed.

"You're supposed to hold it in."

I gave it back. She moved closer, right up against me. She was huddled inside an enormous winter coat. She slipped her arms out of the sleeves and put it around me, too, sheltering us. It was that heavy blue cloth kind, with a big collar and anchors on the buttons. I was in my jumpsuit.

"Is that all you're wearing?"

"I don't get cold."

She sucked at the pink cigarette. I watched her, how she held it in her lungs instead of letting go. She tried handing it to me, but I shook my head.

"What's the matter?" Her voice came out in this cloud of green. "You won't get high with me? You wanted to, before. At work."

"Before, you were smoking tobacco."

"No, I wasn't." Her hand kept holding it out. "I've been up there, honey. I've seen what you're going to see. And believe me, you need this."

Fall had blown away the last shreds of her youth. But somehow that made her even more haunting, her eyes, this gray-blue distance in them, the way her face was stamped on, slightly crooked, at an angle. This is what's left, I thought, once all the surface stuff is gone, the things you think are so important at the time, this is the essence, what lies underneath, driving you. I watched the tight circle of paper flare as I breathed in. Almost immediately I wanted to cough, but somehow I mastered the urge and sat there, motionless, my lungs inflated like a hot-air balloon. She took it back from me.

"What do you mean, you don't get cold? You were freezing a minute ago, walking down the street. You just want to look good."

"So?" I found I could talk, by moving my lips and thinking what I wanted to say out loud. I didn't need air. It was highly overrated, breathing. "What's wrong with wanting to look good?"

"You'd look good no matter what you wore, at your age." She brushed ash off my leg. "He's there."

"Well, of course. It's his Opening."

"So is she."

"Who?"

"I don't know her name."

I nodded. Marron.

"You look like you're about to pass out."

I let my breath go right in her face. I hadn't meant to. She blinked and coughed. We laughed.

"So what do you think?" She posed for me, struck an attitude, without really moving. "No makeup. Well, hardly any. And I stopped dying my hair."

That's what it was, I saw now. All this gray.

"You look great."

"And I got a job in an office. Can you believe it?"

"Viktor attacked me, I think."

"You think?"

She shook the joint impatiently, for me to take it from her again.

"Well, I thought he attacked me. He acted more like it was another marriage proposal, but when I said no, he took it back. So I guess the wedding's off."

You can't flee the Devil, I remembered. You have to sleep with him. No, that wasn't right, was it?

"Eve."

I grabbed it and inhaled, then started talking while not letting my breath out, talking in that high, tucked-up voice.

"I mean, who *is* the Devil? That's the big question, isn't it? It's almost like he descends on men and possesses them for short periods of time. And then, just when you think you know who he is, he flies away and they're this normal guy again, the one you started out liking. But by then it's too late, because you've turned around and he's right behind you, fluttering over your shoulder like a bat, waiting to take over whoever's nice to you next."

"Have you ever gotten stoned before?"

"And you know what else I've begun to doubt? This whole idea of winning. When you win, when you come out on top, what do you exactly feel? Nothing! I mean maybe you're happy, but you're not thinking, you're not actually learning from life. At least I'm not. And then, right after, there's this incredible letdown, like you were fooled, like you didn't really win at all. But when you lose, that's something you take with you, that becomes part of your experience. So really you haven't lost anything. What do you mean 'stoned'? You mean like the woman who committed adultery? John 8:5?"

"Did you really want to get married?" she asked.

"I don't know. I thought it might be fun. I like the dress,

that part of it. Walking down the aisle. Plus I needed the documentation. Viktor could make me a real person."

"What about him? The guy upstairs?"

"Horace? He could make me a woman," I heard myself say, and then was so shocked and embarrassed I tried explaining it away. "I mean, not that I'm not a woman already. But he could give me the illusion of being a woman that would actually make me feel more like what I already am, apparently. Does that make sense?"

"I wouldn't be in any rush."

"To get married?"

"To be a woman."

"That's easy for you to say. You *are* one. I don't know what I am. It's like I keep waiting for someone to tell me. Or maybe tell me that I'm not. That I'm a new species, instead. That would explain a lot."

She put out the joint.

"No more for you."

We were each holding up a side of her coat. Together, they formed the door of a tent. I dropped mine, stuck my head out, and saw the sun had broken through. The wind was still blowing, but the last rays had slid beneath the clouds and, with this slicing angle, made everything realer than real.

"Look," I said, except there was nothing to see, just gilded trash, floating frozen in the sky, my hand, the way my five fingers were cut from one sheet of smooth, soft, fresh pie dough rolled out by my mother. Suddenly everything felt so hopeless.

"What should I do, Nora?"

I wasn't even going to tell her about the third man in my life, a middle-aged, wife-beating, crooked policeman who wanted to dress me up like his daughter. The funny thing was, he really cared. More than the others. I knew it. The wind found the place where his lips had kissed mine. And where his hand had hit my cheek. I touched to see if they felt any different.

"Don't ask me for advice. My life's a disaster." She shivered. "I'm just the opposite of you. I'm cold all the time. You should know, though . . ."

"Know what?"

I could see she was weighing in her mind whether I really should know or not. Whatever it was. People came out, walked past us, laughing. We watched. They seemed so young, even though they were older than me. I was seeing them through Nora's eyes.

"You should know there's other stuff going on," she finally said. "Other people. That no decision is entirely yours to make."

"He doesn't love her."

She gave me this puzzled look, then took back her coat and buttoned it up, snuggling into it.

"Whose is that?" I asked.

"What do you mean, whose is it? It's mine."

"It's so big."

"It used to be someone else's." She took out a cheap plastic compact and examined herself. "I still find stuff in the pockets."

"You were talking about Horace, right? He doesn't love her. That girl. Marron. Is that who you meant?"

"God, I look like shit. Why didn't you tell me?"

I was eating up her face, I was so hungry. You must have been beautiful once, I wanted to tell her. I can see the traces. She powdered parts of her forehead, then her nose. My eyes had forgotten how to blink. I saw deep into her.

"How did you even know this was happening? That it was tonight?"

"From that postcard he was passing around at the bar. I remember things." She made it sound like a problem, a curse. "Besides, I like art. Don't you?"

"Not especially."

She got this sly smile, putting away the makeup. She looked more like herself now. Her old self.

"You'll like *this* art. Go see."

I got up, expecting her to follow. But she started off in the other direction, down the steps.

"Aren't you coming?"

"I've already been."

She swayed off, the way I'd seen her do a million times, leading customers to their table, not turning. I couldn't help noticing, looking around, how guys on the steps, even though her body was completely hidden, even though they were sitting with pretty girls half Nora's age, followed her with their eyes.

I was glad I hadn't worn a coat. There would have been no place to hang it. People stood casually in the packed, airless room. I hesitated, trying to swallow down a metallic taste until I realized it was my heart, racing. But any anxiety I felt wasn't connected to the rest of me. I was sheltered. I regarded everything from a booth. The occasional look bounced off me with the heavy thud of a rock hitting clear plastic. "Stoned." Was this what Nora meant? I smiled and willed myself into the thick of things, heard this familiar voice and steered myself toward it. At that moment, another group came and bulldozed the people ahead of me sideways. I went straight. There was a path, then it closed behind. I couldn't tell what I was making happen and what I was reacting to. Either way, I was in it, deep inside now, the crowd and the event itself. All around me I glimpsed Horace's paintings, these dense canvases of numbers and letters and symbols, with strange spectrums washing over the dry formulas, making them shimmer. They were shapes, abstract patterns, but inside was all calculation, so you felt they actually meant something, that they weren't just pretty. They were the answers to secrets. Trying to be, at least. I suddenly thought, seeing one longer than I meant to, actually making contact with it, he really is a good *painter*. The way he paints. Even if they're not of anything in particular. And then I jumped away from that, because I didn't want to think of him that way, the way other people thought of him. Still, it was strange, that for once I had seen what I was supposed to see.

"It's about the non-linear nature of time. I mean, I had seen this portrait before it was painted. That's how powerful it is. It shows the Female Psyche overcoming the patriarchal, cause-and-effect way we look at our lives. And what's so amazing is that he comes from such a male perspective. I mean that's the story of it. After all these references to rational science, to this very Western mode of trying to make sense of things, he finally lets go and breaks through to something feminine and unquestioning. See, she's *dreaming* us watching her."

Marron was standing in front of a huge painting that took up the whole back wall. I made my way closer, prying apart people the way I had tried to pry apart the bricks outside the bar.

I remembered that trick of her having these ready-made speeches she would slip into.

"It worked backwards through my life. I thought I had

seen the person before, but really I had seen her portrait, in my future. I had seen what she was going to become."

She had these killer boots that went past her knees, ribbed stretch pants, and a black sweater. She had let her hair grow out so that, for the first time, I could see the dark roots. It's fall, I thought. It hadn't really hit me until now, but the way she dressed made it clear, somehow. Not only that it was fall, but that fall was almost over.

Where is he? I wanted to ask. Why are you standing in front of his painting like you own it? Like only you understand?

It was the big one, that I had touched, laid my palm flat against. Except now it had that magic buffer zone. It was a Work of Art. People gave it this respectful distance. Everyone but Marron. She straddled the invisible line. You couldn't look at it without looking at her, too. She was the tour guide, museum guard, and wife, all in one.

"The others are just exercises," I heard her explain. "This is what they were all leading up to."

. . . my suede boots, I completed the sentence in my head. My hundred-dollar pants. My cashmere turtleneck.

I finally saw Horace across the room, standing as far away from the action as possible. Someone was talking to him. He had found this patch of wall and was up against it, cornered, even though there was no corner. He had brought his own corner with him and was in it, now. His shoulders were hunched. I had never seen him looking so vulnerable. So exposed. Before, there had been this edge of smugness to him, he was sure of himself, but now, with his paintings on the wall and his name printed just inside the door, he looked pale and thin and I knew that, given the chance, he would make a dream lover. I felt this enormous need rising out of him,

I could almost see it, this aura of who he was that even he didn't know, but I did. And I could show it to him. That's what made him so appealing. He could be my mission.

"Eve," Marron finally noticed.

Shut up, I thought, staring at my future life. I'm having a moment, here.

"I can't believe you came."

Shut up, shut up, shut up.

"Horace," she yelled.

Everyone turned.

"It's Eve!" She pointed, like he wouldn't recognize me, like she was his social secretary, and waved for him to come over.

They're not really staring, I told myself. It's an optical illusion. But just in case they were, I tried that Brandy trick of standing straight, like I thrived on attention. I threw my shoulders back. Marron pretended to admire my outfit.

"Cool jumpsuit."

"Thanks."

"You have great nipples."

But I wasn't going to let her make me feel like an idiot this time. Horace's job was working his way across the room. People kept stopping him. This tall handsome stranger. Stranger? Yes, stranger to himself. And I thought, just like that other time, why not? I know that sounds lame, but maybe the strongest argument in someone's favor is the absence of any objection. Why not? Maybe love wasn't a giant step you took but something you unblocked, that you allowed to happen. You lowered your defenses. You stopped doubting. Yes, he'd space out and be cold, cruel, even. Yes, he had the power to make me feel foolish. Sometimes I'd want to crawl under a rock and die. But the person he'd mistreat would be *me*, not her. Because there was always a her. That seemed to be part of love, too. A necessary ingredient. And for all my talk about how much more interesting it was, I was tired of losing. I had learned enough for one life, that's how it felt, watching him come toward me. I was tired of painful lessons. How about a little mindless happiness? It was a wedding, in my head, except something was screwy because he was the one coming down the aisle and I was standing there with my rival sister, my best woman, who couldn't shut up, who kept explaining to all these onlookers:

"When a thing is so big, it makes this depression in the fabric of your existence, so you gain momentum, heading toward it. You actually see it before it happens. That's why it seems so right when it does. It fits into a space that was already there for it. A space *it made*. Because really everything happens all at once, or is happening and unhappening at the same time, in a kind of flux, and it's only the guy thing of needing to make it ABC or 1, 2, 3 that leads to this crazy construct we try and lead our lives by."

He stood in front of us. He didn't look nervous anymore. He looked goofy. Maybe he's drunk, I thought. No. The one time he drank with me, he just got more himself, more serious and intense. But now he was loose-limbed, a marionette with its strings cut.

"Well?" he asked.

"Congratulations." I didn't want to say anything stupid like, It looks great, since I couldn't really see anything.

He put his hands on my shoulders. It was so public. I didn't have time to step back. He spread his palms. He is going to hug me, I thought. Here, in front of everybody. In the center of the Art World. Then he was turning me around. He wasn't hugging me, he was turning me like I was on a pedestal, except I wasn't, so I moved awkwardly, on stiff legs, until I faced the painting.

"What do you think?"

I wasn't really looking. I was trying not to look, like I'd done before, but this time because I didn't like what I saw. It was different from the others. It was *of* something. A woman. Her head splashed down. Her eyes closed. Her mouth open. You could almost hear her snore. She was naked, of course. They're always naked. There was all this skin, it took up much more of the canvas than her face, and because it was close up you saw how vast it was, the shape of her body, how much effort he put into displaying it. All the formulas were there, the same things he'd been using before, foreign alphabets, maps, and lists of words, crazy equations, but this time they all fit together and really added up to something, a picture of a person, this monster girl, this goddess, this mountain of flesh.

"It's you."

"I know," I said, even though I hadn't, and still didn't . . . didn't want to, even though it had been seeping in all this time, through Marron, through the way other people were looking at me, through the words I had somehow managed not to read, the lettering right in front of me, on a clear plastic label stuck to the wall: *Eve Asleep.*

He had painted my portrait.

"This is what I was trying to tell you about at the bar. It was that morning. When you passed out at my studio. I saw exactly what I wanted. I worked the whole time you were asleep. Then I left. That's why I didn't come back. I couldn't see you awake, once I got started. It would ruin everything. I didn't want to be confused by reality."

He waited, I guess for me to say something, but I couldn't think of what. All I could compare it to was the way a dog comes into the house with a dead bird in its mouth, these bloody feathers, and expects you to be proud, laying it at your feet, with his paws spread out, his tail thumping.

"That's why I didn't call. I got the outline, but I still had to work in all the detail. I had to imagine you. To create you."

"She's ugly," I finally said.

"No she's not," he answered quickly. "She's beautiful. As soon as I finished, I came to see you. I tried to explain, but you wouldn't let me. Then I figured it would probably be better anyway if you just came here and saw it. I knew you'd understand."

Whoever she is, she's not me, I thought. Not anymore. He stole my soul. He did what I said he could do. Maybe what I wanted him to do. He took advantage of me while I was asleep. So I had no one to blame but myself. But now I was somebody else. All he got was a person who wasn't there anymore.

"Listen." His hands were still on my shoulders. He bent down and talked from behind. I felt his gaze, shooting past, admiring his own work. "Will you come to Tuscany with me?"

"What are you talking about?"

"I want you to come to Europe."

"Come to Europe and do what?"

"Paint. Well, I'll paint. I'll paint you. Don't you understand? I love you."

After all these times of him being tight-lipped, he was finally talking to me, making this declaration, and the only thing I wanted was for Marron to butt in, to stop this hideous moment. But of course it was the one moment she had chosen to disappear, to give us some space.

"Where is this coming from?" I demanded. "I mean, for weeks now you haven't been calling me. Every time we get close you find a way to back off. And now you're saying . . . all this stuff."

"You wanted to know, that other time, if I had any fantasies. It took me a while to figure one out, but this is it."

"Going to Europe is not a fantasy. It's taking a vacation together."

"I'm not talking about a vacation."

By now I had turned. He was looking at me, but I could still feel the presence of the other me, the image he'd stolen, looming behind.

It was wrong. I mean, parts of it were right, like the idea of being taken care of—loved, even—but I couldn't be this girl who took off her clothes and made him feel like an artist. It was too nutty. And even if I could, even if I could be his muse or his inspiration, whatever he was looking for, what was in it for me? I mean who would I be, apart from that? But I was also mad because he had stolen my dream! He had turned it into something I didn't want, although when I thought about it, which I was trying with all my strength not to do, what he described was almost exactly what I had wished for. But now that there was an opportunity to make it happen, all I could think about was how to get away.

"So will you come?"

The crowd was pressing in. More were waiting. I stepped back and let them come between us. He looked at me.

"Stay," he said. "Give me a minute."

"Of course."

. . . not, I added silently, waited, and then slipped out.

But there were so many people. This time they weren't magically parting. It was the opposite. They were preventing me from leaving. I kept trying to go around them and ended up back where I started. Finally, I felt the cold breath of the open door. I was sweating. I was glad, all over again, that I hadn't worn a coat, although now I'd be freezing. But just when I was about to make my escape, Marron appeared, blocking my path.

"Hey," she said, suddenly serious. Not chatty.

"I have to go." I tried to think of some lie, some excuse. "I have to meet someone."

"I know. You have to meet me."

"What?"

"You have to meet me. My dad said so."

"Your dad?"

She looked different. It wasn't just her hair or her clothes. She was standing differently, in a way I remembered from someplace else.

"My father." She searched my eyes, trying to see how much I understood. "Carl Van Arsdale? He said you wanted to talk."

CHAPTER
NINE

"Are you going to eat your fries?"

She shook her head. I speared some with my fork. She was only eating her burger, not even the bun.

"I love meat," she said.

It wasn't a coffee shop I knew. The booths were small. We sat opposite each other. Our knees touched. I could see, now that I'd been told, how that radical yellow hair Marron had the first, well, the second time we'd met, covered a dark brown appearing at her roots. It was her real color, the one that went with her eyes.

"So I went back there a few days later, when he wasn't around, and checked his desk. I knew he'd have that policeman keeping track of everyone."

"You wanted to see if the man you stabbed was OK?"

"Him?" She was chewing. "I couldn't care if he lived or died. But I did see a copy of that report you made. It gave your name and address. Except I figured your name wasn't really 'America.' People are so dumb. And it told what you saw. Or what you said you saw. So I decided to put you on my mailing list. Just 'Eve.' "

"That's how I got the invitation."

She nodded.

"But why?"

"Because you lied. I liked that."

"I didn't lie. I just didn't know what I saw." I looked at her. I still couldn't get used to it. She was the girl on the street! It was so obvious. It wasn't just the hair. Her whole manner had changed. She had dropped this mask and was the true Marron, one I'd had glimpses of before, but never so completely. Not since that night. "I still don't know what I saw."

"Want me to tell you?"

"No."

"I have a problem," she admitted. "I overreact, sometimes. I've seen a million doctors about it. Apparently I have intimacy issues. It would probably help if I talked about it."

"Please don't."

"I was with a guy that night, one I'd just met, and he wanted to do it. And I didn't. I mean I did, at first, maybe, but at a certain point I didn't. Does that make sense?"

"But your solution was a little extreme, don't you think? I mean, why carry a knife around with you in the first place?"

"Because I know what happens if you don't."

I reached over and took more of her fries. There was a wedge of lettuce, too. I was taking everything. I was starving.

"How come your name isn't Van Arsdale?"

"I changed it. McKee is my mother's maiden name. I

know that's just her father, but at least I didn't know him. Not the way I know mine."

"Your dad seemed all right. I wonder how come he never said you were his daughter? He has a really nice apartment."

"It's not an apartment. It's a penthouse."

She made it sound like an important distinction. An apartment was middle-class, someplace where you'd have a husband and raise a family. Where right and wrong applied. A penthouse was up in the stars, above all that.

"He was protecting you," I realized. "That's why he didn't say who you were. Even if it made him look like a pervert. He wants you to be safe."

"His idea of safe. Safe in a padded room. Taking pills that make you stupid. I need to know what you saw that night, Eve. What you're going to *say* you saw."

"Not you, too," I groaned.

"Listen to me. It's important that you understand what really happened."

I didn't want to hear any more. I let my head fall forward and caught it. I covered my eyes with flat palms and tried blocking out all the light that streamed in. But even the colors I saw when my eyes were closed seemed more vivid. Marron talked, and, gradually, without my wanting it to, her intimacy crept past all my defenses.

"My father was this incredibly handsome man. Women used to go crazy over him. I remember, when he would pick me up at school, or take me out to a restaurant, just us, the look on their faces. To me, that was love, this longing for what you can't have. I saw it on my mother's face, too, because she never had him either. He was always leaving us, for work, or business trips, and finally for another woman. He was this powerful unreachable creature. And mysterious. He had that penthouse for years before we even knew about it. It's where he disappeared to. So when I started dating, I didn't want to be one of those women, 'in love' with some guy. I'd seen how that turned out. Instead, I wanted to be him, walking away. I hated the idea that I could need someone to complete me. I wanted to be an animal. I wanted to do things out of biological necessity, then forget all about them."

"That's impossible," I murmured.

"You're right. It is. But I didn't know that. Not at first. Then I began to realize that every guy I saw was really him. They were all these cheap little plastic imitations of my father. I thought I was rebelling, but really I was just following in everyone else's footsteps, all these women I was so contemptuous of."

"Didn't he care?"

"He only cared about me when I screwed up. So that's what I started doing, more and more. I took really stupid chances, to get his attention. And it worked. That's the amazing thing. Suddenly, one day, he was there. Taking care of me. I guess he felt responsible. Or maybe he just noticed me, now that I wasn't a child anymore. Maybe it took my being a woman for me to even appear on his radar. I don't know. But instead of ignoring me, he got incredibly controlling. He started wanting to know where I was going every night. Who I was seeing. He went from not being there for me at all to demanding the ultimate say over every aspect of my life. It was this complete turnaround."

I smiled. It didn't sound so bad. I mean, it did, but . . .

"For a while I went along with it. I was totally submissive. I let him tell me what to do. I mean, I was his daughter, after all. Then, one day, when I was wondering what he would say about something, whether he would approve or disapprove,

I looked in the mirror, and saw my mother! This was exactly what happened to her. I was tiptoeing around, hearing his comments even when he wasn't there, imagining his will and then obeying it. Like this slave girl."

"So what were you doing the night I saw you?"

"Trying to get away! It didn't start out being so dramatic. I just got dressed up and went to a bar. I wanted to have a good time. Like I used to. At first everything went fine. There was this guy. There always is, if you set your sights low enough. I told him I knew a place. He probably thought I meant I lived around there, but he was so wasted he would have followed me anywhere. We walked around a bit. Then I led him back to the building. I don't know what I was thinking. I *wasn't* thinking. And then . . ."

Her voice trailed off.

"You saw me."

"I saw you *before*."

"Before when?"

"Before you saw me. I looked over, and saw you coming down the street. I know this sounds corny, but I saw myself through your eyes: this neurotic little girl showing off for Daddy. That's when I freaked. Suddenly I didn't want to be her anymore. I wanted to grow up. Or I *had* grown up, that's what was so scary, but I was still doing this, still repeating the same mistake, over and over. It was terrifying. I hadn't gotten clear of anything at all. With every move I made I was getting even more tangled up in this web of craziness I'd spent my whole life trying to escape. And I wanted to stop. But he wouldn't let me. He wouldn't let me go."

I opened my eyes. She was leaning forward. The world was completely different. But not in a way I could explain.

The colors, the shapes. Some lens had been twisted while I wasn't looking, making everything unbearably sharp and tight.

"Who?" I was confused. "Who wouldn't let you go? You mean your father, or the guy you picked up?"

"What does it matter? The important thing is that I cut myself free."

"But, Marron, did you ever actually tell him you wanted to stop?"

"Well, I certainly *thought* it."

"Oh."

"Then I dyed my hair, right before the Opening, in case you came. Everyone said how good it looked. Sometimes I think that's the reason the show was a hit. Because of my hair. So I owe it all to you, in a way. My success."

"I can't believe I didn't recognize you."

"You weren't ready. Not then." She wiped her mouth. We were down to our plates. "So are you going to do it? Are you going to help them lock me up?"

Our kneecaps were flat against each other. I could feel her bones through the suede. On the tabletop, in the debris of the meal, a balled-up paper napkin was slowly expanding, like a white rose.

"I knew my father would try to use you. That's how he works. That's why I had to get to know you. So we could talk. So you could hear my side of it."

"You stabbed that man for no reason?"

"I stabbed him for every reason in the world! You saw what he was doing."

"But you said—"

"It doesn't matter if I wanted it or not. He shouldn't have been there in the first place. A woman takes her chances every time she goes out the door with some guy. Why shouldn't a man take his chances, too? I really don't see what all the fuss is about."

Then she reached out and touched her finger to the center of my forehead, as if she was tapping into my thoughts.

"How much did he offer?"

"It doesn't matter." I swallowed. "I said no."

"You said no, but you meant yes. That's why you told him you'd meet me. So you would be convinced. So you would say, She's crazy. She *should* be locked up. So you could pretend you didn't have a choice. See, in this society it's OK to be a slut about money, just not about sex."

That got me mad. I hated it when people used the special insults only I was permitted to call myself.

"You know, you're the kind of person who gives women a bad name."

"I try." She smiled. "After all, who wants to be a good girl? They're the worst."

"And for a while there, I actually thought I liked you."

"You didn't like me. You wanted to be me. That's different."

I thought about it. She was right. Buying the knife. Wearing her clothes. I envied her. I even envied what I'd seen on the street that night: someone freeing herself. But at what a price.

"What about Horace?" I argued. "He's not your dad. You don't want him the way you want those other guys. You love him."

She faltered. There was this crack in her confidence.

"Horace is just a friend. He loves you."

"No he doesn't. He paints me."

"That's love, to Horace."

I shook my head. I never understood what Marron said.

No, I did. It just seemed so obvious, once she explained, something we all knew but didn't want to hear. It made sense, but was embarrassing. She's a genius, I remembered people saying, and thought, God, maybe she is. Maybe that's being a genius, seeing the obvious.

"What's in it for me? If I don't tell?" I tried making it a joke. "You never got me a present, remember? You said you would find me the perfect thing."

She stared.

"Maybe I already have."

After, I walked, trying to find my way back in, back to that feeling I had when I first came to the city. But the streets seemed familiar now. Instead of sounding the pavement, listening for a secret passageway, stepping sideways into a parallel universe, I was going over everything in my mind, seeing it from the perspective of a person who'd been through something, though what I still couldn't say. On the way home, I passed the newspaper vendor dragging the last of his bundles inside. He nodded, then came back out with a piece of carpet and a portable radio. I watched as he carefully oriented himself in a direction that had nothing to do with city blocks, and kneeled.

"One God?" I asked, remembering a prayer from *The Penguin Guide to Islam.*

". . . and Muhammad is His prophet," he answered automatically.

The muezzin's broadcast call bounced off buildings.

It wasn't until a few days later that I thought I understood.

Marron's words came back to me. "That's love, to

Horace." Was she giving me her blessing? Was she explaining, Yes, he did love me, and so I was allowed to love him back now? After all, hadn't the only thing missing from my wanting him been that I was pretty sure he didn't want me? That maybe he didn't even know how to want someone? And now that he'd proved he could, even if it was in this typically sick, boy way, by painting a huge privacy-destroying picture instead of just being nice to me personally, what exactly was left to hesitate over? It's not like I couldn't imagine being with him. As a matter of fact, that's about all I could imagine. It was the position my mind occupied when nothing else was going on, this daydream that was always playing and that I only occasionally—say, ten or fifteen times an hour—checked in on. Even my anger was just another excuse to think about him. It was so deep, the urge. Maybe that was the problem. In which case all I had to do was decide it wasn't a problem. Decide I loved him. But can you decide that?

I called the Port Authority Lanes and asked to speak to the manager. Viktor sounded nervous. I told him I wanted my passport and I wanted it now, that I was leaving the country, going as soon as possible. There was this silence. I heard voices in the background. Women's voices. I realized he had a whole little circle of worshipful admirers working for him there, too. Just like at the bar. It didn't make me mad. It made me nostalgic. It also increased my determination. He couldn't get around me the way he used to. I told him that if the things he'd said meant anything, then he should do what he promised. Anyone would have thought I was pitiful, this jilted girlfriend trying to make him keep his word. But I didn't let my voice break, or ask any questions, or allow him to talk at all. He couldn't. I saw him there, surrounded by these wounded, jealous girls, each feeling she owned a piece of him, that she had some special relationship going, all of them listening while pretending not to, while he shifted nervously from foot to foot. He's a bully, and bullies are really cowards, I told myself. If I put it just right, he would do anything I said.

But when he did, I was completely shocked.

"Yes, why not?" he sighed.

"What?"

"One Centre Street." He was using his bored, business voice, talking to a salesman or a collection agency, someone he wanted to hustle off the phone. "This afternoon. Four forty-five."

"Today?"

"You say it is urgent, yes?"

"One Centre Street, that's . . . Is that the big building next to City Hall? Is that where people get married?"

"As you know, I can refuse you nothing."

"Wait a minute," I said. "I just wanted the documentation. Does this mean we're actually—?"

But he had hung up. He started to hang up before he said whatever his last words were going to be, so they came simultaneously with the click. The phone was still in my hand, this clunky engagement ring. Four forty-five. I wanted to write it down, so I wouldn't forget, even though there wasn't much chance of that. No, to make it more real. One Centre Street. So I could look at it, over and over again, on a piece of paper. I wanted to get up, but I couldn't. I was sitting cross-legged on the floor, absolutely still and yet ascending, blasting off. Even though it was fake, even though it was just to get him a green card and me a passport, it meant something. That's what surprised me. I straightened my back, improved my posture, practicing for life as a married woman. And I had managed to do it without saying yes!

That's what I wanted to tell Mother. This wave of sweet sadness washed over me. I intensely missed everything. My innocent girlhood days . . . which are these! I laid the receiver gently down.

Hey, guess what? I'm getting married!

That's what I wanted to say. To anyone I met. But since I didn't have anyone to meet, I just kept it inside, where it bubbled away, fermenting, until it changed, so when it finally did come out, it was something else entirely:

"I'm here to see Mr. Conover. About a job."

They looked at me.

Do what I say, I smiled, and no one gets hurt. I'm a woman with a wedding date and I'm not afraid to use it.

"Mr. Conover? In Human Resources?"

"That's right."

They had said they were interested. They had told me to check back with them. And here I was. I didn't know what the lie-detector man wrote, but I talked my way past that, too. I talked my way past all their hesitations. I think it was my manner, this mix of enthusiasm and fanatical sureness. I showed initiative. There was never a second's doubt they were going to hire me as a salesgirl. I made it seem like the only thing they could do. I kept waiting for this voice inside me to object, but there were no voices anymore. I was solid. All one piece.

BLOOMINGDALE'S, EVE SMITH, TEMPORARY EMPLOYEE, it read, this card they gave me. It was much fancier than what I used to dream of, working in a drugstore, having one of those cheap badges with my name in green label tape. This was so official. Too bad I was only going to use it once. I went to the bridal shop. The same woman was in charge. I didn't think she recognized me. I got her to let me take it into the changing room this time, the dress I had been so knocked out by. It fit. I could go into ecstasies about how it remolded my entire body, not in some pinching, suffocating way, just the opposite, how it gave me this hidden ease I never even suspected I could have, how I slouched and it turned even that into a kind of gesture, what you'd see in a fashion magazine. But all that I noticed later. Looking into the mirror, I was in too much of a hurry to wonder anything more than, would I be late? The saleslady, buttoning it from behind, breathed, "Oh God, it's perfect." She must have been waiting for me to cry or faint, because she seemed disappointed when all I did was ask what time it was.

"Ten to four."

"I'll take it."

She tried explaining about the special box it came in, how I couldn't possibly wear it out of the store, that there were all these booklets and flyers about proper care, showing how you could preserve it for years to come. "So your daughter can use it." I didn't have time for any of that. I whipped out my employee identification card and then almost all the cash I had left in the world. It felt good, instead of going broke by dribs and drabs. This was more like gambling. I was putting all my money on me. Me and my dress.

"Oh, you work here."

"I just started."

"Didn't they tell you? Employees don't become eligible for the discount until they've been here a month."

My heart sank. We both looked down at the money I'd heaped by the register. A moment ago it seemed like so much. Now it wasn't nearly enough. Then I saw she did recognize me, or recognized something in me.

"It's OK, honey." She started pressing the machine.

I watched her. At first I didn't know what she meant. Then I saw she was copying numbers off her own ID card, the one she wore on a clip off her shirt pocket. The drawer popped open. She started sorting the cash. She glanced at me once, surprised I was still there.

"Go," she said.

She didn't even give me a receipt. She knew I wasn't coming back.

The express was out of service. That's how I ended up on the number six train again, going downtown, to City Hall this time, in my wedding dress. Now, *this* is how it's supposed to be, I thought, looking at the stations as we slowed for each, taking on more and more passengers. This is the aisle and I'm coming down it and all these strangers are my relatives, the people I haven't seen in years but who show up at occasions like this. They all looked vaguely familiar. Uncles, aunts, cousins, grandparents, nieces and nephews. Citizens. My accidental family. The dress was a white waterfall. But short. I could still see my sneakers. I had forgotten about shoes. It didn't matter. There was also, instead of perfume, this nauseating new-car smell rising off the fabric. The sizing, I guess. But it all came together. I was as beautiful as I was ever going to be.

Once upon a time, I wanted to be someone else. Anyone else. I would pass a person on the street and think, I want to be her. For no reason. Just because it would relieve me of the burden of being me. They were closing the door to the Marriage Bureau. I was the last one in. I thought if I had a part to play, instead of just being who I was, I could do it better. Start fresh. Be less messy. That's what this felt like, wearing white, heading for the altar. A new beginning.

"Eve." Viktor was wearing a tie. It made him look very European, and nervous. "You came."

"Just," I breathed. "Did you see? They almost didn't let me in. You said four-forty-five, right?"

"Yes. They stop taking applications then. So the office can close at five. It is the only time the line moves fast. Civil servants, you know."

He had shaved and cut himself. I could see the small slash under one ear. So what do you think? I was about to ask, and model the dress, do a little spin, but he went on, in this urgent whisper, "I did not think you were coming. I kept trying to call you back. I could not talk, before. There were too many people around."

"Why were you trying to call me back?

"Hey, Eve. Is that a wedding dress?"

Crystal was standing next to him. I hadn't seen her at first. Or I had, but I didn't think it was her. I rejected the idea. She looked different, somehow. She didn't belong with the rest of the picture.

"What are you doing here?" I asked.

"We are getting married," he said. "Crystal and me."

"Crystal and I," I corrected automatically.

"No. Not you."

"I know. But you said, Crystal and me. It's Crystal and I."

"Don't be silly. How could you marry her? You are a woman." It was like our language had completely broken down. "I am marrying Crystal. That is what I was trying to tell you."

"When? When did you try and tell me?"

"When I called your number repeatedly. Where were you?"

"Out." I pulled back my sleeve. She was trying to touch the material. "It's not a wedding dress. It's just a dress."

"I'm pregnant, Eve."

"Of course you are. That's obvious."

It was, now that I looked. She was huge. I just hadn't seen her in a while. Viktor was kicking the floor.

"You said you needed your passport so urgently," he complained. "And my friend was delivering them to me here just now. There were items I needed as well, to go through with the ceremony. But after I got off the phone, I realized you might think—"

"Oh no." I laughed. "I didn't think that at all. That *we* were getting married? Give me a break!"

"Is it silk?"

"I don't know what it is. I got it at a thrift shop. It cost ten dollars."

"Then how come the price tag says—?"

"It's a *look*," I said witheringly.

"Kholmov?" a voice called.

"Come." He put his arm around her.

I had seen him do that probably a hundred times before. There was no personal space with Viktor. He grabbed you to get your attention, rubbed against you, moving behind the bar, started massaging your aching shoulders when you were tired. It was partly working together, the familiarity, but also that he liked women. All women. It was deceptive because you could churn up this whole romance in your mind, based on these touches, and really they didn't mean anything. But the way he touched Crystal then, put his arm around her in this caring, shielding way, as if she was already the child she was going to have, that's when it hit me.

"You're getting married?" I screamed.

They both looked dazed. I guess they thought we'd been

over that. It was this big day in their lives and there I was, ruining it, standing in front of them, feeling so wronged.

"I did not know, Eve. Not when I asked you. Then, later, after I found out, it still wasn't clear what we were going to do, Crystal and me."

He seemed stuck on the phrase, like the bad English made it special. I could see them changing, right before my eyes, into a couple, like in a horror movie.

"We weren't sure we wanted to keep it," she explained.

Yeah, right, I thought.

"I believe in accepting responsibility for my actions." He sounded so full of himself. So admiring. And completely without humor. Why had I ever liked him?

You knew, I glared. You knew she was pregnant when you asked me. That's why you did it. Not to get a green card. You would have gotten one of those no matter what, no matter who you ended up with. You asked me because you were scared and wanted out. Even as late as the other day. That's what you meant by me "saving" you. I was Plan B. The escape hatch. But I could have told you Crystal would never let that happen. She's the kind of girl who goes from one person to the next. She decides when to make a move. Not you.

"Once Crystal made her decision, my way was clear," he went on gravely. "The child needs a father."

And the bully needs to be bullied, I thought. She'll be better at it than I am. By far.

They called him again. Crystal and I were alone for a minute. She looked tired and scared.

"Have you been sick?"

"I was at first. Now I'm better."

"That sure was a nice bridal shower you threw me."

"It wasn't my idea. The girls wanted to do it and I couldn't say no because then I'd have to explain what was going on with me."

"Where's Brandy? Your partner in crime."

"She's pissed. She wouldn't come. She kicked me out of the apartment."

"Good for her. So you're going to be living under a bowling alley?"

"We found a place in Staten Island. Viktor can drive. I'm going to fix it up. Make it nice." She sighed. "I didn't plan it this way, you know."

"No kidding! That time you talked to me, when I was in the bathtub, you made it sound like . . . I guess I didn't get it."

"There's lots of ways two people can live together."

"Does Viktor know?"

"Know what?"

So he didn't. I nodded. So he was getting what he deserved. But then she said something that made me see I didn't know anything at all.

"You think I could do this if I didn't . . . love him?" She stumbled on the word, like it was a tippy rock in a stream, but kept going. "Besides, I—"

I never found out what she was going to say next, because he came back in a panic.

"Eve, you must come with us right away."

"I'm not going anywhere with you."

. . . you baby-making rapist foreigner.

"Go where?" Crystal asked.

"To the chapel. It is the one thing I forgot. Only a single secretary is left. The clerk says we need another witness."

"A witness? No way."

I had already witnessed enough, thank you very much. Crystal looked at me.

"Oh, all right," I grumbled.

It seemed to be the only thing I was good at, watching other people make big mistakes. They led us into a room that had all the hideous trappings of a church but was careful not to show a cross or star or part of any specific religion. Instead it was the worst of all, that phony holy atmosphere where everything's just a little bit special, extra-curvy or made of super-polished wood. But for no reason. The window would have had a great view but was blocked by this abstract network of poured cement. It was the single ugliest thing I had ever seen, except for the man standing in front of it, this young guy with his belly sticking out of a suit, holding a vinyl booklet like it was the menu for a bad restaurant.

He looked at the three of us.

"Who exactly is getting married?"

"Oh. Her." I tried moving back and stepped on Viktor's foot.

"Are you sure?" he asked.

"This? I got it at a thrift shop."

"It is Kholmov." Viktor was trying to get me off him. "Mr. and Mrs. Viktor Kholmov."

We were tangled up somehow. Crystal waited patiently until he got free. I stood off to the side.

They were the last couple of the day. The clerk read in a hurried drone. I looked around, not just at the sacred office furniture, the artsy light fixtures, but at them, Viktor and Crystal, at the man's stomach, hanging over his belt, and finally at myself, my worn sneakers attaching me somehow to the wall-to-wall carpeting. What are we? I asked, annoyed that this was where thinking always took me, to more questions, never an answer.

"Miss, you have to sign."

"Sign?" I echoed blankly.

He had one more form.

"Sign where? What do I write?"

"Your name. And I need to see some identification."

I looked around. The man didn't notice. He was putting things in his folder, ready to get out of there. Viktor dug into his pocket and slipped me a driver's license, a Social Security card, a birth certificate, and a shiny blue passport. I opened the passport, saw me, and gave this little squawk of delight. My face was half-embossed by the Seal of the United States, and then after that there were all these blank pages, all these places I could go, a book yet to be written.

I flipped to the front.

"We did not know what to put," Viktor mumbled. "You said this name was common. I looked it up. It means 'maker of horseshoes.' I hope it is all right."

"Smith," I read out loud. "No, that's . . . that's perfect, Viktor. Actually, it's amazing, because I just—"

"Miss?" He looked at his watch.

"Oh. Right."

I wrote carefully, I didn't want to misspell anything, and stood back to admire my signature. Then he said it, something like: "By the power vested in me by the state of New York, I now pronounce you man and wife."

I found Mingrelia, I wanted to tell him, but they were kissing. I looked it up. It's part of Georgia. The Republic of Georgia. And the Euxine Sea, that's just the Black Sea, right? But they were kissing. They were kissing. I tiptoed out of the chapel. I could go anywhere now. I had a passport. I had documentation. Proof I was a real person. I knew because—I didn't realize it at first, not until a few drops fell on my dress—I was crying. I was weeping uncontrollably.

It was one of those sunsets when the streets lined up perfectly. Rays fell pure and straight. I looked into them so my tears would have a reason for being. Why was I so upset? I had gotten what I wanted, and didn't give up a thing in return. I had never loved Viktor. I was always fighting him off. I was still fighting him off, flailing at this person who wasn't even there anymore. Why did I feel hurt? Rejected? He had picked somebody else, not me, thank God. I still had my plan. I was still on course. I took a deep breath. Viktor, the bar, the girls, were gone, leaving me light, almost weightless. Because I was blinded, my footsteps sounded unnaturally loud. I listened to that slight crunch, the grit of the city, lubricating things, sliding us all along.

Detective Jourdain opened the door to Horace's studio.

"Oh Jesus," he said. "This is just what I was afraid of."

I looked past him. The lamps were down. Those long shallow fluorescent rods that hung from chains. They were laid out on the floor, taking up almost all the space. Which they could, because there was nothing else. He stepped aside. The studio was empty. Out the window, on the highway, cars whizzed by. Most had turned on their headlights, even though you could still see, as if they were trying to bring on the dark.

I had stood across the street for twenty minutes. I wasn't sure which windows were his. I wanted there to be some sign this was my true fate. Of course there wasn't. The sign would be me, walking up those steps. Finally, I looked down and noticed the price tag still dangling from my dress. I tore it off, crossed over, and pushed the buzzer. There was a pause, the pause between when you know you're going to kiss someone and you actually do, then this low buzz back, with the click of a lock unlocking itself. I hiked to the second floor and was ready. Love. It was automatic, simple as a buzz and an answering click.

"Well, don't just stand there."

I walked in. Just a few steps, the same as the first time I had come, so he could close the door behind me. It made that important-sounding boom of steel slamming shut. Like a bank vault. This finality. I squinted to the far side.

"What happened to the bathroom?"

It wasn't there. The toilet and sink and shower head were, but without a wall. They huddled all by themselves at the end of the room.

"Why? You have to use it? The water's still on. I could go out in the hall and wait."

"No, no. I was just wondering."

"They're doing a gut renovation. Making the place nice. This neighborhood's taking off, apparently. Lofts like this are going to be worth a lot."

"Oh."

"The workmen just started today. I was supposed to come by and make sure no personal belongings were left behind. Cleaning up." He shrugged. "Same as always."

"I don't get it. Where's Horace? What are you doing here?"

"Mr. Van Arsdale owns this building. Didn't you know that?"

I looked for the bed, the mattress on the floor, but that was gone, too. Everything was gone. I could feel myself closing in on the memory, preserving it. Some part of my mind was already doing that, instinctively, even though the rest of me hadn't accepted the fact, hadn't even figured out what was going on.

"You really put the fear of God into those two. I've got to hand it to you. Mr. V. couldn't believe you weren't jumping at his offer. And that daughter of his was just as terrified you were going to turn her in."

"He owns the building?"

"Finally got them to agree on something. Which is a first."

"They agreed on what?"

"This." He motioned to the empty space.

I took a deep sniff, to suck back any tears that might make a reappearance. But I was all cried out. Instead, I got a lungful of dry desert smokiness. Sandalwood. Or sawdust.

"Mr. V. got that boyfriend, what's-his-name, Dean? He got him to take her on. They left for Europe yesterday afternoon. Rome, I think."

"Rome? No, Horace wouldn't do that. He was going to go to Italy with—"

I bit my lip.

"Most people aren't as hard to convince as yourself," he said gently.

"I don't believe it." I tried hitting him. I went up and hammered away at his chest. "What did you do? How did you get Horace to go with her? Did you threaten him?"

"Me? Threaten? That boy was bought and paid for a long time ago. Cut it out, Eve!" He held my fists until I stopped. "What do you think he was doing here in the first place?"

I just stood there.

". . . wouldn't be too hard on him. Most people don't even realize it when they're selling themselves. It's second nature to them. I mean it's what we're all supposed to do in life, one way or another, isn't it? Sell ourselves? Just got to make sure you get a good price."

"I should go."

"If you want."

We stared at the crumbled stumps where things had been. Wood and nails. That white board that turns into chalk.

"And this was all right with you?" I asked suddenly. "That she gets away with it? What if she does something else? I thought you were so concerned about justice."

"Well, she won't be doing it in my backyard. Which means it can't come back to bite me, that I didn't lock her up. And who knows? Maybe she'll get better. You got to have a little faith. Besides, that boy's going to look after her. She's his responsibility now."

I couldn't imagine what her father had possibly offered. I mean, I couldn't see Horace taking money. He wouldn't sink that low.

He cleared his throat and went on, "Speaking of backyards. If you need a place to stay, I've got this room, this whole house, practically. It wouldn't be any kind of a situation. I mean, you wouldn't have to pay."

His side was a wall, a wall you could lean against that wouldn't disappear from one day to the next. A wall you could shelter behind. You wanted a part to play, I thought; well, here's one. Maybe not what you fantasized about, but a role, ready-made, waiting. One you know you could do.

"I suppose it's kind of silly, but ever since I saw you that morning, in front of your apartment building."

He stopped.

"What?" I asked impatiently. Make a case, for God's sake. Make an ass of yourself. I need to be convinced.

He forced the words out, "Listen, whatever it is you want, that I can give. All you have to do is ask."

And he can kiss, a voice reminded.

I jumped. I thought I was done hearing voices.

"So . . . what?" I asked. "It's like the dust has cleared and you're the last man standing?"

"Huh?"

"You hit me!"

"When?" He looked confused. "You mean when you jumped right in front of my car?"

"No. That time in the elevator."

"Oh, then. Damn right I did. Because the situation called for it. And then you marched into that room and told off one of the most powerful men in the city. You don't remember that part, do you?"

I was standing a few steps away. I wasn't just going to melt into somebody. Some body.

"I hit you and you got strong," he went on. "Your problem is you don't give yourself enough credit."

"That's my problem?"

He took my arms but didn't pull me to him. We stood there, an in-between distance apart. I remembered before, how this irresistible force lifted me, how I had stretched higher than I thought I could, to reach him, to follow his lips, until my feet were about to float free.

"You can't go on the way you've been. Writing those letters to your mother. Telling her about walking the streets at night, about that boss of yours, how he tried to grab your private parts."

"What?" I asked.

"You know."

I felt his fingers, pressing into my forearms, weaken.

"Yes, I know. Because it's my life. But how do you know? I never told you any of that."

"I guess I was just jealous."

"You read my composition book. How did you even find it?"

"Eve—"

"You're the one who broke into my apartment!"

"You were crying out for help. Don't you see?"

"But why did you have to trash the place?"

He frowned. I guess it was the most obvious thing in the world. But I still didn't get it.

"So you would call, of course. I needed you to need me."

"Oh, I could never go back home with you. You're far too weird."

It was out of my mouth before I even knew what I was saying. And then there was that same look on his face as before. This deep hurt. Except this time it didn't pass. It stayed, and deepened.

I wish I could say it felt good to give someone else the big kiss-off for a change, instead of being the one to have their heart broken. But it didn't feel good at all. I left the studio, and walked. I walked all the way uptown. It was late and I was tired. By the time I got home, I couldn't stop yawning. I stumbled up the stairs. All I could think about was sleep. Somehow, I had gotten myself off nights.

"Let gel remain in hair one hour."

"One hour!"

"Or until desired color is reached. Rinse and dry naturally. DO NOT BLOW-DRY."

I looked in the mirror. I couldn't see anything, yet.

Brandy was really into reading the instructions. It's like she had found this sacred text.

"The longer gel remains in place, the deeper color will be."

"So how do I know when to wash it out?"

"It's up to you, I guess."

The kittens were playing with her outfit. She grabbed it. They thought she was part of the game, and jumped high in the air, trying to get it back.

"How cold is it out there?" she asked.

"Freezing."

It was actually kind of wild this way, with my hair sticking straight up, all swathed in evil-smelling jelly. The rest of me was in the white terry-cloth robe. What would happen if I never washed the stuff out? What would the directions say about that? DANGER: WILL CAUSE PERMANENT BRAIN DAMAGE.

She came out of the bedroom in two sweaters and sweatpants. She was dressing more like me. And here I was, primping and preening. It was this weird transformation we'd both noticed, each borrowing from the other.

"Do we need anything?" I asked.

"You're not going out again, are you?"

"I might."

She looked at herself in the mirror. The Bikini Bar didn't have a room in back. I'd been, once. Just to see. It was definitely a step up from Viktor's. At least it had a name, and a sign, and a door on the street.

"Milk, I guess. For the cats."

It's not like we talked. I mean, we did, but that wasn't what was nice. It was the silence, actually. This homey sensation. What I imagined home was like, never having had one before. The apartment was always different when I got back at the end of the day. It didn't have that dead feel that things were exactly as I'd left them. The smell of cooking. The radio. I wasn't alone. Even when she was gone, there was this presence. I slept on the couch, and would wake up in the middle of the night and see all these things around me, rugs and chairs and lamps, little end tables, the cats, their green eyes. It felt real. Not like my old place. I wasn't in hiding. On weekends, we'd make popcorn and watch TV.

Brandy's hair was trapped inside her sweatshirt. She bunched it up and shook it loose so it bounced and arranged itself over her shoulders. Then she gave herself this one rapid, admiring look. Some things never change. She noticed the dress I was still wearing every day, hanging in the bathroom.

"No wonder you were cold. In that."

"I know."

I wore thick woolen leggings with it now, which made me look even more like a demented bride-to-be.

We never talked about what had happened. It was this hurt we were both trying to layer over. Before leaving, she gave a last critical glance at my hair.

"Not much longer."

"Good."

Still, it made me jumpy. I was afraid of leaving the dye in too long, afraid of not leaving it long enough. I didn't know what to do. How to pass the time. I could eat, but that wasn't very appealing, crouching in front of the refrigerator, wolfing down food, watching the seconds tick by. I could read, but then I might look up two hours later and discover I was bald. I was standing there, in the middle of the room, totally indecisive, when the phone rang.

"I am looking at a very beautiful young lady," a voice said.

I turned to the window. It was already dark. There were curtains, but I hadn't pulled them. Somehow that meant I was in for the night, and I wasn't sure I wanted to be. Not yet.

"It's Carl Van Arsdale." He realized I still didn't know. "Marron's father."

"Oh. Right."

"It's a large portrait of you. Done by a promising artist, I'm told. I never actually met the young man in question."

"I have."

"Well, yes. That's obvious."

"Wait, how are you looking at Horace's portrait of me? It's in a gallery."

"The show came down several days ago. It certainly alters the focus of the room. Which is why I called."

"You bought it?"

"I purchased it, yes."

For some reason that sounded more delicate. No, you purchased him, I thought. That's what you had to offer, the one thing Horace wouldn't have considered a bribe. Because it wasn't. It was just an artist, selling his work. For a ton of money, plus the buzz of being collected by someone so rich. It was a good career move. And who did he have to thank for it? The girl lying next to him right now. In some bed. In Tuscany. Was this the gift Marron had promised me? This cold freedom?

"Do you like it?"

"I'm not sure. It's disturbing. You're disturbing."

"What are you talking about?"

"You disturb me."

"I'm sorry," I said absentmindedly, although really, why was I apologizing for being in a painting that nobody asked him to buy? Well, she asked him to buy it, of course, but that didn't mean he had to ruin the pristine beauty of his penthouse with this mammoth nudie shot. I'd be disturbed, too. "Is that why you're calling? Because you don't like the picture?"

"I'm calling to see how you are."

"I'm fine. I got a job at—"

"Bloomingdale's. Yes, I know. Arthur has kept me current on your progress. And it is progress, Eve. I have a copy of an evaluation here from your supervisor. You're doing well. I'm proud."

"You bet I'm doing well. Because I'm working like a maniac, that's why. They're already talking about moving me to the second floor. That's where the designer fashions are."

"Is that what you really want to do?"

"I don't know. It might be. It's a start."

"Because there are college programs you could enter. I would be willing to—"

"The point is, I'm making it on my own. So don't start acting like you have anything to do with it. Why are you even calling?"

"I was wondering if you'd eaten yet."

"Look, if this is to threaten me with getting fired, because I never told what I saw that night, go right ahead. Have them fire me. I don't care. I'm good at what I do. That's what I've been finding out. I can be good at anything I want. God put me on this earth and I belong here. I am His Daughter. We all are, all women. And I am tired of you trying to make me feel like some kind of inferior creature."

"Eve—"

"What did you say? Before?"

"I asked if you'd eaten yet. I am threatening you with dinner."

"Oh." I looked down at my robe. I loved that soft belt. The big floppy knot. Had I just been preaching, back there? That's what it felt like.

"There are restaurants," he began. "I know some good ones. Or, if you prefer privacy, we could have food here."

"Takeout."

"Not exactly. A chef arrives, and—"

"Excuse me, no offense, but I can't even do the math. Are you three, four, or five times older than I am?"

"We're talking about dinner, Eve."

I passed the mirror.

"Oh my God."

"What's happening? Are you all right?"

"Nothing. Nothing's happening. Listen, I have to go."

"So you're not free tonight?"

I poked at the gel, revealing this seam of amazing color. Like finding gold.

"I *see* you," he complained. I thought he meant from his window, that he could see everything, he was so high up, before I realized he meant the painting. "It's an amazing likeness, but, as I said, disturbing."

"I have to go," I repeated. "I have something very important to do. I just remembered."

"Can't it wait?"

"No."

"I want to talk about your future."

I hung up. I had never done that before. Hung up on someone. It was strange, because the connection wasn't really broken. I hadn't said good-bye. So bits of him were still with me, in the apartment, in the bathroom, as I rinsed out all the junk and towel-dried my hair. He was the Devil. I knew that. He was my devil, and I would have to deal with him, but not now. Blond was never an option. Everyone was blond. I considered black, jet-black. I liked its mystery. I thought if I changed the way I looked on the outside, then change would work its way in. But Brandy said it was the other way around, that I had to find the inner me and bring her out. "Face it"—she picked a box off the drugstore shelf—"you're a Flaming Redhead."

Outside, a blizzard was beginning, filling every inch of sky. New York City. It's just not what I expected, I thought, then remembered, milk, and went down the steps, feeling each snowflake, as it landed on my hair, sizzle and hiss.